ALL FOR ONE

"We've got them. Push them back!" Thorn shouted, using his big Mameluke sword with skillful accuracy until the remaining attackers turned, ran and leaped over the cliff edge into the darkness.

Sam advanced, firing his big Colt as the Desert Weasels made their howling, screaming retreat. At the edge of the cliff, he stared down, seeing only black shadows dart back and forth as they fired wildly up at him and the bounty hunters.

"Ranger, look out!" shouted Sandoval.

Sam turned in time to see a warrior wielding a long war ax. But upon hearing the bounty hunter, the warrior turned quickly and swung the ax in Sandoval's direction.

Sandoval dodged the powerful blow from the ax. He spun with his sword and laid the *Comadrejas* open with a deep, lethal slash across his sternum. As the warrior staggered backward, Sam grabbed him by his wrist and swung the man out over the edge of the cliff. The darkness swallowed him, leaving only a long scream resounding down the black hillside.

BLACK VALLEY
RIDERS

Ralph Cotton

A SIGNET BOOK

JA, 12

SIGNET
Published by New American Library, a division of
Penguin Group (USA) Inc., 375 Hudson Street,
New York, New York 10014, USA
Penguin Group (Canada), 90 Eglinton Avenue East, Suite 700, Toronto,
Ontario M4P 2Y3, Canada (a division of Pearson Penguin Canada Inc.)
Penguin Books Ltd., 80 Strand, London WC2R 0RL, England
Penguin Ireland, 25 St. Stephen's Green, Dublin 2,
Ireland (a division of Penguin Books Ltd.)
Penguin Group (Australia), 250 Camberwell Road, Camberwell, Victoria 3124,
Australia (a division of Pearson Australia Group Pty. Ltd.)
Penguin Books India Pvt. Ltd., 11 Community Centre, Panchsheel Park,
New Delhi - 110 017, India
Penguin Group (NZ), 67 Apollo Drive, Rosedale, North Shore 0632,
New Zealand (a division of Pearson New Zealand Ltd.)
Penguin Books (South Africa) (Pty.) Ltd., 24 Sturdee Avenue,
Rosebank, Johannesburg 2196, South Africa

Penguin Books Ltd., Registered Offices:
80 Strand, London WC2R 0RL, England

First published by Signet, an imprint of New American Library,
a division of Penguin Group (USA) Inc.

First Printing, November 2010
10 9 8 7 6 5 4

For Mary Lynn . . . of course.

PART 1

PART 1

Chapter 1

The Cuban Dee Sandoval sat perched high atop a towering pine overlooking the small badlands mining town of Minton Hill, which lay a good thousand yards east of him. But from this height, through his brass-trimmed naval telescope, he held an unobstructed view of the dirt street and the familiar faces of the three riders entering the settlement at a loose gallop.

On the rocky ground below, the older man, Cadden Thorn, sat on his horse, staring up at him. When Thorn saw Sandoval lower the battered telescope, he called up to him, "Are those our targets, Sandy?" A long scimitar-style Mameluke sword hung from a metal clip down the left side of his saddle horn.

"Yes, it is them," Sandoval called down to him in English as good as any Thorn was used to hearing. "There is one rider following them, less than a mile behind." He swung a big Swiss rifle from his shoulder by its strap and began to make adjustments on its raised sights as he judged the wind, the sway of the pine and the slant of the afternoon sunlight.

"I had a hunch there would be someone on their trail," Thorn said. Uncrossing his wrists from his saddle horn and adjusting the reins in his hands, he murmured to himself, "A lawman, I have no doubt."

"Yes," said Sandoval. "It's the ranger, the one who wears the gray sombrero."

"The ranger, of course," Thorn said under his breath. He paused only for a second, then called up to Sandoval in a resolved tone, "He'll have to be reckoned with." He turned his horse to the thin trail reaching down the hillside to the main trail. "You know what to do. Carry on."

Without looking down from his swaying perch, Sandoval only nodded as he wrapped his left forearm into the leather rifle strap and raised the butt into the pocket in his right shoulder. *Yes . . .* He knew what to do, he reminded himself. He relaxed over against the trunk of the pine and let his body take on the tree's back-and-forth rhythm. He squatted deep on his right leg, his knee almost to his chin, his left leg hanging loose down past the bough beneath him, in order to serve as a counterbalance when the recoil of the big rifle punched his shoulder.

He had learned this type of shooting by wrapping a safety rope around the mast of a ship and tying off before making his shots. But not these days. Tying off was for beginners. He knew the rifle and its recoil—how to rock back with it just enough, and not let it unseat him. This weapon had become a part of him over the past year. It was not his first long-range rifle.

He had equally given service to the Spencer tin-plated carbine and the Springfield Trap Door rifle over the years. But he had come to know the feel and force of the big Swiss Husqvarna precision rifle as he knew his own heartbeat.

Beneath him, the Cuban rifleman caught a peripheral glance of Thorn riding down the steep hillside and out across a rocky stretch of flatlands leading toward town. Sandoval pinned the rifle against the tree trunk with his knee and raised the telescope to his eye for another look before his shooting began.

Young Arizona Ranger Samuel Burrack saw the rise of trail dust coming toward Minton Hill from the west, beneath a line of hills on the opposite side of the sandy flatlands. It could be anyone, he told himself, letting the big Appaloosa stallion pull the trail beneath them at a fast, strong pace. Taking on a gang the size of the Black Valley Riders had him looking over his shoulder a little more than usual.

A gang that size was capable of anything, he thought, riding on. A haze of dust still loomed in the evening air from the three riders who had stirred it up only moments before him. As he neared the edge of town, Sam slowed the stallion to a walk and whispered down to it, patting its sweaty withers, "Easy, Black Pot. You got us here. We're in no hurry now."

The stallion chuffed and cantered down, slinging its wet mane back and forth.

The ranger eyed the wide dirt street ahead of him and realized what a perfect setup this would be for an ambush—late afternoon, the empty street, a town of workingmen resting from the heat of the day before venturing out to the cantinas and gambling parlors.

He saw no sign of the three men's horses at the hitch rails along the street. He might not have been on the job long, but he could recognize when things weren't quite right. And this was one of those times, he knew. Yet, in spite of a nagging feeling in the pit of his stomach, he proceeded on, keeping the stallion at a walk rather than stopping altogether and tipping his hand.

In preparation he slid his Winchester rifle from its saddle boot and carried it in his left hand, his thumb over the hammer, his finger inside the trigger guard. *Let the play begin,* he told himself, feeling the prickly sensation of being watched down the length of a gun barrel as he glanced along either side of the street.

It was with almost a sense of relief when he saw two of the three men step out of an alleyway and move to the middle of the street facing him. But the appearance of only two of them presented a whole new situation— where was the third? He stopped the stallion, swung down from his saddle and swatted his gloved hand on the animal's wet rump, sending it out of the street. The big Appaloosa loped into a nearby alleyway, turned and stood staring out at him through its dark eyes.

"Step away from me, Riley," one of the gunmen, a wild Wyoming outlaw named Virgil Bates, whispered to the other, a West Texan killer named Bertram Riley. "Let's get him standing still, talking, while our shooter draws a good bead on him."

"You've got it," answered Riley. "I can't wait to see his brains hit the dirt, this sumbitch." He spat in the ranger's direction and sidestepped out across the street. "I've never been dogged so long, nor so hard in my life."

"Then pay attention," said Bates. "It's time we stuck this ranger underground."

From the middle of the street, the young ranger watched as the two eased forward like two stalking wolves, their hands poised beside their holstered Colts.

"You are a case to beat all others, boy, you know that?" Virgil Bates called out to the ranger. He stopped forty feet away and planted his feet firmly. "I can't tell you how many times I have wanted to stop and choke you to death with my bare hands this past week."

"You are one annoying little *law dog*, Ranger," said Riley, also stopping, standing with twenty feet between him and his partner.

Sam could not shake the feeling that he was being sighted down on at that very moment. But he had a job to do. He stopped and planted his feet shoulder width apart. Ignoring their taunting, he called out to them in an official tone, "Virgil Bates and Bertram Riley, you are both under arrest for murder, robbery and arson. Loosen your gun belts and let them fall to the ground."

The two killers chuckled. "Hear that, Riley?" said Bates. "He wants us to drop our gun belts in the dirt, like common saddle tramps."

"I heard it," said Riley. He called out to the ranger, "We'd get our nice, clean guns all dirty if we did like you said, boy. Did you even consider that before you asked?"

"I didn't *ask*," Sam said calmly, but with iron in his voice. "I'm taking you both in to stand before the territorial judge."

As he spoke, his right hand went matter-of-factly around the big Colt on his hip and raised it deftly from the holster as if he'd only brought it up to show it to them. Then his thumb pulled back the hammer with a resolved click. In his left hand, the barrel of his rifle tipped upward slowly at the same time, making the same sound as his left thumb cocked it.

"I'll be damned . . . ," Bates murmured.

Both outlaws gave a strange, dumbfound look, seeing the two open gun bores staring at them, both hammers back, ready to fire. Somehow the two gunmen had allowed this pup of a ranger to get the drop on them. It was that simple and smooth, no warning, no threat. All in clear view, as easily as if he'd drawn a pipe from his pocket.

"You ain't taking me no-damn-where," Riley shouted, angered that he'd been caught off guard even with his eyes on the serious young man. "You've been wanting to take a bite out of the Black Valley Riders. Here I am!" He stepped forward; his hand went for his gun. But even as he made his play, his eyes took a fast glance upward along the roofline.

From that roofline, the ranger caught the flash of sunlight on a gun barrel as he pulled the trigger on his own Colt and felt it buck in his hand.

Here it comes, ambush. . . .

His shot hit Riley dead center and sent him spinning backward as his Remington slipped out of its holster and fell from his hand.

There was no time to turn away from Bates long enough to deal with the hidden rifleman. The ranger fired his Winchester one-handed, and noted a look of satisfaction come over Bates' face, as if the outlaw knew that even as he died, the ranger was dying with him.

Bates staggered backward as the rifle bullet caught him squarely in his chest, and the ranger spun toward the roofline. He knew beyond hope that he was too late, yet he had to play it out. There stood the third man, Bobby Boy Parsons, who had stepped boldly out of the shadow of a roof facade, knowing he had the advantage—and making the best of it.

The ranger made his move in spite of the futility of it. His hand snapped the big Colt upward, expecting Parsons' rifle shot to hit him any second. He braced himself. But instead of seeing a blast of fire and smoke erupt from Parsons' aimed gun barrel, he saw the gunman jerk straight up onto his toes and appear to hang suspended in thin air for a moment.

Then Parsons' head exploded silently in a red, bloody mist, and his body crumbled. He fell from the rooftop like a broken child's toy as the sound of a distant gunshot caught up with itself and rolled like thunder across the badlands floor.

Sam spun in the street, guns in hand, prepared for anything, not knowing what to expect.

"Hold your fire, Ranger!" a voice called out.

Turning toward the sound of the voice and a rumble of a horse's hooves, he saw a single rider come rounding out of an alleyway at a fast gallop. Sam held his fire, but he remained poised and ready. The rider reined the horse down less than ten feet from him, and the ranger couldn't help noticing the Mameluke sword hanging from the man's saddle horn.

"Stand down, sir," the man said as if issuing an order. "We mean you no harm."

We . . . ? The ranger gave a quick look around.

"I'm Cadden Thorn, bounty hunter," said the rider, holding his empty hands chest high in a show of peace. He gestured toward the body of Bobby Parsons, most of the top of his skull missing, lying in the dirt where he'd fallen. "We're claiming the bounty on Parsons. I charge you to give witness to his death."

We, again . . . Sam cut another glance along the empty street—empty, save for the curious heads of wary townsfolk beginning to poke forward from store doorways along the boardwalk.

Seeing the ranger's apprehension, the tall, lean, older bounty hunter said beneath a straight-trimmed graying mustache, "At ease, Ranger. If I meant you harm, you wouldn't be upright at this moment."

The ranger didn't like what he took to be a veiled threat, or at least a declaration that this bounty hunter had some sort of an advantage over him.

"But I am *upright*, Mr. Thorn," the ranger replied, cocking the Colt menacingly in his right hand. "If you want to remain *upright* yourself, you best explain what's going on here." As he spoke he gestured toward Parsons' body in the dirt.

The bounty hunter gave a tight smile of admiration, liking the way the young ranger handled himself. "Never back an inch, eh, Ranger?"

"I'm not in the backing business, mister," Sam said. He stared, awaiting an answer.

"Well spoken, *Ranger Burrack*," said Thorn, letting the ranger know that he realized who he was talking to. He gave a slight nod toward the hill line where the shot had come from and said, "That was my man's shot. He's on his way here right now. We came here for these Black Valley Riders. Had you not killed those two, most likely we would have. As it turns out, we're claiming the five-hundred-dollar bounty on Bobby Boy Parsons." He paused, then added, "That is, if you have no objection."

Sam looked out and saw the rise of dust coming toward town from the hill line. He eased the hammer down on his Colt. Settling, he let out a breath and said, "No objections. The fact is, your man might have saved my life."

"Might have?" Thorn said wryly.

Sam nodded. "All right, he *did* keep me from taking a bullet . . . obliged," he said. He lowered the Colt into his holster without replacing the spent cartridges, but he kept his Winchester in hand, ready, but not at high guard.

"Our pleasure, sir," said Thorn. He touched two fingers to his hat brim, almost in a salute. Sam noted the small brass eagle that pinned the front of Thorn's hat brim up against its battered crown. The Eagle stood spread-winged, atop a globe and anchor.

The Marine Corps emblem . . . , the ranger told himself.

"That's right, Ranger," said Thorn as if reading the ranger's thoughts. "I'm Captain Cadden Thorn, United States Marines . . . *emeritus*, by choice, of course." His right hand touched the handle of his sword in a sign of respect.

"Of course," said Sam. Now that he'd noted the eagle globe and anchor, Sam also noted the big military-style holster strapped across Thorn's abdomen, its leather flap closed over the butt of a big Colt horse pistol.

"Ranger Burrack!" the town sheriff called out from

the boardwalk. "Pardon me for barging in if you two are not all finished shooting the living hell out of my town, but just what the blazes is going on here?"

Sam turned to the boardwalk as the sheriff stepped down and walked forward. "Mr. Thorn, this is Sheriff Paul Braden," Sam said. To the sheriff he said, "Sheriff Braden, this is Cadden Thorn, a bounty hunter trailing the same gang I'm after."

The sheriff and the bounty hunter gave each other a respectful nod.

"Those damn Black Valley Riders," said Braden, looking away from Thorn and down at the bodies strewn on the dirt street. "I should've known."

"I would have come to you first if I'd had the time, Sheriff," Sam said. "But while I had these three gathered close, I figured I best get it done."

"Except for Parsons, Sheriff," Thorn cut in. "*We* shot him."

"We? Who's *we*?" Braden asked, looking all around.

"My partner, Sheriff," said Thorn. He gestured a nod in the direction of the rise of dust as it neared the dirt street from the stretch of sandy flatlands. "Here he comes now."

Chapter 2

As the younger bounty hunter rode up onto the dirt street, Sheriff Paul Braden said in a lowered voice just between himself and the ranger, "Who are these two *bounty hunters*, Burrack? Why have I never seen them before, or at least heard of them?"

"You know as much about them as I do, Sheriff," the young ranger replied. "I've never laid eyes on them before." He nodded at the man riding toward them. "I only know that this one kept me from catching a bullet." Having noted the sword hanging from Thorn's saddle horn, he now saw the handle of a shorter sword sticking out of the younger man's bedroll.

"Well," Braden said with resolve, "bounty money is payable to whoever earns it." He looked at the bodies on the street. "I still don't like the notion that somebody can ride into my town, rub out three men and leave here with a poke full of cash for doing it."

"Two of those dead men I killed, Sheriff," Sam replied quietly.

"That's different," said the sheriff. "You've got a

badge given to you by the Territory of Arizona, giving you the authority."

"And they've got a bounty *poster*, which guarantees any man a reward for bringing these outlaws to justice, Sheriff." Sam met the sheriff's eyes as the young bounty hunter reined his horse down a few feet from his partner. "When the territory puts a price on a man, they know somebody's going to try to collect it."

"Point taken," said the sheriff, turning his attention to the bounty hunters as the two stepped down from their saddles.

Sam noted that the young bounty hunter waited until Thorn's boots touched the ground before swinging down himself. When the two stood facing the ranger and the sheriff, the young Cubano stood a step behind Thorn, the big Swiss rifle in hand.

"Gentlemen," Thorn said proudly, "I'd like you to meet my associate, Mr. Dee Sandoval." To the Cubano he said formally, "Mr. Sandoval, meet Sheriff Paul Braden and Ranger Samuel Burrack."

"Sheriff Braden, I am pleased to make your acquaintance, sir," the Cubano said respectfully, touching his gloved fingertips to the brim of his dusty hat.

Braden returned Sandoval's greeting, touching his own hat brim in response.

Turning from Braden to the ranger, Sandoval said in a quiet voice, "Ranger Burrack, I have heard much about you. It is an honor to meet you."

"The honor is mine," Sam said in the same courteous tone. "I'm obliged to you for saving my life." He gestured toward the body of Bobby Parsons lying in the dirt, where a wide puddle of blackening blood surrounded his head. Then he looked out at the distant hill line a good thousand yards away. "That was some good shooting," he added.

Sandoval only nodded.

The sheriff stepped in closer to admire the big Swiss rifle in the young Cubano's hand. "That must be some special kind of rifle, making a shot like that," he said. As he spoke he reached out as if asking Sandoval to hand the rifle to him.

But Dee Sandoval held on to the rifle. "Are you asking me *officially* to surrender my weapon, Sheriff Braden?" he asked somberly.

"Well, no, not *officially*," Braden said. He looked a little embarrassed. "I just thought I'd take a look at it, is all."

Sandoval looked to Thorn as if for guidance.

Thorn ignored the matter altogether and said to the sheriff, "Will there be any difficulty in us taking our reward today?"

"None that I can see," Braden said. "I can sign off on an affidavit, send you to the bank, get you paid and on your way, if that's to your suiting."

"It is," Thorn said. "Some towns get a little edgy if we stay around after our work is finished."

"Not my town," Braden was quick to inform him. "But if you two are ready to push on, I'll accommodate you as best I can."

"Obliged, Sheriff," said Thorn.

Braden looked to the ranger and said, "It hardly seems fair. You shoot down two killers face-to-face and get *no* reward."

"I get paid to do my job. It's fair," Sam said, in a voice that asked for no further discussion.

"But still . . ." Braden let his words settle for a second, then nodded at the other two bodies. "What if I signed off on these two as well?" He looked back and forth between the ranger and the bounty hunters. "The three of you could settle up the reward money to suit yourselves."

Before Sam could reply, Thorn cut in, saying, "Mr. Sandoval and I take no pay for work we didn't do. Parsons is the bounty we have coming."

"I understand," Braden said quickly. He looked to the ranger. "I was only suggesting that the three of you, and even myself as far as that goes—"

"Sheriff," Sam said, cutting him off, "these gentlemen want to get on their way. So do I, for that matter."

Braden took on a sullen look. "In that case I'll just trouble you three to give me a few minutes while I take care of the paperwork." He said to the ranger, "I'll need you to come with me, Samuel, to witness what you saw and help identify these Black Valley gunmen."

"All right," said the ranger, "anything to help." Along the boardwalk he saw townsmen beginning to move forward, looking at the dead bodies strewn about in the dirt street.

"Obliged to both of you," said Thorn. He stepped back to his horse. "You'll find us at the Big Winner, after we attend to our animals," he said, gesturing toward the big clapboard saloon occupying half a block along the dirt street. A giant hand-painted mug of foamy beer stood beckoning from a large sign. Beneath the frothing mug a giant pair of painted dice lay as if tumbling toward the street below. Through the open doors of the saloon, a stream of townsfolk filed out onto the street looking all around at the dead.

"Make yourselves to home," said Braden. Looking at Thorn and Sandoval, he said in a warning tone for the benefit of the gathering townsfolk converging now from every direction, "But keep your guns holstered and your manners in check."

Cadden Thorn gave a thin trace of a smile as he and Sandoval turned their horses to lead them toward the saloon. "Sheriff, you'll hardly know we're here," he said over his shoulder.

As the two walked away toward the saloon, Sheriff Braden said to two of the gathering townsmen, "Jake, you and Charles line these bodies up. Let everybody get a good look, then haul them over behind the barbershop."

"Sure thing, Sheriff," answered one of the men.

Looking back toward the two bounty hunters, Braden said to the ranger, "Isn't that a marine eagle on Thorn's hat?"

"Yes, it is," Sam said. "He called himself a captain, *emeritus*."

"Meaning . . . ?" the sheriff asked.

Staring after the two bounty hunters, noting the tall leather leghorns reaching up to Thorn's knees, the ranger said, "Meaning, he retired his marine commission but doesn't want to give it up just yet."

"Yeah, I think I understand what you mean," said Braden, also staring as the two walked through the approaching onlookers to the hitch rail out in front of the Big Winner Saloon. "It must be hard walking away from that kind of a life. I'd like to know what his story is."

"Sandoval's too," said the ranger, watching the young Cuban walk three steps behind Thorn into the saloon, the big Swiss rifle still in hand.

Now that the gun battle was over, the bodies in the dirt street had drawn the afternoon drinking crowd away from the Big Winner Saloon. The only remaining patron, a thin, pale-faced gambler, sat at an empty gaming table idly shuffling a deck of cards. He looked toward the two bounty hunters when they stopped and stood at the bar, looking back and forth for the bartender.

"It appears that you gentlemen may have passed the bartender on his way across the street," the gambler said in a whiskey-tilted voice. "Speaking on behalf of the Big Winner Saloon, I bid you both *help yourselves*."

"Obliged," said Thorn.

Sandoval reached across the bar top, took two shot glasses from a row of clean glasses and stood them in front of Thorn and himself. Instead of walking behind the unattended bar and taking down an unopened bottle of rye, he uncorked a house bottle the bartender had stood to the side for his single-shot customers.

Thorn picked up his glass and tipped it toward Sandoval in a toast. "Here's to keeping up the good work, Sandy."

Sandoval nodded. "To the good work."

Both men raised their glasses to their lips. But before the two could take a drink, above them on the second landing a door flew open and a bare-chested gunman charged out, his big six-gun blazing.

From his empty table the lone drunken gambler sat watching as both bounty hunters spun from the bar toward the upper landing. Thorn's big horse pistol came out of its flapped holster in one long, sleek motion. Sandoval's Army Colt came up from a shoulder rig worn high under his left arm. Both men fired as one as shots from the gunman above them zipped past their heads.

In the room behind the gunman, a young woman let out a scream, the bounty hunters' bullets splattering her with blood from the two exit wounds in the shirtless man's back.

The gunman, a thief and killer named Earl Baggett, broke through the second-floor handrail and crashed headlong onto the plank floor below, the impact of his fall jarring the entire building. His Remington revolver spun three full circles on the sawdust floor like an instrument in some deadly game of chance, then stopped and lay two feet from his fingertips. Smoke curled up from the long barrel.

"My, my," the lone gambler said, watching quietly, not the least rattled by the roar of gunshots, the screams or the flying bullets.

Along the bar top a mug of foamy beer had exploded from one of Baggett's shots. The impact of it had knocked over an open whiskey bottle. Beer and whiskey ran over the edge of the bar to the dirty floor. A spittoon that had been knocked over onto its side rolled back and forth on its belly until it settled against the iron boot rail.

Baggett's dead eyes stared wide and aimless across a spreading sea of sawdust and blood. The gaping exit wounds in his back revealed fragmented remains of heart and bone matter. A cloud of gray powder smoke loomed above the bounty hunters and rose slowly into the rafters.

"Adios, Early . . . ," the gambler said under his breath. He tipped his glass toward the limp, bloody body, then tossed back a drink of rye and went back to idly shuffling a deck of cards atop his empty table. He gave a slight shrug as the two bounty hunters turned toward the sound of his hushed voice in the ringing silence.

"I'm just paying my final respects, sir," he said in a refined Southern accent. His words did not hint at the large amount of rye he'd drunk throughout the day.

"Friend of yours?" Thorn asked. He held a bone-handled Colt horse pistol in hand, its barrel raised upward, but poised and ready.

"My friend? Not particularly," the gambler said. "Yet by no means would I call him *my enemy*."

Thorn took note of the man's pale skin, his loose-fitting black linen suit—a string tie above a silk brocaded vest. Near the edge of the table stood a tall, dark green top hat; a rip along the edge of its high flat crown had been repaired with black thread.

"But you *do* know him?" said Dee Sandoval, the younger bounty hunter. He stood three feet from Thorn, scanning along the second-floor landing as he spoke. A women's frightened face peeped out of a narrowly opened door, then jerked back as she shut the door quickly.

"Indeed I *did* know him," the gambler replied. "I daresay every reprobate on this godforsaken Western frontier knew *Early* Earl Baggett." He looked down at

Baggett's body and said in a tone of regret, "I planned on getting to know him *much better* once he finished satisfying his more *primal* needs." He sighed and laid the deck of cards down between his clean pale hands. "You appear to have put the hiatus on that plan."

"Earl Baggett . . . ," Thorn said, recognizing the name. "When did he ride in here?" he asked. As he posed the question, he walked over to the gambler's table.

"How might *I* know such a thing as that?" the gambler asked in reply. He cleared his throat, reached over and refilled his empty shot glass from a bottle of rye. He tipped the bottle toward Thorn and glanced toward a chair across the table from him.

Thorn declined the drink, but he pulled out the chair and seated himself. "It strikes me you would know just about everything that goes on around here," he said. Raising his holster flap, he slid his big horse pistol into a belly-style rig running across his lower abdomen, leaving the flap open. Leveling a curious gaze, he added, "As a matter of fact, you look awfully familiar yourself."

"Don't try buffaloing me, sir. It won't work," the gambler said. "And be careful saying that you've seen me before. That would imply that you have been in the same places I've been—something you might not want to freely admit in Christian company."

"I meant it," said Thorn. "You look familiar, though I can't say from where."

"I might look familiar, sir, but I am not," the gambler said with finality on the subject. He gave a faint smile and said with satisfaction, "I watch and I listen, as my vocation requires." He raised his glass, sipped at the rye, then set the glass down. "I'm Tinnis Lucas, at your service," he said. "And you . . . ?" He gazed expectantly, awaiting a reply.

Thorn just stared at him.

The gambler gave up. He made another shrug and looked the bounty hunters over.

Military man . . . , Lucas said to himself. He knew their type. Oh yes, he thought, he knew their type all too well. . . .

Behind Thorn, Dee Sandoval remained standing, positioned quarterwise to the second-floor landing. He kept a watchful eye along the line of doors beyond the broken handrail, particularly the one where he'd seen the women's face, as he punched out the smoking empty cartridge from his Colt and replaced it.

"So, you two are *soldiers of the sea*, I take it," the gambler said, seeing the same bearing, the same preciseness and economy in the young man's demeanor that he saw in Thorn's.

Without answering, Thorn stared straight into Tinnis Lucas' eyes and went back to his original question in the same tone of voice. "How long ago did Earl Baggett ride into town? Which way did he come from?"

The gambler shrugged and said reluctantly, "Earlier today. I'm afraid I neglected to check either my watch or my compass." He avoided Thorn's stare, as if avoiding it might make it go away.

But it didn't. Thorn's eyes demanded more answers.

Lucas put him off, gesturing a nod at Thorn's hat brim. "I'm familiar with that eagle and anchor insignia from back in Charleston Harbor."

"Good for you," Thorn said. "Who rode in with Baggett?"

"My goodness, man!" said Lucas. "How many questions are you going to ask me?"

"As many as it takes," said Thorn. "I don't want to think you knew that man was going to try to kill us and you weren't going to warn us he was there. That would be upsetting."

"Yes, I can allow as how it would," said Lucas, his face looking more and more concerned, as if his whiskey was suddenly leaving him flat.

"Who rode in with Earl Baggett?" Thorn asked again. He slipped the long horse pistol back out of the belly holster and laid it atop the table pointing at the gambler.

"Come, now, Mr. Thorn," Lucas said drunkenly, "you wouldn't harm an unarmed man, would you?" He started to reach up and open the lapel of his black linen suit coat. But Thorn leaned forward, reached over the table and stopped him.

"I don't know any *unarmed men*," said Thorn, opening the gambler's lapel himself and pulling a short Colt Thunderer from a shoulder harness beneath Lucas' left arm.

"I was going to take it out and disarm myself," Lucas said, his cool demeanor starting to change, grow less confident, a little edgy and unsettled.

Thorn inspected the Thunderer, hefted it in his hand as if to get a feel for it. He looked the ivory-handled gun over. "Who rode in with Earl Baggett?" he persisted.

"Come on, gentlemen, please," said Lucas, raising

his hands chest high in a show of peace. "A fellow can get himself killed spreading too much information around in this blasted hellhole."

"A fellow can get himself pistol-whipped with his own gun too, if he's not careful," said Sandoval.

"I'm through talking," Thorn said.

"Bravo, sir. I feared the end would never come," the gambler said.

Chapter 3

Inside the sheriff's office, the ranger had just poured himself a cup of strong coffee from a pot on the wood-stove when the gunshots resounded from the Big Winner Saloon. He set the steaming cup down and picked up his rifle from where it stood leaning against the sheriff's desk.

Braden, seated at his desk, stared up at the ranger for a second through a thick pair of reading spectacles. He stuck his ink pen back into the inkwell and stood up.

"Here we go again," he said, taking off the spectacles and laying them down on the half-completed affidavit he'd been writing. He and Sam headed out the door.

"Sheriff, Sheriff!" a woman shrieked tearfully, her hands pressed to her cheeks in fear and despair. "What's happening to our town?"

Seeing the gathered townsfolk turn their attention from the bloodstained street to the big clapboard saloon, Braden ignored her and said to the ranger over his shoulder, "I'm starting to wonder if these two sailors are going to be more trouble than they're worth."

"Not sailors," Sam corrected him, "marines."

"*Whatever* they are," Braden grumbled.

Inside the Big Winner Saloon, Lucas held out as long as he could. He didn't know if Thorn was bluffing or not about pistol-whipping him with his own gun. But he was sobering fast and he didn't like his odds. "All right," he said, speaking faster, seeing Thorn's hand tighten around the butt of his own shiny nickel-plated Colt. "Early Baggett rode in with Elmer Fisk and a couple of bummers I've never seen before. Baggett hitched his roan out front. The other three rode on to the water trough, watered their horses and themselves and headed north straightaway. That's the gospel on it."

"Elmer Fisk, also known as *Crazy* Elmer Fisk," Thorn said in recognition, "owing to how easily he loses his mind and kills people."

"That was him all right, Crazy Elmer in the flesh," said Lucas. "Now, gentlemen, are we all finished here?" He summoned enough drunken courage to start to rise from his chair. "Because if we are, I'd like my pistol back—"

"Almost," said Sandoval. "Sit down."

"*Almost?*" The gambler sighed and gave them both a dubious look. He sat back down. "This is a dangerous thing I'm doing," he said. "Leastwise, it's far too dangerous to be doing for free." He looked back and forth between the two of them.

"Tell us what you know about the Black Valley Riders gang," Thorn said undeterred.

"Whoa!" said Lucas. A wary look came to his caged eyes. "When it comes to *those* outlaws, I know less than a monkey knows about soap." A sheen of sweat seemed to appear out of nowhere across his forehead. He gave a guarded look toward the open doors, making sure the conversation wasn't being overheard. "No amount of pistol-whipping is going to change that."

"In that case . . ." Thorn reached into his duster pocket, took out a bag of coins and shook it enough to raise a sound of ringing silver. Then he dropped it onto the tabletop. ". . . you can start telling us everything you *don't* know about them," he said.

"Gentlemen, you can save your money," said the drunken gambler. "There are some things even a callous reprobate such as I will not discuss—"

From the open front door, Sheriff Braden's voice cut in, saying, "I can tell you about the Black Valley Riders. They're a bunch of murdering, thieving dogs."

Dee Sandoval's Colt had already swung to the sound of the voice. But upon seeing the sheriff and the ranger, he lowered the revolver an inch and stood back to allow them both closer to Thorn at the gambler's table.

Sam stopped and looked down at Baggett's body, the two bullet holes gaping up from the bloody, hairy back.

"Well, well, if it isn't our good Sheriff Braden," Lucas said, "and just in time." To the bounty hunters, he said, "There's nothing like the sound of money rattling in a bag to bring out our trusty law-enforcement officer."

"Shut your mouth, Lucas," the sheriff warned the gambler. He looked first at Sandoval, then at Thorn, and said, "I'd hardly know you are here."

"My sincere apologies, Sheriff," Thorn said. He gestured up at the broken handrail. "As you can see, we were put upon by surprise."

"I understand," said Braden. He looked at the Colt still in Sandoval's right hand. "You'll find I work better without a gun cocked at me, Mr. Sandoval."

Sandoval looked back and forth between the ranger and the sheriff, but he didn't lower the Colt any farther until the sheriff lifted his hand from the butt of his holstered pistol and stooped down over the body on the floor.

Raising the dead man's limp wrist, the sheriff pressed two fingers to it, found no pulse, then let the hand fall heavily back to the floor.

"He's dead," he said, out of habit, staring at the gaping hole in Baggett's hairy, naked back.

Lucas shook his head. "Congratulations, Sheriff. Care to take a guess at what might have killed him?"

The sheriff ignored the drunken gambler's remark. He stood up and gave Thorn a questioning look. "All right, what was *this one* about?"

"Same thing, Sheriff," said Thorn. "I take it that Baggett has partnered up with the Black Valley Riders. He rode in earlier and took a room. I figure he was waiting for the others to get here."

"Imagine, Sheriff, all of these desperadoes congregating in *your* town. How well does this bode for our law enforcement?"

"You're drunk, Lucas," the sheriff said, "and I don't

even like you when you're sober." He gave the gambler a hard stare. "Now keep your moth shut or I'll throw you in a cell for public drunkenness—"

Braden's words were cut short when the door on the second floor creaked open slowly and a half-naked young woman stepped out and looked down at them. "Sheriff, can I come down now?" she asked shyly, wearing only a pair of short pantaloons and clinging to a thin towel she held pressed to her breasts.

"Well, certainly you can, little darling," said Braden. To the ranger and the bounty hunters, the sheriff said, "Easy, fellows, that's just Mona Blaine. She's a good gal."

They watched as the woman walked along the landing and stopped atop the stairs. "He was in my room, you know," she offered quietly, looking over at the body lying on the floor. "He said he was supposed to be meeting some men here—supposed to be watching for them. But he wasn't. Instead he was all over me." She jerked a thumb toward the room she'd come out of. "His saddlebags are up there. His rifle is leaning beside the window."

Thorn, Sandoval and the ranger looked at one another.

"Gentlemen, let's go see what we can find out what this snake, Earl Baggett, was up to," said Braden. To Thorn and Sandoval he said, "You two cause a lot of commotion, but you do have a way of trimming back the rodent population."

"May I come along too, Sheriff? Lucas asked. He stood up.

Braden looked at him. "Can you walk?"

Lucas sat down. "Perhaps our darling Miss Mona will be kind enough to inform me afterwards," he said. He poured himself another glass of whiskey and drank it straight down.

Inside the room on the second floor, Sandoval walked straight to a window that looked onto a narrow alleyway running alongside the building. The girl, the sheriff and Thorn looked on as Sandoval raised the window and stuck his head out and looked back and forth. Beside the window a Winchester rifle stood leaning against the dingy flowered wallpaper.

"He didn't have much of a view from back here," Sandoval said. Gazing toward the front of the building, the young bounty hunter saw only a sliver of the dirt street they'd ridden in on.

"Once he got here, he seemed to lose interest in watching the street," said Mona with confidence, one hand propped on her well-rounded hip, her other hand holding the thin towel in place over her breasts. "You might say I saved you fellows' lives."

"Obliged, ma'am," said Thorn. He picked up Baggett's dusty saddlebags from the floor, opened them and dumped the contents out onto a small wooden table.

Braden leaned over and said discreetly into Mona's ear, "Maybe you'd like to put on some clothes, little darling."

Mona smiled and walked over to a robe hanging from a peg on the wall. She inspected it quickly for any blood splatter, then put it on, tossing the thin towel aside. Braden stared intently until her ample breasts disappeared behind the robe. "How was that, Sheriff?" Mona said softly.

"Tha-that was fine," Braden said, seeming to snap out of a light trance.

Rummaging through a pile of wadded-up dirty clothes, loose ammunition and various personal items, Thorn stopped and picked up a silver emblem, a sliver of a moon with a star hanging from it.

"Here we are, Mr. Sandoval," he said, holding the silver moon up for Dee Sandoval to see. "Every Black Valley Rider carries one."

Sheriff Braden and the woman stepped in closer for a better look. "You're right," said the sheriff. "I should be ashamed to admit it, but I've seen lots of trinkets being worn in my town of late. But if the man wearing one hasn't broken a law, there's really nothing I can say about it."

"I've seen some of my customers wearing them," the young woman offered. She shrugged. "I just thought they were the latest things in men's style."

The three men looked at her.

"It's starting to look like they are around here anyway," said Thorn, closing his fist around the gold ornament and giving Sandoval a knowing look.

Braden took exception to the bounty hunter's words and said, "Now, look, Thorn. I run a good clean town here. I can't keep men from riding in just because I don't like the accessories they're wearing."

"I never said you could, Sheriff," said Thorn.

"It sounded to me like you were implying something," said Braden, his hand falling deftly to his gun butt. Thorn's eyes followed the move, then went to meet Braden's gaze. The sheriff noticed the change in Thorn's expression, and quickly removed his hand and kept it clear. "Maybe I was a little too quick to take offense."

"Maybe you were," Thorn said.

Braden cut a glance to the ranger, who stood watching and listening, his Winchester rifle cradled in the crook of his arm. "Samuel here can tell you. I do the best I can to keep out the trash."

"You don't need me to speak on your behalf, Sheriff," the ranger said quietly.

"Especially not to us," Thorn put in. "If I made a careless choice of words, I take them back," he said to the sheriff. "No offense intended." Yet as he spoke to Braden, he stared straight at the ranger.

Sam returned the bounty hunter's flat stare, doubting if Cadden Thorn had made a careless choice of words in his entire life.

Braden appeared to consider Thorn's apology for a second, if indeed it were an apology. "In that case, no offense taken," he said, finally, cooling down as quickly as he'd flared up. "We're all on the same side of the law here. I expect we are all looking for the best way to go about doing our jobs."

"Yes, we're all the on same side of the law," Thorn said to the sheriff. "That being understood"—he turned his gaze back to the ranger—"what say the three of us throw in with one another for a time, Ranger Burrack? After all, we seem to be trailing the same men."

"I work alone," Sam said, leaving no invitation for further discussion of the matter.

"I know," said Thorn, "and I find it admirable that

you do." He gave a thin, tight smile. "Mr. Sandoval and I are much the same way. But with a gang this large and this spread out, maybe it would be more prudent of us to join our—" His words stopped short as he and the others turned toward the sound of boots pounding up the stairs.

"Sheriff, come quick!" a short red-faced man wearing a leather apron shouted as he charged into the open doorway and room and caught himself on the door frame with both hands.

"Good God, Clarence, what is it?" asked Braden, his hand once again snapping around his gun butt in reflex.

Clarence Bowes, the town blacksmith, blurted out in a voice full of rage and bewilderment, "Has our town gone completely to hell on us?"

"Well, I don't know, Clarence," Braden said stiffly. "Why don't you settle down and tell me what's going on? Maybe it's something—"

"It's that drunken gambler!" said Bowes. "Bad enough we've had two gunfights in less than an hour! Tinnis Lucas run out of here and stole a woman's day rig right out from under her!"

"Damn it all!" said Braden. "We just left him downstairs, too drunk to climb the stairs!"

"Then he wasn't as drunk as he let on," said the blacksmith.

The two bounty hunters and the ranger looked at one another knowingly.

"Damn it!" Braden shoved the blacksmith aside and walked out the door. "Lucas is a drunk and a cardsharp! He's no horse thief."

"By God, he is now," said the blacksmith, hurrying along behind him.

"Every time we turn over a rock, another Black Valley Rider jumps out," Thorn said, following the sheriff and the blacksmith out the door. On his way down the stairs, he said over his shoulder to the ranger, "Consider my offer, Ranger Burrack. It may well work to both of our advantage."

"I'm considering it," Sam replied. When he reached the bottom of the stairs, he spotted a woman standing just inside the saloon doorway, her hat lying lopsided atop her head, a long streak of dust on the side of her dress where she'd landed on her behind.

As the lawmen, the blacksmith and the horse theft victim walked out onto the street, Mona stood at the open door on the second floor and smiled down on the empty saloon and the body of Earl Baggett lying sprawled in blood on the sawdust floor. *So long, Early . . . ,* she said to herself.

Chapter 4

———◆———

Crazy Elmer Fisk sat atop his horse overlooking the trail that meandered across the stretch of flatlands into Minton Hill. With his naked eyes he watched Tinnis Lucas stand crouched above the buggy seat. The long tails of his swallow-tailed coat stood straight out behind him, flickering on the wind like the forked tongue of some deranged serpent. His tall top hat bounced and rolled on the buggy floor.

"Jesus!" Fisk murmured, watching the gambler fly up off his feet and come back down in place as the buggy bounced over a deep rut in the rocky trail. The impact launched a bottle of rye upward from within a wooden crate that sat beside Lucas on the driver's seat. The bottle came down midtrail and crashed in a spray of whiskey and broken glass. Back along the trail Fisk saw dark wet spots where other whiskey bottles had crashed in the buggy's wake. "And they call *me* crazy." He shook his head.

To the two men beside him, he said, "Get down there and stop that fool."

"I'll stop him," said Rudy Duckwald, an ill-tempered, off-and-on member of the James-Younger Gang. "I'll stop him on the end of a rope." He looked at the man beside him and said, "Come on, George. Let's get him and string him up."

"Whoa, hold on," said Fisk, stopping the two. "Just out of curiosity, why would you want to hang this drunken fool?"

Duckwald gave a mindless shrug. "I just like watching people hang." He spread an evil half grin. George Epson, his brother-in-law, gave him a strange puzzled look and backed away from him.

"I don't want Lucas harmed," said Fisk. "Just bring him up to me. Maybe he can tell us what's come over Minton Hill. I'll meet you farther along this high trail."

"What if he puts up a fight?" said Duckwald, sounding disappointed. "Can we go ahead and—"

"Damn it, he won't put up a fight, Rudy," Fisk spat. "Lucas is on our side. He keeps us informed on what's going on out here." He gave the burly gunman a stern glare. "Do you understand what I'm telling you?"

"Yeah, I got you," Duckwald said sullenly. "Let's go, George."

Fisk started to turn his horse, but he stopped again and called out, this time singling out Epson. "George, make sure you don't break any of that whiskey."

"Right, Fisk," said Epson. He gave a worried nod back over his shoulder and rode on.

"Since when did you become the one he puts in charge?" Duckwald grumbled, riding along beside him.

"I don't know," said Epson, "but I didn't ask for it and I don't like it."

"Neither do I," Duckwald said in his usual ill-natured growl.

In the open-topped buggy, Tinnis Lucas continued standing, racing and bouncing along for the next mile. When he rounded a turn in the trail and saw the two gunmen seated atop their horses facing him, he let the whip fall from his hand. With a loud *"Whoaaaa!"* he pulled back hard on the traces and brought the buggy to a sliding sidelong halt. Dust billowed and swirled.

"Holy Moses!" said Lucas. "Am I glad to see you gentlemen!" He looked at the coiled rope in Duckwald's hand and the sour expression on his face and said, "I see you're as warm and jovial as ever."

"You don't know half of it," Epson said. He stepped his horses forward and looked down to make sure not all of the bottles of whiskey had broken along the trail. "He wanted to hang you."

"Still do," said Duckwald.

A worried look came upon Lucas' face. "What is going on, gentlemen?" he asked. "Where's Fisk?"

"Fisk sent us to bring you up and meet him," said Duckwald, gesturing a nod toward the hill line.

"You left a string of broken whiskey bottles for the past five miles," said Epson, leaning over into the buggy and eyeing the open crate with a few unbroken bottles still inside.

"Not that this should mean anything to you," Lucas said, turning sarcastic, "but I took a big risk sneaking out of Minton Hill just to come warn Fisk and the rest of you."

"We appreciate it all to hell," Duckwald said in a flat

tone. "Now get moving before I can't help myself with this rope."

Lucas shook his head, picked up his top hat and put it on. "I don't know why I bother . . . ," he murmured under his breath. He settled onto the buggy seat, feeling better now that two gunmen were flanking him. "You know Clato Charo and his band of *Comadrejas* roaming out here.

"Clato and his Desert Weasels?" Epson looked all around, concerned, as if just saying the name might conjure up the band of desert killers. "Those sonsabitches give me the willies."

"Where'd you hear that?" Duckwald asked. He stepped his horse in closer beside his brother-in-law.

"The army came through Minton Hill a week ago," said Lucas. "They said they'd been hunting Charo and his warriors the past month." Lucas grinned, liking the way he'd unsettled the two gunmen. "The *Comadrejas* would slit a man gills to gullet to get their hands on a crate of this pure Missouri Red Rye whiskey."

"Rudy's right. We should get moving," Epson said, growing more wary at the thought of a band of wild-eyed *Comadrejas* riding down on them from the hill line.

"Indeed *we should* . . . and indeed *we will*," Lucas said. As he spoke, he reached into the crate, pulled up a bottle and jerked the cork from it. "First, let's get ourselves a little shot of grit and determination, just to keep our devils settled, eh, George? In case Charo kills us in our sleep." He raised the bottle and took a long swig.

"I don't like that kind of talk," Epson said, still looking all around. But as soon as Lucas lowered the bottle from his lips, George reached out to take it, only to see Duckwald snatch it from Lucas' hand.

"Sorry, George," said Lucas with a shrug as Duckwald took a long pull on the fiery rye, "*age before beauty*, as they say."

When Duckwald lowered the bottle and let out a hard belch, he passed it on to Epson. "Hurry it up. We're in a bad spot here for an ambush."

Epson took a long drink and passed the bottle back to Lucas, who looked at it and shook his head. Then he corked the nearly empty bottle and put it back inside the crate. "Gentlemen," he said, "let us proceed."

"After you, I *insist*," Duckwald said in a mocking surly voice, letting the gambler know that he didn't trust him riding behind his back.

Lucas gave a slight chuckle and sent the buggy horse forward with a quick cluck of his cheek and a touch of the reins. They rode on in silence.

A half hour later as the assemblage of buggy and horsemen rode upward on a path leading to a higher trail, Elmer Fisk stepped his horse from behind a white oak and waved his hat toward a hillside covered with saguaro and juniper. When Lucas and the other two joined him there, Fisk reached out expectantly for the bottle of rye as Lucas stopped the buggy horse.

"What the hell is going on in Minton Hill?" Fisk asked as he jerked the cork from the bottle and took a long drink. He lowered the bottle, let out a hiss and said before Lucas could answer, "Where's Baggett? Where's Parsons and the others?"

Lucas stared at him. "Good afternoon to you too, Elmer," he said. He held his hand out for the bottle.

But Elmer Fisk ignored him. He raised the bottle to his lips again, finished off the rye and tossed the empty bottle aside. "I don't waste my time on worthless formalities, gambler," he said, gruffly, wiping his shirt cuff across his lips.

"In that case, let me tell you straightaway," said Lucas. "Parsons is dead, so is Baggett . . . so are Bates and Riley." He gave the outlaw a reproachful look. "There, now, is that *informal* enough for you?"

"Damn!" said Fisk in surprise. "I heard all the shooting. I figured somebody was sucking air. But both Baggett, and the men he went there to meet? *Damn!* Who killed them, a railroad posse?"

"No posse," said Lucas. "It was that young ranger everybody's been talking about. The one who killed Junior Lake and his gang."

"Samuel Burrack . . . ," said Fisk. "I might have known they'd be sending that one after *me* before long. They want me awfully bad."

They . . . ? Lucas thought. *After him . . . ?*

Epson, Duckwald and Lucas all three looked at one another.

"The ranger killed them—all four?" Fisk asked the gambler.

"No," said Lucas. "The ranger had two marine bounty hunters with him."

"Two what?" Fisk asked.

"Two United States *Marines*," said Lucas. He stared, waiting for Fisk's reaction.

"Marines?" Fisk gave him a strange look. Gazing all around the dry desert hills in bewilderment for a moment, he finally said, "They've sent the *navy* after me?"

"No, not the *navy*," said Lucas. He sighed, reaching for another bottle of whiskey. "The *marines*."

"Either way, why'd they do something like that?" Fisk asked, still bewildered.

"I can't *begin* to guess," Lucas replied, uncorking the bottle, realizing it was going to take a while before Crazy Elmer understood that this was not entirely about himself.

"You said these two men are *bounty hunters*?" Epson said.

"That's right. They're bounty hunters," said the gambler. "I don't think the *navy* sent them." He gave Fisk a sarcastic look. "They didn't ride in with the ranger. I believe the three just come upon one another in their quest for you Black Valley boys." He turned his gaze back to Elmer Fisk. "They weren't after *you* alone, Elmer, if that's any consolation."

"Oh . . ." Elmer considered the matter, then said, "How come four good men are dead, and you're still alive, gambler?"

"Because I am not one of your gunmen, remember, Elmer?" said Lucas. "I only keep you informed." He paused, then added, "For *a price*, of course."

"Don't worry. You'll be taken care of," Fisk said grudgingly.

"I suppose we'll ride on back and kill these three, huh?" said Duckwald.

Fisk looked contemplative. "Damn. We've got four men dead, and we were all supposed to meet up and join Shear and the others for the train job." He rubbed his forehead beneath his hat brim.

Duckwald looked at Epson and Fisk and repeated, "I suppose we'll ride back to Minton Hill and—"

"No," said Fisk, cutting him short. "We're going on and meeting up with Big Aces. It's his gang. Let him decide what we need to do next."

Listening, Lucas looked away and shook his head. "I take it I won't get paid anything for my services until we meet up with Shear?"

"You've got that right, gambler," said Fisk. "You're Big Aces pet snake, not mine. Now strip that horse down and leave the buggy sitting. We're crossing hard country. A buggy won't get it."

"Where are we going?" Lucas asked.

"Don't worry about it," said Fisk. "You'll know when we get there."

"Of course, how *unthoughted* of me," Lucas said under his breath. "What about this whiskey?" he asked.

Looking at Epson and Duckwald, Fisk said, "Stuff the bottles in your saddlebags. We'll drink as much as we can to keep the rest from going to waste."

"Smart thinking," said Lucas. He stood up from the buggy seat and climbed down, lifting the whiskey crate and carrying it with him.

At the battered oak desk, the ranger and two bounty hunters watched Sheriff Braden sit down with the federal bills and gold coins he'd brought from the bank. When he'd counted the money, he placed his palms down on either side of the desk and pushed himself to his feet. Looking wistfully down at the cash, he said, "That's a powerful lot of money, gentlemen."

Thorn picked up the bills and thumbed through them. "It was a *powerful* job we did to earn it, Sheriff," he said. Beside him, Dee Sandoval raked the coins into a leather pouch and pulled its drawstring tight.

"I meant no offense, sir," Braden said to Thorn.

"I took none, sir," replied Thorn. He stuffed the folded bills into a pocket inside his duster and looked to the ranger, who stood cradling his Winchester, watching.

"Ranger Burrack, we are ready to leave, if you are, sir."

"I'm ready," said the ranger. The three had agreed to ride together as far as the hill line on the other side of the flatlands surrounding town. From there they would split up and ride the high trails separately, knowing that in all likelihood their paths would cross again, most any time.

"As much as I'll miss good company," said Braden, as he followed the men out the door onto the boardwalk, "I'm glad to see the three of you clear on out of here. Minton Hill is not used to this kind of action. I left Dodge City for this very reason."

Stepping down to the hitch rail, Sam and the bounty hunters touched their hat brims toward the sheriff, mounted their waiting horses and rode away. Along the street, townsfolk stared as if watching a short parade as the three filed past. Riding a few feet ahead of Sandoval and the ranger, Thorn took off his battered hat and dipped it with an air of modest grandeur toward the onlookers.

"It is his way," Sandoval said quietly, as if Thorn's behavior needed explaining. "We are bounty hunters now, but we're still marines through and through." He touched his gloved fist to his heart. *"Semper fidelis,"* he murmured in Latin, booting his horse forward.

Always faithful . . . , the ranger reminded himself. He rode alongside Sandoval, the three of them following the fresh buggy tracks the gambler had left in the dirt street.

When they had ridden out of Minton Hill, onto the rocky flatlands, the three stopped their horses and formed a huddle over the first broken whiskey bottle lying in the trail. Thorn sat with his left hand resting on the butt of his sword. He looked back toward town, then down at the broken bottle.

"We were right about the gambler, Sandy," he said to the younger man. "We squeezed him, turned him loose and he flew right on away."

"Good move," said the ranger. "No gang this size can stay in business without eyes and ears like Lucas telling them where it's safe to be."

Looking at the ranger, Thorn said, "Did you have any notion this place would be crawling with Black Valley Riders when you rode in?" As he spoke he pulled a pouch of chopped tobacco from inside his duster. He took out a plug between his thumb and fingers and passed the bag on to Sandoval.

"No," said Sam, "but this territory is full of surprises." He looked the two bounty hunters up and down. "You two are a good example. I'm used to most bounty hunters stopping short at the badlands."

"Oh . . . ?" Thorn shoved the plug of tobacco into his

jaw. "You'll find we are not timid, Ranger. We never stop until a job is completed."

"Then you'll do well here," Sam said, taking the tobacco pouch as Sandoval handed it to him. "Or else you'll end up dead." He took out a small plug of chew and handed the pouch back to Thorn.

The two bounty hunters looked at each other. "No gun work is more fair than that," Thorn said dismissingly. He took the pouch and put it away. "What do you think of Sheriff Braden?"

"He's always been a good man," the ranger said. "Not the best, but good."

"Is he a part of this bunch we're after?" asked Thorn.

"I doubt it," said Sam.

"But you won't say he's not," Sandoval cut in.

"I said 'I doubt it,'" Sam repeated.

"He talked like a man willing to bend things around for a taste of money," Thorn said.

"It didn't happen, though," Sam said.

"Because he saw none of us would go for it," Sandoval countered.

"Right," Sam said, "we showed him we all three walk straight. Sometimes that's all a man needs to hold himself together." He looked back and forth between the two men. "A man like Braden works out here alone, nobody like himself around. Sometimes he loses sight of what he's supposed to be doing. Once a man gets off his axis, he starts thinking money will get him back on. It never does."

Thorn chewed his tobacco, spat and contemplated the matter. "So Braden's offer of padding the reward money was just his way of asking us to lead him?"

"Yes," said Sam, "and us turning him down was our way of leading him right." He turned his stallion back to the trail at a walk. The other two did the same. "But I get the feeling you already knew all that, Thorn," he said, "as many men as you've commanded."

The two bounty hunters looked at each other and rode on. Thorn smiled to himself. Looking all around in the failing light, he said, "This is a big, wild, dangerous place we're in, Sandy." He took a deep breath and let it out freely. "It's good to be here."

Chapter 5

By dusk, the ranger and the two bounty hunters had followed broken whiskey bottles and buggy tracks to the empty rig sitting beside the trail. From there they had followed hoofprints upward to a higher trail overlooking the darkened flatlands. In the light of a half-moon, the three built a fire on a flat cliff that cut deep into the hillside.

Sheltered by towering chimney rock, they ate a meal of jerked elk, hardtack and hot coffee. When they'd finished eating, Sandoval pulled the short sax-style sword from his bedroll and laid it under his saddle alongside his Army Colt. On the other side of the campfire, Thorn laid his long Mameluke sword out alongside his bedroll, picked up his Spencer rifle and his tin cup of coffee and walked away into the darkness without a word.

"I can stand first watch," Sam said to Sandoval as Thorn disappeared into the night.

"Not in his camp," Sandoval said. "Captain Thorn always stands first watch. It is his way."

"Captain Thorn?" Sam said, hoping for an opportunity to find out more about the two.

"Yes," said Sandoval, "even though his rank is now honorary, he is still Captain Thorn to me."

"How long did you serve under Thorn's command?" Sam asked.

"All my life," Sandoval said quietly. "My full name is Dee Espinaz Guerrero Sandoval. Do you know what that means, Ranger?" he asked with a level gaze.

"Yes," Sam replied. "*Espina* is Spanish for *Thorn*. So, *Espinaz* means *son of Thorn*."

"Very good," Sandoval acknowledged.

"*Guerrero* means warrior," Sam continued.

"Yes," said Sandoval, "I am Thorn's son, the Warrior. Sandoval is my mother's surname, as is the custom of my people." He raised a finger for emphasis. "I am his *legitimate* son."

"I understand," Sam said. "I wasn't going to pry."

"No, I did not think you were," said Sandoval. "Yet I tell you this because I am proud to be the *legitimate* son of my father, Captain Cadden Thorn."

Sam noted the slightest Spanish accent slip into the man's voice as he spoke about his heritage.

"My mother and father met in Havana while he was on his first duty in Cuba as a young lieutenant. Neither of their religions would allow them to legally wed. When I was born the captain had left Cuba and returned to the United States. He did not know he had a son until I was eleven years old. That is when my mother died and the priest of my village wrote to the captain and told him about me."

Sam only watched and listened.

Sandoval continued. "But when the captain took leave and came for me, I had run away. I worked on the cracker cattle boats from Havana to Florida. The captain found me at the cattle chutes in Punta Rassa four years later. When I turned fifteen he signed me on as a marine into the Spartan Regiment. I learned to shoot at the enemies of my country from within the topsails of a moving ship."

"I saw some of that fine shooting," Sam remarked. "And I have never seen any better."

"Thank you, Ranger," Sandoval said modestly. "All marines are crack shots. But in my case it was most important that I be the best." He gazed off toward the darkness Thorn had walked into. "Captain Thorn had legally given me his name, and the marines had made me a citizen of this country." He smiled proudly. "I had to be the *best of the best*, for the sake of my father, and for my beloved United States of America."

At the edge of the firelight, Thorn cleared his throat and said quietly as he walked back into sight, "I see Mr. Sandoval has told you a little about us, Ranger. I hope it hasn't been too boring to suit you." He puffed on a briar pipe. Smoke wafted away on a night breeze.

"Not at all, Captain Thorn," Sam said respectfully. "I'm privileged to have heard it."

"Oh, it's *Captain* now, is it?" Thorn said. "Careful, Ranger. We might have you counting cadence before this pursuit is over."

The ranger gave an easy smile. "I have the highest regard for the military, Captain Thorn."

"The *marines*," said Sandoval as if correcting him.

"Yes, the marines too," Sam said. He looked at Sandoval, estimating the young man's age to around the same as his own. "You left the military."

"Yes," said Sandoval. He gave Thorn a look, then replied to the ranger, "My hitch ran out a year ago. But soon I must make a decision to either go back to duty or forfeit my rank and leave the Marine Corps for good—"

Sam started to say something, but Thorn cut the conversation short with a raised hand and a gesture toward the sound of something moving on the brushy hillside beneath them. The three stared into the darkness in silence until they all heard the unmistakable sound of a horse chuff as it moved through the creosote brush.

"Hey, you *damn white men*," a voice called out in stiff English, giving away any chance of surprise. "We have you surrounded, you damn white men. Now you must give me all of your whiskey and your horses for crossing my *disierto*. You must do so *mas pronto*."

"What is this? Who's out there?" Sandoval asked the ranger in a whisper. He stooped and picked up his short sword from beside his bedroll, letting the studded leather sheath fall from the gleaming steel blade. With his free hand he drew his Colt from its holster. Near the fire sat two unbroken bottles of whiskey they'd salvaged from the brush alongside the trail.

"They're called *Comadrejas*," the ranger whispered in reply, slipping along in a crouch. Both he and Sandoval left the glow of firelight, Sam's rifle ready in hand.

"Weasels?" Sandoval asked.

"Yes, Desert Weasels," Sam replied in a hushed tone,

readying himself at the edge of the firelight. "Their numbers have grown bigger and bolder of late."

"Then we must do something about that," Sandoval said matter-of-factly.

Thorn also stepped out of the firelight, yet he did so standing tall, his big horse pistol out at arm's length, cocked, his feet planted firmly beneath him. "You there," he demanded in a booming voice, "advance, and be recognized." He held the big Mameluke sword in his left hand, the blade dipped back, ready to strike.

"Ha, you make me laugh, you damn white man," said the voice.

Thorn homed his senses toward the strange sounding voice. "I'm happy that I amuse you, sir," he said, the big Colt horse pistol tensed in his hand as he searched the cliff line in the darkness. "Now do as you're told," he said forcefully. "Come forward and be recognized. That is an order." Behind him Sandoval cocked his Colt quietly.

"You give me no order! You do not tell me what to do," said the enraged voice. "This is *mi desierto*. I tell you what to—"

Thorn locked on to the sound of the voice. His pistol bucked in his hand and silenced it. "This is *my desert* now," he shouted.

A thrashing of brush and rock resounded as the man tumbled backward down over the edge of the cliff into the engulfing blackness. A cacophony of war cries rose from the brush alongside the trail. Thorn took a quick step to the side as a long spear sliced through the air past his ear. His thumb cocked the pistol again as the ranger and Sandoval unleashed their Colts toward the flashes of gunshots in the darkness.

The ranger fired repeatedly into a flood of ragged warriors who stormed upward over the edge of the dark cliff onto the flat rock plateau. Bullets zipped past him. Yet, even as he fired and moved sidelong farther away from the glow of the campfire, he saw Thorn raise the sword and wave it forward. As if following an order to charge, Sandoval pressed forward, firing as a hail of bullets sliced past him.

Sam stopped and moved forward with them as he fired, seeing that the three of them had actually begun to press the stunned *Comadrejas* back over the edge and down the steep rugged hillside. In the dim edge of firelight, he saw Sandoval drop his empty Colt. He quickly switched the sword into his right hand and put it into play. Sam swung his rifle in reflex and fired in time to keep a screaming warrior from firing a pistol into the young bounty hunter's face at point-black range.

Sandoval moved forward into three warriors, swinging the short deadly sword with expert precision, each slash leaving behind it a trail of blood.

"We've got them. Push them back!" Thorn shouted, dropping his empty horse pistol and using the big Mameluke sword with skillful accuracy until the remaining attackers turned, ran and leaped over the cliff edge into the darkness.

Sam advanced, casting his empty Winchester to the ground and firing his Colt as the Desert Weasels made their howling, screaming retreat. At the edge of the cliff, he stared down, seeing only black shadows dart back and forth as they fired wildly up at him and the bounty hunters.

"Ranger, look out!" shouted Sandoval.

Sam turned in time to see a warrior run toward him from behind wielding a long war ax. But upon hearing the bounty hunter, the warrior turned quickly and swung the ax in Sandoval's direction.

Sandoval dodged the powerful blow from the ax. He spun in a full circle with his sword and laid the *Comadrejas* open with a deep lethal slash across his sternum. As the warrior staggered backward with a loud scream, Sam grabbed him by his wrist, below the war ax, and swung the man out over the edge of the cliff. The darkness swallowed him, leaving only a long shriek resounding down the black hillside.

"Hold fast, men," said Thorn, still standing tall and straight, his bloody sword high in hand. "They're retreating."

The ranger looked all around in surprise. A haze of gun smoke loomed eerily in the glow of firelight. Dead *Comadrejas* lay strewn on the rocky ground.

On the dark hillside, gunshots still popped and blossomed wildly as the warriors bounded down on foot, their horses tumbling and sliding along with them. But the fight had ended as suddenly as it had begun. Sam held his fire, hurried back and picked up his Winchester from the ground and called out to the bounty hunters, "Are either of you hit?"

"Yes, I am," said Thorn, "but nothing serious. Sandy, how about you?"

"Same here," Sandoval said, his sword hanging loosely in his hand. "Ranger, what say you?" he asked.

"I'm all right," Sam said, ignoring a bullet nick on his forearm, another on the left side. "We best reload and be ready, in case they come back at us."

Thorn and Sandoval gave each other an approving look in the dim circling glow of firelight. "Indeed, Sandy," said Thorn, the bloody Mameluke sword still raised in his fist, "Ranger Burrack knows these weasels' ways better than we do." His voice sounded rejuvenated by the short, fierce battle.

"Behind you, Captain," said Sandoval, seeing a wounded *Comadrejas* struggle to rise to his feet.

Thorn stepped over and drew the sword back, prepared to deliver a hard fatal swing. But he stopped as he looked down into the man's frightened face.

"Please do not keel me, *monsieur, mon ami, por favor!* Please do not keel me," the man begged with tear-filled eyes, in a delirious mixture of bad Spanish, bad French and broken border English. He squeezed his right hand around his left forearm, squeezing a bloody gash made by Sandoval's short sword.

Thorn gave him a curious look; Sam watched to see what the bounty hunter would do.

Instead of swinging the big sword, Thorn flashed it back and forth quickly, skillfully, and rested its sharp tip against the *Comadrejas'* chest. "Get up," he commanded.

He held the tip of the sword in place as if it were raising the struggling man to his bare feet. "Who is your leader?"

The frightened man looked back and forth warily

among the three before answering. "He—he is *Charo* . . . Clato Charo," he said.

"You go tell Mr. Charo that Captain Cadden Thorn and his expedition will be using this *disierto* for as long as we choose to, without paying him in either horses or whiskey," Thorn said. He gave a faint grin. "*Comprenez? Comprede?* Understand?" he asked in French, Spanish and English.

"Yes, I will tell him, *mon ami*," the man said, eager to leave now that he saw his life being spared.

"Do not call me *your friend*, in *any* language," Thorn said, slapping the sword blade flat-sided against the man's shoulder. "Now go on. Get out of here."

The ranger and the two bounty hunters watched the wounded *Comadreja* stagger and limp over to the edge of the cliff. He climbed down out of sight through a sound of breaking, thrashing brush and sliding rock. When they knew he was far down the hillside, they walked over and stood near the edge of the cliff. Gazing down at the dark flatlands below them, in the pale moonlight, they watched as tiny dark silhouettes moved out of the black shadows on the hillside and gathered and rode off across the grainy purple night.

"That was interesting," Thorn said with a sigh as the last of the *Comadrejas* vanished from their sight. "From the direction they are riding in, I take it they won't be coming back tonight," he offered.

"Not tonight," Sam agreed, his Winchester hanging from his hand, reloaded, as was his holstered Colt. "But I doubt we've seen the last of them. Lucas and his buggy load of whiskey had gotten them stirred up. They're not the best of fighters, but they are determined, especially when it comes to acquiring whiskey or horses."

"They didn't have the fight in them that I expected," said Sandoval. "That many men should have dispatched us handily." He looked to Thorn for comment.

"Right you are, Sandy," said Thorn. "They were nothing like some Turkish pirates I could name."

"Or some Portuguese *Proscritos* I might mention, or some Korean mountain bandits we've run into," said Sandoval. He had finished reloading his Colt. He shoved it into his holster. "Fortunate for us," he added, looking at the dead lying on the ground.

The ranger watched and listened; the two bounty hunters did not talk with the surprise of men who had expected to be overrun and killed. Nor had they fought like men too outnumbered to survive. They'd fought like men who'd accepted the odds being against them and had managed to turn those odds to their advantage. They had not taken a defensive position, he noted to himself. Instead they had rallied instantly and *attacked* their attackers.

Now, in reflection, the ranger noted that there had been no boastfulness in their recounting of the battle, only comparisons of past opponents, made for the sake of future skirmishes.

"We hit them harder than they expected," Thorn said quietly. "The next time they will know us better. They won't overestimate themselves."

"How far do they range across these badlands?" Sandoval asked the ranger.

"As far as they choose," Sam said. "If they think we have something they want, they'll hound us until they get it . . . or until we kill enough of them to change their minds."

Thorn said, "Well, we can't have them diverting us from our business at hand, can we, Sandy?"

"No, sir, Captain," said Sandoval, inspecting his rifle, "we can't have that."

Chapter 6

Tinnis Lucas had stopped the bareback buggy horse and turned on the narrow trail, forcing Rudy Duckwald and George Epson to have to stop abruptly behind him. "Damn it to hell, gambler!" Duckwald cursed. "Either keep up or drop the hell out."

Ignoring the angry gunman, Lucas said, "Listen . . ." He'd gazed back through the darkness back toward the distant sound of gunfire. "Bless their hearts." He gave a wicked grin in the shadowy moonlight. "That's the sound of Charo and his *Comadrejas de desierto*. They're killing our enemies for us."

"Says you," Espon growled. He'd had to jerk his horse to the side to keep from bumping into Duckwald or the gambler.

"Yes, *says I* indeed," Lucas retorted. "Planting that whiskey along the trail, I put the *Comadrejas* right up the three law dogs' shirts for us, gentlemen."

"I thought they were two bounty hunters and the territory ranger," said Duckwald, as if skeptical of Lucas' whole story.

"Jesus, what's the difference?" said Lucas. "Bounty hunters, rangers. They're all law dogs if they're out to nail us to the wall."

"I wouldn't brag about anything I did with the Desert Weasels," said Duckwald. "They are about as low and cowardly a bunch as hell ever collected."

"But good at killing law dogs," Lucas pointed out, not the least fazed by the burly gunman's sarcasm.

"Like hell you planned any of that," Elmer Fisk said over his shoulder, stopping when he'd heard the three horses bunch up behind him. "You got drunk and lost most of your load. Now you say this so you don't look so foolish." He spat to the side in contempt. "Damn the *Comadrejas*." He turned back to the dark trail ahead.

"Yeah? Well, anyway," said Lucas, "they just took care of our trail hounds for us. No need to thank me, though."

"From what I heard, it couldn't have been much of a gun battle," said Fisk without looking back. "It didn't last as long as a shirt in a bear fight."

"That's right," said Lucas, heeling his bareback horse on in front of Duckwald and Epson. "Clato Charo has too many warriors for a couple of bounty hunters and a ranger to stand up to."

"Says you," Epson repeated behind him.

Lucas shook his head. Grinning to himself, he lifted a shiny metal flask he'd filled from one of the bottles of rye. In a toast to himself, he raised the flask and drank from it. Without offering the flask to the two riding behind him, he capped it and put it away.

"Gentlemen, I see that this lackluster conversation is going nowhere," Lucas said, adjusting himself on the buggy horse's back. "Please awaken me when we get to where we are going."

"Like hell, I will," said Epson. "I ain't your manservant."

"God forbid." Lucas grinned.

"Leave him be, George," said Duckwald. "When the drunken sumbitch walks his horse off a cliff, let him fall."

"Yeah, George, let me fall. . . ." Lucas chuckled to himself behind closed eyes as the four rode on through the grainy night.

At the lead, Elmer Fisk led the three men a full hour farther along the high trail. As Lucas slept, Fisk turned onto a narrower winding trail and continued downward in the darkness. When another hour had passed, the riders meandered with caution around the side of a steep craggy hillside until they stood before a tall, thin crevice at the end of a sloping cliff overhang.

"Man, oh, man," said Duckwald, staring out through cloud-swept darkness. The sloping cliff fell away sharply for forty feet, then lay broken off above a yawning black hole. "If a man's horse lost its footing up here, it'd be a week before he'd hit bottom."

Epson said, "I best wake this fool before we ride around this edge." He reached out and started to shake Lucas by his arm.

But Fisk grabbed his hand and shoved it way. "Let's let him sleep."

"But what if—?"

Duckwald cut his brother-in-law off, saying in a whisper, "You heard him, George. Let the man sleep."

George heard the two give a dark chuckle. Beside them Lucas snored softly.

Elmer grabbed the reins to Lucas' bareback horse and jerked it forward onto the steep sloping cliff. The animal protested with a loud whinny, but bolted forward as Duckwald slapped its rump with his leather riding quirt and shouted, *"Hee-iii!"*

"Jesus!" said Epson, watching the frightened neighing animal make a short circle in the pale moonlight, its ironclad hooves slipping and clacking, raising sparks on the stone cliff.

Lucas let out a yelp as the animal began to quickly lose it balance. But he had no time to hurl himself from its back before it started a wild, deadly dance off into the bottomless blackness.

As the three sat staring in the darkness, the clacking of the horse's hooves fell silent. A short scream came from Lucas; a terrifying neigh resounded from the animal as it plunged downward through thin air. For what seemed like a long time, they heard only the waning scream of the horse as it thrashed and twisted futilely in thin air. Then they heard the cracking, splitting, breaking of pine boughs echo up to them from a thousand feet below.

"I bet that sobered him up some," Fisk said quietly, a cruel grin on his stony face.

"You'd think," Duckwald said.

"Jesus . . . ," Epson repeated, his gaze fixed on a wisp of low cloud looming at cliff's edge.

"I never liked the son of a bitch much," Fisk said, turning his horse carefully to the dark crevice.

"Me neither," said Duckwald. "I've wanted to kill him ever since I first laid eyes on him." He turned his horse behind Fisk and followed him into the thin black crevice.

"But what about Shear?" Epson asked, turning his horse and booting it along behind Duckwald.

"What about him?" Fisk asked over his shoulder.

Before Epson could answer, Duckwald said, "It would be different if we left the gambler lying on the flatlands with his belly in his hands." He chuckled. "But hell, any drunk can ride his horse off a cliff in this kind of country."

"Yeah, besides," said Fisk, "everything he told me, I can tell Big Aces myself. I could have shot this turd anytime. I just thought hearing him scream might be a little more fun."

Stopping his horse a few feet inside the narrow pitch-black crevice, Fisk said, "Give me your reins. Get back there and sweep out our tracks with some brush."

"This rock shelf doesn't leave much tracks anyway," said Duckwald.

"Are you going to argue with me?" said Fisk.

Duckwald and Epson handed him their horses' reins and did as they were told. When they returned, tossing aside their handful of dried brush, they stepped back into their saddles. "Good enough?" said Duckwald.

Fisk didn't answer. He struck a long hearth match and spotted a row of three short-handled torches leaning on a rock ledge. He took one down and rolled its blackened tip back and forth in the match's flame until the fire took hold.

"Holy Moses . . . ," Epson said, awestricken, he and Duckwald looking past Fisk and forward down a steep rock path. The corridor of rock lining the trail was barely wide enough for the horses to pass through. "I've heard rumors about this place, but I never thought I'd see it."

"Neither did Lucas," Duckwald said with a dark laugh, his voice sounding strange rolling along the rocky passageway, "but he was right."

"Hold this," said Fisk, handing Duckwald the burning torch.

Duckwald held the flickering light while Fisk rummaged through his saddlebags. Fisk took out a fresh short-handled torch and laid it up on the ledge beside the other two for the next Black Valley Riders who rode through the crevice entrance toward the Black Valley hideout.

"How far is it from here?" Epson asked, staring along the crevice, the closeness of it causing an unsteady feeling in his chest.

"It's still better than a day's ride once we reach the end of this path," said Duckwald.

"Does it—does it get any wider than this?" Epson stammered, trying not to sound too concerned.

"No," Duckwald replied over his shoulder to him with a dark grin. "But don't worry. It doesn't get any *tighter* either."

"I wasn't worried," Epson said grudgingly, "just curious is all."

"Hear that, Elmer?" Duckwald said to Fisk riding along slowly, ahead of him.

"Shut up, both of yas," Fisk said almost in a whisper, watching a rattlesnake wind its way out of sight when the glow of torchlight crept onto it.

The three rode on, circling downward on the narrow path for over a half hour before Fisk stopped and put out the torch and laid it on another rock shelf at shoulder level. Heeling his horse forward, the two men close behind him, he stopped a few yards ahead as Duckwald and Epson felt the coolness of fresh air on their faces.

"Lord, I'm glad to get out of there," Epson said, gazing out across a wide rocky valley in the dim silver-blue morning light. The valley lay harsh and foreboding before them, strewn with towering chimney rock, looming saguaro cactus, breakaway cliffs and cutbanks. A wind roared in off the valley floor, filled with stinging sand and bits of sharp brush stems.

"Yeah, me too," said Duckwald. He raised his bandanna from around his neck up over the bridge of his nose and gave another dark chuckle. "It's a stroll through a garden from here on."

Mingo Sentanza spotted Elmer Fisk and the other riders in the early-afternoon sunlight through a long Union army telescope. "Crazy Elmer . . . ," he remarked more to himself than to the other guard, Ben Longley, who sat atop the rock perch beside him. He had ridden with Fisk long enough to conclude that the man would be no match for him with gun or knife. As with all men he'd ridden with, Sentanza had sized the gunman up early on.

"Yeah?" said Longley. "Who else?"

"I can't make them out, their faces are covered," said Sentanza, still gazing out through the wavering heat.

"Let me see," said Longley, reaching out for the telescope.

"Take it easy," said Sentanza. "I'm making sure they're not being followed."

"With all that dust boiling behind them, how could you tell if they are?" said Longley.

"I can tell," Sentanza said absently, "provided everybody shuts up and lets me look."

Longley settled down and waited in silence.

"Good enough," said Sentanza after a few moments of checking along the trail behind the riders. He lowered the lens from his eye and passed it over to the waiting outlaw's hand. "It'll still be hours before they get over here to us."

"I know that," said Longley, grasping the telescope. "I just like looking." He took the lens and raised it to his eye.

"Happy to oblige," Sentanza said flatly. He looked the outlaw up and down, judging how easy Longley would be to kill should the situation ever arise.

Seeing Crazy Elmer Fisk, riding along in the lead without his bandanna raised against the hot swirling dust, Longley shook his head. "Is he as *crazy* as they say he is, Mingo?"

Sentanza turned from his dark speculations and stared out at the riders, squinting his naked eyes. "Some of the things I've heard and seen, I'd say he's worse," the serious half-breed replied.

Longley scanned the other riders with the telescope, and came back to Fisk. "For instance . . . ?" he asked.

"Never mind *for instance*," said Sentanza. "Why don't you watch him a while? You'll be able to make up your own mind."

"Callahan says crazy or not, Elmer Fisk is one of the fastest guns he's ever seen in his life," Longley said without lowering the telescope. He watched as the other two riders drew closer up behind Fisk.

"Yeah, well . . ." Sentanza spat and ran the back of his hand over his mouth. "Dolan Callahan is easily impressed, in my opinion."

"He's from Missouri," said Longley. "He knows all about them big gunslingers."

"Suit yourself," said Sentanza. He reached over for the telescope. "Come on. Let's go tell Shear they're coming. I don't know about you, but I'd ready to go rob something."

"I always am ready, amigo," said Longley, handing him the telescope. "What about you?"

Amigo . . . ? Sentanza made no reply, but he decided that if it came down to it, Longley would be an easy kill. Like Fisk he would be easily caught off guard, and he would die quickly. He would fight back, of course, as all men would, Sentanza told himself. But in the end he would be no contest for a skillful killer like himself.

The two scooted down the side of the rock, stepped up into their saddles and turned their horses toward a trail along the edge of the valley floor. Sentanza let Longley ride ahead of him a few feet on the tough rocky trail, the clack of their horses' hooves the only sound to be heard save for a low whirring wind.

As the two rode, Sentanza lifted his Colt from his holster and leveled it at the center of Longley's back. If Longley looked around at the sound of the gun cocking, he would kill him, plain and simple, Sentanza told himself.

Yet, as the trigger came back beneath Sentanza's thumb, the unsuspecting Longley rode on staring straight ahead.

For just a split second something in Sentanza's mind urged him to pull the trigger and watch the man drop dead to the ground. But then he would have to answer to Brayton Shear for his action, and explaining himself to Big Aces was something he never wanted to do. Besides, Ben Longley wasn't so bad to ride with. He'd ridden with worse—for a short time anyway.

He lowered the Colt, uncocked it, holstered it and heeled his horse forward up beside Longley. It was easier riding with a man once you reminded yourself that you could end his life any time you chose to.

On a plank front porch out in front of a low-standing earth, sod and pine log cabin, a rifleman, Ballard Swean, watched the rise of dust move toward him from across a wide wasteland of brush, rock and cactus. When the outline of the two guards rose into sight, he reached sidelong and kicked the boot of the man slumbering on a wooden bench.

"Hey, Pickens, wake up," he demanded. "Go tell Big Aces our guards are riding in." He stared hard across the wasteland. "One of them is waving his hat." He jacked a round into his rifle chamber. "You know what that means?"

"Yeah . . . ," said Dave Pickens, waking up quickly and bolting onto his feet. "It means we've got company coming." He turned to the open doorway.

"Stay where you are, Dave," said Brayton Shear who stood in the open doorway, a large black cigar hanging between his fingers. "I've been watching their dust myself." He studied the two guards through the wavering heat and the hot gusting wind. "If the *company* is Fisk and the others, we'll be taking the train down quicker I expected."

Chapter 7

The first dim gray light of morning had brought with it a stirring in the upper bough of a tall, sparse pine whose roots clung to the rock hillside. As Tinnis Lucas' senses came back to him from within a deep, mindless darkness, he raised a careful hand and felt the thick-crusted blood on his right cheek. His body throbbed all over with pain. Somewhere in the distance he heard thunder roll on the horizon. *A storm? Now . . . ?*

The memory of what had happened came back to him slowly—the cliff, the doomed and neighing horse, the scraping of hooves on stone, the plunge and the endless falling through the purple night. "Lord God . . . ," he moaned quietly.

His trembling fingertips followed fresh, wet blood upward from the crust on his cheek until he found the open flap of scalp hanging down from atop his head.

"You're . . . still alive," he managed to say to himself as if in awe of his discovery. Then he gazed down the sheer rock hillside that stretched hundreds of feet below him. He winced and shook his aching head. *For whatever that's worth. . . .*

In the distance, lightning twisted and curled. The mindless darkness crept back in and surrounded him.

When he awakened again, the midmorning sun lay buried in a black-gray swirl. As the pine swayed on the air, he clutched the tree's bough and realized for the first time what had happened to him. In his fall, he had landed twenty feet farther up against the tree and slid down into a triple fork of limbs that wasn't about to drop him.

That's good news, at least . . . , he told himself. Then he gave a dubious look upward at the low, swollen sky.

He searched himself and came out with the battered whiskey flask. He shook it a little, uncapped it and raised it to his lips. "Here's to . . . *weather*," he said, glancing up with wry defiance. Thunder rumbled as if in reply.

When he'd swallowed a drink, he looked down and all around at the harsh rocky terrain, the deep abyss below and the thin air surrounding him. A hundred feet down the falling rocky slope, he saw the body of his horse hanging limply, impaled on the broken tip of another shorter, swaying pine.

The sight of the ill-fated animal made him look away. He hurriedly swigged more whiskey and clung against the rough tree bough until he felt his mind and innards settle. Then he looked down again at the distant rocky ground swaying back and forth beneath him.

"Now, how will you get yourself down from here, Tinnis?" he said to himself, capping the flask and putting it away.

Realizing that the soft soothing glow of whiskey

wouldn't last long, Lucas looked down the tree at the next limb sticking out ten feet below him. *Here goes. . . .* Without thinking too long about it, he slid carefully off the edge of his safe forked nest, wrapped his low-cut town boots around the rough trunk and slid himself down until he felt the broken limb firmly beneath his feet.

"My God, sir," he said aloud to himself, wheezing, gasping for breath as he looked down and realized how much farther he had to climb. "This simply will not do." He noted that the closer he got to the ground, the farther the protruding limbs would be spaced apart.

You have no choice . . . , he told himself. Taking a few deep breaths, he lowered himself onto his rump, slipped off the limb and shinnied on down, this time fourteen feet before finding safe purchase. As he hunkered down to catch his breath on the next limb, he felt the first drop of rain land atop his bare head.

Over the ridge above him, Lucas heard a hard-blowing rain march across the hillside and begin to pound down onto him as if with a vengeance. *What did I ever do . . . ?* he asked with an upward glance, taking out the flask with a sigh. He uncapped the battered flask, drank it empty and let it fall from his hand. He wiped a dripping strand of hair back from his forehead and slipped himself down off the limb, back around the rough, wet tree trunk. "While lightning licks boldly in the sky . . . ," he said, as if quoting the scene in a story of his life.

On the trail a half mile away, Cadden Thorn lowered the naval telescope from his eye and gave the ranger and Sandoval a bemused look. "I have found the gambler," he said, handing the lens over to Sam.

The ranger took the lens and aimed it in the direction Thorn had pointed. Through the obscuring rain traveling toward them, he spotted Lucas shinnying down the pine like some slow, methodical man-ape. Without lowering the lens he moved it to the left and saw the buggy horse hanging limply on the shorter pine. Sam winced at the sight of the horse, but continued searching back and forth on the hillside for signs of any other fallen riders. Seeing none, he lowered the lens and handed it on to Sandoval.

"He rode off a high trail in the night," the ranger said, with no need for further speculation on the matter.

As Sandoval raised the lens and looked out through it, the wall of heavy, blowing rain reached them, announced by a clap of thunder that shook the hillsides like cannon fire. "It looks like it'll be a while before he touches ground," he said, framing Lucas' wet, blood-streaked face in the circling lens.

"We'll want to be there when he does," Sam said, turning his stallion's reins back onto the slick narrow trail. Rivulets of water were already braiding their way downhill toward them. "Whatever hoofprints this rain washes out, maybe he can fill in for us."

"Right you are, Ranger," said Thorn, swinging his horse around behind him. Sandoval collapsed the big naval telescope and heeled his horse along behind them.

A half hour passed as the storm continued to rage. When Lucas reached the lowest limb, he straddled it, exhausted, and let the rain pour down on him, without so much as raising a tired raw hand to wipe his face. Only ten feet to his right, the vertical rock wall stood facing him. But there was no handhold, no foothold, no crack or crevice in reach. Even if he could hurl his spent and aching body that far, there was nothing to stop him from plunging another forty feet straight down the wet rock hillside to the stone trail below.

"All right, I give up . . . ," Lucas gasped, the loose flap of ripped scalp bleeding anew, the rain having washed away the dried, crusted blood. Tears fell with the streaks of water and blood down his face. "Lord, what the hell do you want from me?" he said, pleading to the swollen black sky. "I'm ragged, bloody, done in, and I'm all out of whiskey." He raised his hands in submission. "What am I to do? Tell me something here!"

Lucas' sobbing voice grew in intensity as he spoke, yet a passing streak of lightning followed by a waning sound of thunder was the only reply he heard. Shaking his head, he wept openly. "No wonder I never believed in you," he shouted at the low, growling sky.

On the trail below, Thorn, the ranger and Sandoval looked at one another as their horses walked into sight around a blind turn in the trail and stopped. "Then who are you talking to, Lucas?" Sam called out through the storm.

The gambler's bloodshot eyes turned straight up in reflex, momentarily believing that he had heard this voice being called out from an angry sky. But then he turned, following the voice to its origin, and saw the three men staring up at him from the turn in the trail. "Oh my, Ranger Burrack, and the *soldiers of the sea* . . . ," he said with relief. He quickly wiped his eyes with the back of his hand.

"Marines," Sandoval corrected him.

"Yes, *marines* indeed," said Lucas, recovering quickly from his hopelessness and getting back to his scheming self. Even the storm seemed to lessen its intensity. The rain slacked off, if only a little; the thunder had moved past overhead and began to slowly drift off across the hillsides. "How fortunate you three are to have found me out here," he said with a tone of arrogance.

"Oh, how so?" Sam and the two bounty hunters sat with their wet gloved hands crossed on their saddle horns.

"I've decided I might be persuaded to work with you," Lucas said.

The ranger and the bounty hunters looked at one another, unimpressed. Sam shrugged. "We're not interested," he said. "Throw down you gun."

"Don't be ridiculous, Ranger," Lucas said, trying to take control.

Sam stared up at him, then started to turn away.

"Wait, Ranger! I can take you to where the Black Valley Riders are holed up," Lucas called down through the pouring rain.

Sam called up to him, "I suppose you could, if you weren't sitting up in a tree." He paused, then added, "If you don't throw down the gun, I'll have to shoot you down from there."

Lightning streaked, moving away but still too close for comfort. "Ranger, this is not the time for foolishness," Lucas said, sounding serious. "Here is my offer. Get me down from here and I'll lead you to a hidden passage through the hillside. Otherwise you'll never find it on your own."

The three only stared up at him. Sam reached down and drew his Winchester from its boot.

"Wait! I'm trying to make a deal here!" Lucas called out. "Let's talk about this some."

Sam levered a bullet into his rifle chamber, stepped his stallion forward in the pelting rain and said up to him, "Either drop the gun down or I'll shoot you down from there, gambler. I'm placing you under arrest for horse theft."

"Horse theft?" Lucas looked stunned and incensed. "You can't be serious, Ranger. You three have larger issues to address than me *borrowing* that lady's buggy for a limited time." With a look of disgust, he jerked his Colt Thunderer out of his shoulder harness and pitched it down onto the muddy trail.

"Borrowed for a *limited time*?" Sam looked up at the grizzly scene, the dead buggy horse hanging impaled on the pine. "You left the buggy sitting in the trail for the Desert Weasels to scavenge. You rode the horse off of a cliff and killed it." As he spoke he stepped down from his saddle, picked up the gambler's Colt and shoved it down behind his gun belt. Then he opened his saddlebags and pulled out a coiled vaquero-style rawhide lariat.

Seeing the lariat, Thorn cut in, saying loud enough for Lucas to hear, "Are we going to hang him now, Ranger Burrack? Isn't that what they do to horse thieves out here?"

"Often, yes," Sam said. He looped the leather lariat from one hand to the other, gauging its length and limbering it in the falling rain. "But in weather like this, we always wait until after coffee," he said, dropping the coiled lariat over his saddle horn. He took the stallion's wet reins and turned him on the trail.

"*Coffee . . . ? Wait*, Ranger!" Lucas shouted above the rumble of dissipating thunder as the three men turned their horses as one and rode back out of sight around the turn in the trail. "Drop the stolen horse charge and I'll take you to them! This is no joking matter! Look at this lightning! I'll get struck dead up here, Ranger!" he called out. "Throw me the *damn* lariat. That's all I ask. You've got my gun! I'm harmless. Just throw the damn lariat up here!"

Harmless . . . ? Sam wondered. He and the two bounty hunters stepped down from their saddles and led their tired, wet animals under the partial cover of a cliff overhang, still hearing Lucas pleading from around the run in the trail.

A half hour later, Lucas still sat huddled against the trunk of the tree, his arms wrapped around his knees, shivering, wet and streaked with blood. The rain had all but stopped; the thunder had rumbled off into the west, taking the remaining streaks of lightning with it. Runoff water had slackened to thin streams alongside the trail and down the hillsides.

"Hello, the tree," Sam called out to the trembling gambler as he stepped his big stallion back around the trail. Even as Sandoval had boiled a pot of coffee, the ranger had remained within sight of the gambler stuck up the tree. But he wasn't about to let Lucas know. "Are you about ready to come down now?"

Lucas raised his trembling face and stared down at him. Forcing himself to speak in a calm, even voice, he said humbly, "Yes, Ranger, I am. If you will throw me up the *godda*—" He stopped and got himself back under control with a deep, calming breath. "That is, if you will *please* throw up the lariat?"

"My pleasure," said Sam, stepping down and walking over beneath the tree, the coiled lariat in hand. "I might be a few feet short. But it's closer to the ground than you'd be without it."

"That's most comforting," Lucas replied, careful of what he said, least the ranger go back around the turn in the trail for another half-hour wait. He stood crouched out on the wet limb, steadying himself with one hand on the tree trunk. The ranger tied one end of the lariat around the rest of the coil to hold it together and threw it upward with all of his strength.

From the turn in the trail, Thorn and Sandoval watched the gambler fumble with the lariat but manage to catch it on the first try. While the three watched, Lucas tied a neat foothold loop in the end of the line. He made a single wrap around the limb.

Thorn and Sandoval gave each other a look, impressed by Lucas' skill with the lariat.

"Ahoy below," Lucas said down to them in a mocking tone. He lowered the loop enough to step off the limb into it and began lowering himself easily down the tree trunk.

"Not bad," Sam said under his breath, equally impressed by the gambler.

When Lucas' hands reached the end of the line, he looked down with relief, seeing that he was only five feet above the trail. He turned loose of the lariat and dropped to the ground. With a jerk on the line, he let the rope fall unfettered to the ground at his feet.

"Looks like luck is with you, gambler," Thorn said.

"My luck is dubious at best, sir," Lucas replied, wet and shivering. The wound to his scalp was bleeding again.

"Well done," Thorn said. He held a cup of steaming coffee in his gloved hand; Sandoval stood with a folded blanket over his shoulder.

"Yes, for a drunkard," the gambler said wryly. He deftly coiled the lariat in hand. "Obliged, Ranger," he said, handing him the coiled line. The pain in his torn scalp came back to him sharply now that he was safely on the ground.

Sam took the lariat and slung it over his shoulder as the two bounty hunters moved in closer and stood around Lucas.

"Have some coffee, gambler," Thorn said, holding the cup out to him.

Lucas took the cup in his trembling hands. "Obliged," he said. "I don't suppose you have anything to cut this with?"

"It so happens I do," said Thorn. He produced one of the unbroken bottles of whiskey they'd salvaged from the brush.

"Sir, you are a living *saint* among men," Lucas said, quickly holding his cup out as Thorn pulled the cork. "I'm starting to think you *soldiers of the sea* are indeed both gentlemen and scholars."

"It's too early for whiskey," said Thorn, "but today we're making an exception."

"And bless you for it," said Lucas, watching Thorn pour the booze into the hot black coffee.

"Drink up," said Sandoval. He spread the blanket across the gambler's wet shivering shoulders and patted a gloved hand on his back. "You'll need the whiskey once I start sewing your scalp on."

Chapter 8

———

Sam looked on, asking nothing of Lucas while Sandoval attended his wounds. Beneath the cliff overhang, the Cuban bounty hunter spent over an hour sewing Lucas' torn scalp back in place. With the skill of a field physician, Sandoval shaved a strip of hair from around the gambler's scalp wound. Using a surgical needle and thread from his saddlebags, he sewed the torn flap of skin back in place and closed or cleaned a half dozen other scrapes and gashes Lucas had acquired during his fall.

Once the sewing was done, and the gambler had drunk nearly the entire bottle of whiskey, Sam scooted over closer to Lucas and handed him the discarded flask he'd found lying on the ground.

"I thought you might like to fill this, to carry on the trail," Sam said. He looked pointedly at Lucas and said, "While you're leading us to this *hidden passage* through the hills you talked about."

"You could have gotten me down from there sooner, Ranger," Lucas said, turning sullen.

"Or I could have left you there longer," Sam countered, holding his gaze, unblinking. Now that the gambler's crisis had passed, the ranger knew he'd try to better his position—get the upper hand if he could.

"Or there's still the matter of the stolen buggy horse," said Thorn. He asked the ranger, "Isn't there a standing reward of a hundred dollars for the capture of a horse thief, dead or alive?"

Sam didn't answer; he kept his eyes fixed on Lucas.

But Lucas replied, saying to Thorn, "That's the most preposterous thing I've ever head of."

"It's true," Sam said.

Lucas looked back and forth between the pairs of staring eyes. Finally he let out a breath. "It doesn't really matter, Ranger," he said. "A deal is a deal. I said I'd show you the hidden passage, so I will. In turn, I trust you will drop the stolen-horse charge." He looked all around and said, "You can trust me. What else would I do, walk back to Minton Hill, through a desert full of *Comadrejas*, cutthroats and rattlesnakes?"

"I want more than your word, gambler," said Sam. "I believe you're slippery enough to twist your word to mean whatever you want it to mean. What I want with you is an *understanding*."

"An understanding?" Lucas said.

"If we ride into a hidden passageway with you and find ourselves riding into a trap, I want you to *understand* that you won't be riding out," Sam said.

"Thank you, Ranger Burrack," said Lucas, "I believe I understand that most clearly. Don't forget that Elmer Fisk and his pards ran me off the trail and tried to kill me. I owe him and the Black Valley Riders nothing."

He raised a finger for emphasis. "But be mindful of this, once I lead you through the hillside to the hideout, I owe you nothing either. I will ride away at my choosing."

Sam studied the gambler's bloodshot eyes, beginning to realize that nothing he said to this man was going to matter. Lucas was a schemer, a player, and a headstrong drunkard who was not accustomed to listening to anyone. No amount of threat or force was going to change that. If anything, pressing him on the matter would only make it worse.

"The horses are rested, Ranger," Thorn said, standing over the two. "It's time we ride on."

Sam looked up at him and realized the older bounty hunter was reading Lucas the same way he was. "You're right, Captain. It's time to ride," said Sam, standing, dusting the seat of his trousers. He'd told Lucas what he'd do if the gambler double-crossed them. Now all he could do was stand prepared to make good on his warning. He lowered his hand to the gambler, who took it and pulled himself stiffly to his feet.

"Now it's *Captain*, is it, Ranger?" Lucas said with a trace of a whiskey slur. He held the filled flask in hand. "Don't tell me that you have become as enamored as I by these two *marine* bounty hunters." He gave a grin and said to Sandoval, who stood staring at him, always ready to correct him, "It is all right if I call you two *marine bounty hunters*, isn't it?"

Sandoval looked at Thorn before replying to the gambler. "We are bounty hunters, Mr. Lucas," he said respectfully, but with restraint in his voice. He turned to Thorn and Sam. "I'll get our horses."

With the land still wet from rain and the trail laced by thin braided streams of runoff water, the riders resumed their upward trek. Following Lucas' directions, they ascended a series of slick winding paths through rock and brush until they reached the higher trail the gambler and his cohorts had ridden during the previous night. Lucas rode behind the ranger on the big stallion until they'd reached a place where the trail became too unsafe on horseback. Once atop the high trail, the gambler looked back and forth with an air of uncertainty. He jerked the flask of whiskey from inside his ragged shirt, uncapped it and raised it to his lips.

"Go easy on that stuff, Lucas," Sam said, "or we'll have to take it away from you."

"You would *have to* indeed, Ranger," Lucas said with defiance. He lowered the battered flask, capped it and put it away. "I drink to ease the pain, sir."

Sam let it go. "Doesn't this place look familiar to you?" he asked, having seen Lucas' lost expression a moment earlier. Knowing that the tracks they'd followed had been washed clean by the deluge, Sam knew that they were at the gambler's mercy. If Lucas misled them, intentionally or otherwise, they would be right back where they'd started, the gang still running free.

"Yes, of course it looks familiar," Lucas said, turning upward along the trail. "Follow me." He stomped off, along the wet rock trail.

Leading his horse up beside the ranger, Thorn asked quietly, "Do you suppose he was too drunk to remember?"

"I don't know," said Sam. "But without tracks to follow, he was our best hope right now."

They walked on in silence, winding behind the gambler single file as the wet path became narrower and steeper with every step. A hundred yards farther up along the rock trail, the hillside to their left fell away sharply and left the path turning around a bald wall of rock.

Stopping, Lucas gazed out over the broken edge at a thousand-foot drop through thin air, jagged rock, wisps of cloud and swaying pine tops. He chuckled under his breath and leaned sidelong against the rock wall to their left.

"How are your wings, Ranger?" he said, gazing out across the open abyss.

"Never better," Sam said, the two bounty hunters bunching up behind him. "Keep going, before your whiskey gives out on you."

"What an ugly thing to say, Ranger," Lucas replied. He squinted and looked all around again. "To tell you the truth, this is as far as my recollection takes me." He gestured out across the steep sloping rock cliff, at the scrapings left by the buggy horse's steel shoes. "There is where the buggy horse did its last dance."

Sam stepped past the gambler and looked farther along the trail. "They couldn't have gone any farther than here," he said. "This is the end of the trail." He looked down from the edge and spotted the tiny dead horse still swaying in the treetop below. "But this has to be where you fell from," he said to Lucas.

"Yes, it is, Ranger," the gambler said. "I was feigning sleep. I heard Fisk tell the other two that this was the place. That's about as much as I can give you."

"Why were you feigning sleep?" Thorn asked pointedly.

"Call me peculiar," said Lucas, "but I do that a lot. It helps me hear what I might not hear otherwise."

"The same as pretending to be drunk?" Thorn asked.

"Watch your language, please, *Captain*, *sir*," Lucas said in his wry, playful tone. "A man should never pretend himself drunk. He should simply *be* drunk and forgo any pretense."

"Still," said Thorn, "I'd like to know why you felt you needed to pretend—"

"Over here," Sandoval said, cutting in before Thorn could continue.

Thorn, the ranger and the gambler all turned as one to where Sandoval stood crouched at a black crevice in the rock wall, his hand on the opening of it as he peered into an endless blackness.

"What have you, Sandy?" Thorn said, stepping over to the young bounty hunter. The trail lay flanked by a wall full of such crevices, all of them tall, deep and jagged, carved into rock by wind and water. This one was no different at first glance, only a bit wider than usual.

Turning his eyes from the blackness to the ground at his feet, Sandoval picked up the short damp stub of a burnt match stick and examined it between the tips of his gloved fingers. "Jackpot . . . ," he murmured as the other three drew closer around him.

"Keep up the good work, Sandy," Thorn said with a thin smile, seeing the burnt match. He patted Sandoval on his shoulder as he stepped past him. "Cover me, gentlemen," he said over his shoulder as he raised the flap on his holster, took out his big horse pistol and walked inside the black crevice. Three feet inside, he stopped and took a match of his own from inside his duster pocket and stuck it on the rock wall.

Sam and Sandoval stepped forward and crouched at the opening, guns in hand, seeing the flare of the match rise, then taper off into a flickering yellow glow.

"Don't you think you should give me back my Thunderer, Ranger?" Lucas asked.

"No," the ranger said flatly, keeping his eyes on the match light inside the crevice.

Lucas shrugged and mumbled to himself, "It's probably broken anyway from being thrown to the ground."

"Quiet, gambler," Sam said over his shoulder.

In a moment the flickering light of the match grew in its intensity as Thorn called back to Sandoval and the ranger, "I've found some torches and lit one." He paused for a few seconds, then called out, "Gentlemen, I think we're onto something here."

"I'll bring your horse, sir," Sandoval called out.

"Yes, please do that, Sandy," said Thorn, "I'll continue on and scout the way."

A moment later, Thorn stopped and looked back, seeing another torch flare up in the darkness and start moving toward him above the clack of the horses' shoes on the stone floor. Rather than wait for the others to catch up to him, the older bounty hunter walked on for a half hour, negotiating the narrow downward-winding rock corridor, until he saw a break of daylight slash sidelong across the darkness ahead. With his horse pistol hanging in his hand, he leaned against the wall and waited until he saw Sandoval's face in the flickering glow of torchlight.

Taking the reins to his horse from the younger man, Thorn let Sandoval take the lead and fell in behind him, followed by the ranger, who kept Lucas walking in front of him inside the glow of the two torches.

"I really think it would be wise of you to give me my Thunderer now, Ranger," Lucas said over his shoulder into the darkness. "What is it you're afraid of?"

"I'm afraid you'll do something stupid and make me shoot you," Sam said.

"I'm touched that you'd go to such precaution to keep from doing me harm, Ranger," Lucas said.

"Don't flatter yourself, gambler," Sam said. "I just wouldn't want the gunshot to warn anybody."

"Of course," said Lucas with a flat grin, "how *presumptuous* of me."

They walked on.

At the end of the long corridor, Sandoval extinguished his torch and leaned it against the wall. Behind him Thorn did the same. The two led their horses out onto a flat cliff overlooking a wide crater valley, Lucas and the ranger following. The four men gazed out as the shadows of evening stretched long across the carpet of cactus, brush and chimney rock a thousand feet below them.

"There's no need in thanking me, Ranger," Lucas said wryly, looking all around, as surprised as the others but trying not to show it. "I'm sure you'd have done the same for me had the circumstances been the other way—"

"We can't stay up here," Thorn said, cutting the

gambler off. "If this is the only way in from the south-east, you can bet they watch this hillside like hawks."

"Right," said Sam, looking down at the same sets of hoofprints they'd been watching ever since they'd entered the crevice. He gestured toward the tracks leading down a thin trail to their left. "We'll follow them on down to the valley floor—manage to keep ourselves out of sight."

Gazing out across the rough windy terrain, Sandoval said, "The ground is still wet enough to hold down our dust up here. Once we're down there, it will be a different story."

"All the more reason to hurry," said Thorn. "When this land is dry and dusty, a jackrabbit can't move without its dust being seen a mile away." He gazed out with the others and said, "What a perfect place for the Black Valley Riders to see their enemies coming without ever being seen themselves."

Without reply, Sandoval turned his horse and led it onto the thin downward path. Thorn followed suit. Behind him, Sam reached over and took Lucas by his shoulder as he raised the flask to his lips and took a quick shot of rye. Giving him a nudge, Sam sent him stumbling on ahead of him in the dimming evening light.

"Ranger!" Lucas said in a mocking, playful tone. "Don't tire of me so soon. We may still yet have a long ways to go."

PART 2

PART 2

Chapter 9

Brayton *Big Aces* Shear was waiting for Mingo Sentanza and Ben Longley when they rode up at a gallop and slid their horses to a halt out in front of the cabin. Stepping down from the porch, flanked by Ballard Swean and Dave Pickens, the outlaw leader grabbed Sentanza's horse by its bridle and watched it saw its head as he rubbed its wet frothing muzzle.

"This is the only hideout in the world where a man can ride a horse plumb to its nubs just getting word back and forth," Shear said with a grin. "Tell me something good, Mingo. I slept poorly last night."

"Riders coming, Big Aces," Sentanza said, staying atop his horse, waiting for a signal from Shear that it was all right for him to step down.

"Now, tell me it's Elmer Fisk," said Shear, "so I'll know it's time we get to work."

"It is Fisk," said Sentanza. "I couldn't make out the other two, but it's Crazy Elmer for sure. They must've made it to the valley just ahead of the storm this morning."

"Nobody trailing them?" Shear asked, watching Sentanza's response.

"We saw no dust across the valley floor," said Sentanza. "But with the rain hitting along there, the dust will stay settled for a day or two."

"Yeah . . . ," said Shear, rubbing his chin in contemplation. "That's the only trouble with this place. It's so damn big, the weather can get ahead of you." He gave a short chuckle as if that was really not much to worry about.

Two other gunmen, Calvin Kerr and Dolan Callahan, relief guards for Sentanza and Longley, walked over from a run-down barn leading their horses behind them. As they drew closer to the rest of the gunmen, Shear called out to them, saying, "Elmer Fisk is riding in. Ride out there. Make sure the other two are men of ours on your way. Then get to your lookout position fast. That storm has left the trail wet."

"We're on it, Big Aces," said Callahan. Stopping to step up onto his saddle, he said to Sentanza, "Nobody behind them, eh?"

Sentanza gave a shrug. "We wouldn't be here if anybody was following them, now, would we?"

Callahan swung up in his saddle; beside him, so did Calvin Kerr. "It never hurts to check," Callahan said with a tight mirthless grin. "No offense intended."

Sentanza aimed his index finger at Callahan like a pistol and clicked his thumb as if dropping a hammer. "None taken," he said, with no grin in return.

"It looks like you two have a lot of steam you need to wear off," Shear said, looking back and forth between Sentanza and Callahan. "The two of yas ride out and meet them," he demanded. "Longley, you and Kerr both stay put here."

All four men looked surprised. Kerr and Longley both backed away. Sentanza and Callahan both stared at Shear in disbelief. It was no secret among the Black Valley Riders that the two men hated each other.

"You've got to be kidding, Big Aces," Sentanza said down to the outlaw leader. "I just finished standing lookout."

Shear's gun hand slipped deftly around the butt of a large black-handled Dance Brothers pistol holstered on his thigh. His voice turned menacing. "Do I look like I'm kidding to you, Mingo?"

Sentanza met his gaze with defiance, yet he kept quiet, backed his horse a step and turned it to the trail without even watering the tired animal. Dolan Callahan only gave a touch to his hat brim as he rode past Shear and the others and rode up alongside the smoldering Sentanza.

"You just couldn't turn it loose, could you, *Mingo*?" Callahan said in a taunting manner.

Sentanza forced himself to cool down. "I have turned it loose now, Dolan," he said. He took a deep breath and let it out slowly, settling his white-hot temper with a thin smile. Beneath him the frothed horse traveled on in spite of its thirst and exhaustion.

The two rode in silence toward a rise of trail dust until they had crossed the valley floor far enough to clearly see Elmer Fisk and the other two outlaws riding toward them. The wind and dust had settled enough for Duckwald and Epson to lower their bandannas from their faces. Recognizing them, Sentanza and Callahan reined their horses down and met the three in the long remnants of harsh evening sunlight.

Callahan called out to Fisk, "Big Aces is waiting to see you. Where's Bates and Riley?"

"Virgil Bates and Bertram Riley are both dead," said Fisk. He stopped his horse and rested his wrists on his saddle horn. "So is Bobby Parsons and Earl Baggett, according to Tinnis Lucas."

"Ah, that's too bad," said Callahan. "How'd that drunken gambler know so much about them?"

"He saw it all," said Fisk, not wanting to tell too much now, knowing he'd only have to retell it once he rode to the cabin. "He was riding with us, but he left all of a sudden." He slipped a faint, knowing grin to Epson and Duckwald.

Sentanza sat sullen, listening, getting a good idea that the gambler was dead.

"What's wrong with you, Mingo?" Fisk asked. "Somebody piss in the *frijoles* again?"

Not wanting to irritate Crazy Elmer, Sentanza held his tongue and allowed himself to give a thin smile.

"Nothing is wrong," he said. "How are you doing, Elmer Fisk?" He touched two fingertips to his battered short-brimmed sombrero and gave a nod to Epson and Duckwald.

Duckwald returned his nod and gestured toward Sentanza's worn-out horse. "If you don't rest that animal soon, we'll be watching him turn over a fire."

"He's okay," said Sentanza, patting the tired horse's withers. "We don't have far to go."

"If Mingo here thinks he's riding double with me,

he's got some bad news coming," Callahan said tauntingly, looking the tired horse up and down.

Your time is coming, you son of a whore pig . . ., Sentanza told himself. Yet he gave only a withering smile and remained silent.

"Speaking of beans and horse meat," said Fisk, "I'm starving here. Let's get on to the cabin."

"You three ride on in. We're headed out to watch the high trail," said Callahan. "I can't wait to build a fire and eat something myself."

Before turning his horse to leave, Fisk gave him a look. "How would Big Aces known if it wasn't us?"

"He'd've heard the shooting by now," Callahan said, tipping his hat brim as he and Sentanza reined their horses back to the trail.

As soon as Elmer Fisk and the other two riders stepped down from their saddles out in front of the cabin, Shear appeared in the yard to meet them. "Swean," he said to the gunman standing nearest beside him, "take Elmer's horse and tend to it. Him and I need to talk."

Walking alongside and directing Fisk toward the cabin door, Shear said, "Where's the others? We're going to need all the men we can rally."

"Hell, they're dead, Big Aces," said Fisk, stepping onto the porch. "I hope you've got something skint and gutted in here. I'm starving." He bounded inside the cabin and looked all around.

"Whoa! What do you mean, *they're dead*?" said Shear, turning Fisk by his arm.

Fisk stared down at the hand on his arm, just enough

to let Shear know that putting a hand on him was a bad idea. "I mean they're dead, Big Aces," he said in a more somber tone. "They messed with the wrong persons."

Shear removed his hand, but persisted. "What on earth happened? You and Baggett were supposed to meet them in Minton Hill."

"I expect Baggett met them rightly enough . . . straight down in hell. He's dead too!" Fisk leaned close to his face and gave him the sort of leering bug-eyed grin that had earned him his name Crazy Elmer.

"All right, Elmer," Shear said, getting impatient with him, "tell me about it."

"What I'm telling *you* is what your pal that drunken gambler Lucas told me," Fisk said.

"Tinnis Lucas?" said Shear.

"That's right," said Fisk, "Lucas was there and saw it all. Two sailors and the ranger who killed Junior Lake and his gang killed all four of our boys. Shot them down in the street, like they were dogs."

"That damned ranger," Shear said. Then he caught himself and said, "Two *sailors* . . . ?" He stared at Fisk.

"Yeah, that's what Lucas told me," said Fisk. "The sailors who wear that new emblem on their shirts—the eagle, the globe and anchor?"

"Yeah, *marines*," said Shear, getting a better grasp on the matter. "The ranger is partnered with *marines*? How much was Lucas drinking when he said all this?"

"About as same as usual, drunker than a skunk," said Fisk. He gave the crazy grin. "Drunk enough that he rode his horse off a cliff on the way here . . . looked like a barn rat learning to fly."

"Jesus . . . !" Shear tried to take in everything Fisk had told him. Drunk or sober, Tinnis Lucas had never sold him bad information. "Why was Lucas coming here? Didn't you give him what he had coming to him?"

"Yes, in a manner of speaking," Fisk said, still with his leering grin. "He said the marines are hunting bounty that's been put on all of us Black Valley Riders."

"Marines, hunting bounty?" said Shear. "I don't get it. Shouldn't they be off settling a war or hanging pirates or somewhere?"

Fisk gave a shrug. "I expect times are tight the world over."

Shear gave a bemused look and shook his head in contemplation. "All right, then. We'll have to pick up some men on our way. We've still got a big job waiting for us." He looked at Fisk. "I had the men start getting ready to clear out of here when I saw Sentanza signal you were coming. You and the other two rest up. We'll pull out first thing come morning."

"You've got it, Big Aces," said Fisk, stepping over to a pot of coffee that hung simmering over a fire in a stone hearth. On a charred mantel above the hearth sat a tin bread pan with a cloth thrown over it. "Meanwhile, I'm going to eat anything that I don't have to chase around the room."

As Fisk walked over, flipped back the cloth and dug up a piece of leftover flatbread, Shear asked him, "Did you see Lucas' body after he rode off the cliff?"

"No, it was too dark," said Fisk taking a big bite of bread as he looked around for a tin coffee cup.

"Then you don't really know for certain he's dead, do you?" said Shear.

"Oh, he's dead, Big Aces," said Fisk. "You can take my word for it—Duckwald and Epson's too. He must've fell a thousand feet." He feigned a remorseful squint. "It was awful, Lucas screaming, the poor horse neighing . . ." He shook his head as if to get rid of the grim picture. "I'm sickened just thinking of it."

Shear just stared at him. "But you didn't see his body," he persisted.

"I told you, Big Aces," said Fisk, getting a bit annoyed, "Tinnis Lucas is stone dead. That's all there is to it."

"I've known that drunken rebel for a long time," Shear said, as if drawing from a deep well of knowledge on the subject of the gambler. "He's awfully hard to kill. . . ."

At dark, Sentanza sat searching upward along the high trail, a canteen of water lying on the ground by his side. Behind him, Dolan Callahan poured himself a cup of hot coffee from a pot sitting over a low flame. With his cup in hand he sat back and picked up a warm, opened can of air-tights he'd set near the fire. "Ah," he said, sniffing the can of warm pork-seasoned beans before plunging a spoon into it. "There's nothing beats pork and beans for my money," he said, taunting Sentanza as he had been throughout the evening.

Sentanza didn't reply. He spat to the side and resumed watching the high trail while Callahan ate.

"Too bad you had to turn around and come back out here, without so much as grabbing yourself some overnight supplies," said Callahan. He smiled to himself. "I feel awful not offering you some of this. But a *wise* man is always mindful of keeping his strength up, out here in the wilds like this."

By the saints, I will kill him. . . . Sentanza smoldered, but said nothing. He studied the high trail, especially a spot where moments before dark he thought he'd caught a glimpse of a man start to step from behind a rock, but then fall back out of sight. He had made no mention of it, not wanting to give Callahan more fuel for taunting him.

"It is dark. Put out the fire, Dolan," Sentanza said over his shoulder. "It can be seen a mile away."

"Not until I'm finished with this *delicious* can of warm beans, *Mingo*," Callahan said mockingly, knowing how badly he was chafing Sentanza.

"You are through cooking. Put out the fire," Sentanza insisted. "You know this is how we always do things on lookout."

"But I find it *soooo* settling," said Callahan, "gazing into the flames over a cup of hot coffee." He spooned up another mouthful of beans and chuckled to himself before taking a bite. "You wouldn't be so tensed up yourself, going around with a mad-on all the time, if you learned to relax a little."

"I'm going to relieve myself," Sentanza said flatly.

"You go right ahead, *Mingo*," Callahan said. "I'll keep an eye on the high trail." He shrugged. "Not that I think anybody would be foolish enough to try to get in here on us."

But instead of turning and even glancing up along the high trail, Callahan sat eating the beans until he finally licked his metal spoon, stuck it into the empty can and set the can down on the wide stone shelf beside him. Moments later when he heard a boot scrape the stone behind him, he said, "I hope you shook it good. You've been gone long enough."

He chuckled and looked down at his shirt pocket as he fished inside it for his bag of fixings. As he did so his breath gasped sharply in his chest. He felt a gloved hand wrap across his forehead. He saw six inches of a blood-smeared steel blade slice through the front of his shirt and stick out from the center of his sternum. The blade sliced back and forth once, expertly, severing his heart.

His eyes stayed fixed downward, but glazed over as the gloved hand guided him forward and sidelong to the ground. The sleek blade disappeared back into his chest and out of his back, beside the sole of Sandoval's black knee-high boot.

Chapter 10

From two different hiding places, Thorn and the gambler slipped over the edge of the smooth rock surface and ran forward in a crouch, meeting where Sandoval stood in the glow of the firelight, bloody ax blade in hand.

"Kill the fire," Thorn said to Lucas.

"Aye, aye, Captain," Lucas replied almost jokingly, but he did as he was told, quickly, as the ranger walked into sight leading Sentanza's tired horse by its reins.

Noting the question in Thorn's eyes, Sam said, "He was gone when I got there."

"To warn the others," Thorn said.

"I don't think so," Sam said. "He could have done that by firing shots in the air. I think he decided it was time to get out of here and save his own skin." He looked at Lucas, who had begun rummaging through the dead man's saddlebags on the ground by the fire. "What are you looking for, gambler?"

"Whiskey," said Lucas. "I'm a drunkard, Ranger," he added. "What else would I be looking for?"

"Take your hands out of those saddlebags," Sam said. "They better be empty," he warned. "Anyway, you've got enough whiskey."

"*Enough* whiskey?" Lucas let out a sigh. "Ranger, a drunkard never has *enough* whiskey." He ignored the ranger and continued to rummage.

"You do," Sam said, reaching a boot over and clamping it down on the saddlebags. "Now take them out, *empty*, like I told you."

"If you insist," Lucas said. He removed his hands as the ranger raised his boot. Holding his hands chest high, he said, "All right, there is a gun in there. But obviously I had no idea when I began searching. I truly was looking for whiskey, on my word as a gentleman."

The ranger stooped down, pulled out a small pistol and stood up shaking his head. "You're getting on everybody's nerves, Lucas," he said, shoving the small pistol into his belt beside Lucas' Colt Thunderer. "Keep it up and we'll be right back to a charge of horse theft and a set of handcuffs."

Lucas sat down and slumped and shook his head. "What do you really think I am, Ranger, a member of the Black Valley Riders?" He held up the lapels of his thin, ragged suit coat. "Look, I don't even have the proper *accessories*. What self-respecting Black Valley member would be caught without his silver quarter-moon and star pendant?"

Sam said, "For all we know you might have had one. You could have sold it for a drink."

"Now, that hurts, Ranger," said Lucas. "I am a gambler, and a damn good one . . . that is, when I'm on my game." He looked up and back and forth among the three as they stared down at him.

"That's the trouble, gambler," Sam said. "I haven't yet figured out just what your game *is*. That's why you're not packing a gun and getting the chance to warn anybody we're coming."

"I would not do that, Ranger," Lucas said. "For reasons you would never understand, I would not warn Shear and his men that you are coming. I do have *some* self-respect left. Not a lot, but *some*."

He looked up at Thorn and saw the questioning look on his face. "Well, Captain, you've studied me awfully close since our paths crossed. What do you say my game is? Have you *figured* me out yet?"

"No, not completely," Thorn said. "But I think I've got you pegged close enough."

"Oh, do you, now, really?" said Lucas. "Then pray tell us, sir. We all want to know."

Thorn appeared to be on the verge of saying something. But he stopped himself, shook his head and said instead, "You're a contemptible drunk who doesn't know which side to be on. You're not a part of the Black Valley Riders, but you beg for crumbs at their table. You sell them just enough of your soul to keep yourself in cheap rye. You ally yourself with *nothing* or *no one*—"

"Because I *like* it that way," Lucas cut in sharply. "I owe alliance to nothing or nobody, sir!"

"No, you don't," said Thorn. Seeing the sting his words had given the gambler, he refused to let up. "That's because you have nothing—you have *nobody*. You're afraid too, gambler. That makes you a *coward*."

"A coward! How dare you, sir!" said Lucas, suddenly coming to his feet, his fists clenched at his side. Sam and Sandoval looked on, witnessing a dark, serious side to Lucas that they'd not seen before. "You know nothing about me!"

"You're wrong, gambler," said Thorn, a look of realization having come upon his face. "I know all there is to know about you. I know everything about you. You've made a lifelong practice of picking the *wrong* side to be on."

"I was not on the *wrong* side, Thorn," said Lucas. "I was on the side that didn't *win*." He glowered. "But enough of that, sir. You have pushed me too far."

The gambler stepped toward Cadden Thorn with fire in his bloodshot eyes, but the bounty hunter didn't back an inch. "I hope you're not demanding satisfaction, Tinnis Lucas, if that *is* your name," Thorn said. "I refuse to waste my time on such a sorry creature as you."

The ranger and Sandoval glanced out across the darkness, then back to the two men standing almost chest to chest in the grainy night. "Easy, men," Sam said. "Whatever this is about, you'll have to take it up later. We're inside the Black Valley Riders' lair. We need to keep moving and get this job done." Even as Sam spoke, Sandoval stood to the side as if prepared to be Thorn's second in a gentleman's duel if need be.

"Right you are, Ranger," Thorn said without taking his eyes off Lucas. "We'll finish our little talk later, gambler . . . sober. That is, if you think your nerves can take it."

"At your pleasure, Captain Thorn," Lucas said with

a newfound strength to his voice. "Whether I'm drunk or sober, my nerves are holding up *remarkably well.*"

The ranger watched with a flat expression. Whatever situation had begun to act itself out between these two was of a personal nature, he told himself. He wasn't sure *how* he could tell, but he could tell.

Stepping closer to the ranger, Sandoval whispered in private, "As you were, Ranger. The captain knows what he's doing."

The ranger only nodded. *So does the gambler . . . ,* he said silently to himself. He hadn't mentioned it, but ever since he'd seen the way Lucas had handled getting himself down from the tree, he'd begun to notice a different side to Tinnis Lucas.

When Mingo Sentanza had reached what he considered a safe distance higher up the trail from the bounty hunters and the ranger, he stopped his horse and looked back across the dark valley floor. He smiled to himself. He liked the idea of taking off on Callahan's horse and leaving the big Irish gunman there alone—him and his warm can of beans. The fact that he'd heard no gunfire the past few minutes told him that by now Callahan was either dead or in irons.

Either way, *good riddance. . . .*

He had been on the verge of easing over and slicing Callahan's throat when he'd realized there were men slipping down around them in the night. But this was better, he thought. Let them kill Callahan, or take him prisoner.

Still, just for good measure, he raised his Winchester from its boot, propped its butt down on his thigh and

levered three shots straight up into the purple sky.
"Who can say a damn thing?" he murmured, rehears-
ing his future explanation, should one ever be needed.
He'd done exactly as he was supposed to do, except for
abandoning his loudmouthed partner. "I warned you
first," he practiced saying to Shear. "Then I grabbed the
closest horse and cut out." He added with a grin, "Oh,
poor Callahan is dead? Captured? That is too bad. . . ."

He stared through the night in the direction of the
cabin sitting across the wide valley floor. Then he slipped
the rifle back into its boot, turned the horse and rode
away.

Across the valley on the front porch of the cabin,
Ballard Swean stood up from his wooden chair with a
blanket wrapped around him, rifle in hand. He stared
off toward the sound of the distant rifle shots and
wiped sleep from his eyes. The sound of voices came
from within the cabin behind him. He searched the
black far-off hill line as if something would reveal itself
to him.

"Did that come from our lookouts?" Shear asked,
stomping out onto the porch, shoving his shirttails down
into his trousers. He stood barefoot. He'd thrown his
gun belt over his shoulder when his feet had hit the
plank floor and drawn his big Dance Brothers pistol
from its holster. He held it cocked and raised in his
right hand.

"Yeah," said Swean, "it's warning shots from Sentanza and Callahan. We've got somebody coming, no
doubt about it." He threw his blanket aside. "Want me
to take some men out and set up an ambush along the
trail?"

"No, not this time," said Shear. "We're all set to move out come morning. We'll just leave tonight instead. There'll be plenty of places to pull an ambush between here and the north wall." He uncocked the big pistol and let it hang in his hand.

"If these sonsabitches want to come visit Black Valley, we'll do our best to take them on a guided tour," he said.

Hearing the signal shots, the rest of the awakened gunmen came running up from all directions to see what Shear would want them to do.

"We're not running, are we, Big Aces?" a thin gunman named Ted Lasko asked, hearing what Shear had just told Swean.

"Hell no," said Shear. "But I want whoever's out there to think we are, for the time being anyway." He looked quickly around at more than a dozen gunmen gathering around him.

"Tell us what you want, Big Aces," said a gunman named Tobias Barnes.

Shear said, "Toby, ride like hell ahead of us to the north wall pass."

"Hatchet Pass?" Barnes asked.

"Yes," said Shear. "You'll find Metcalf and some men there. Tell him to start getting things ready, that we're headed his way. As soon as we ride through the pass, I want him to be all set to close it off behind us."

"How many you figure there are, Big Aces?" Barnes asked.

"I don't know," said Shear. "But it won't matter. You've got enough explosives and equipment to turn back an army out there. Now get moving."

Shear slid his Dance Brothers back into its holster and turned and stomped back inside the cabin, Swean right behind him. Over his shoulder Shear said to him, "We won't be coming back here for a while. Make sure you take all your gear with you."

"Will do, boss," said Swean.

In moments, Barnes had saddled his horse, mounted it and ridden away from the livery barn. The rest of the men had saddled their horses and hurriedly led them back to the cabin. They mounted their animals as Swean and Shear came back out onto the porch.

"Where's Fisk, Duckwald and Epson?" Shear asked in a gruff tone.

From his saddle, Elmer Fisk called out, "I'm right here, Big Aces."

"How many do you say there are out there, Elmer?" Shear asked.

"If it's the same ones who killed our men in Minton Hill, there's just the three I told you about," Fisk replied.

"The ranger and the two sailors?" Shear asked.

"That's right," said Fisk. "The ranger and two *bounty hunters*," he corrected.

"Nobody else?" Shear said, as if making sure.

Fisk looked at Epson and Duckwald. "Nobody else that we saw," Fisk said, getting a little irritated that Shear pressed so hard. "Hell, I can't say who might have come along and joined them."

"You three ride up front with me," said Shear in a sharp tone.

Feeling a tension set in among Shear, Fisk and the other two men, Swean said, "Hell's fire, Big Aces, like as not, with this kind of a head start, they'll be lucky if they get close enough to see our dust."

"I don't like getting up and leaving my bed in the middle of the night for nobody," Shear said. He stared hard at Fisk and the other two as he stepped down from the porch and walked to Pickens, who stood holding his horse for him.

As Fisk, Duckwald and Epson stepped their horses over beside him, Fisk said, "If they get close enough to us, Big Aces, they'll wish to hell they had our names in their mouths."

"If they get close enough to us, I'll hold you to that, Elmer," Shear said, jerking his horse around and booting it toward the north trail.

Chapter 11

"There went your *element of surprise*, Ranger," Lucas said as the warning shots from the escaped trail guard's rifle resounded off the hills and rolled out over the valley. His voice didn't have its usual critical tone, or its whiskey-tinted edge to it. Sam had noted the gambler's quiet sullenness ever since the earlier flare-up between him and Cadden Thorn.

"It makes no difference, gambler," Sam said over his shoulder, him and Thorn riding side by side ahead of Lucas and Sandoval. "We were going in with or without the element of surprise."

Lucas made no reply as they rode through the purple darkness. But over the next half hour, he let his horse stray back a few feet from beside Dee Sandoval. When Sandoval said nothing about him lagging back, he lagged back even farther and rode on. He could tell that the outlaw's horse beneath him was still tired from a day on the wide valley floor. Yet, at a place where a path cut sharply down off the trail, he decided to make the move he'd been planning ever since his heated confrontation with the bounty hunter.

Sam and Thorn both turned in their saddles at the sound of the horse's hoove pounding away through brush and loose rock. Instinctively the ranger started to turn his stallion in pursuit, but Thorn stopped him.

"I'd be obliged if you'd let him go, Ranger," he said, holding a hand up as if to block Sam from turning off of the trail himself.

Sam looked back and forth at the two bounty hunters, who sat calmly on their horses. He understood in an instant what had just taken place. Looking at Sandoval, he said, "You let him ride away, didn't you?"

Sandoval didn't answer; instead he looked to Thorn.

"It's all my doing, Ranger," said Thorn. "I knew Lucas would make a run for it after our talk. But it's all right. He won't go join Shear and his men."

"It's not all right," Sam said. "And you can't say that he *won't* join Shear and his men. Even if he doesn't, there's still the matter of him stealing the horse and buggy."

Thorn said, "He kept his word. He led us here, just like he said he would. As to the horse and buggy, I will see to it the woman is paid for her loss."

Sandoval cut in. "Besides, Lucas can't tip off Brayton Shear that we're coming. The lookout guard's shots have already warned him."

Sam looked at Thorn. "All right, Captain, you seem to know so much about the gambler. Why did he run away from us if not to join Shear?"

"Because there's something eating away inside him,"

said Thorn. "Lucas thinks the only way to get rid of it is to outrun it." He gave a tired smile in the grainy darkness. "I know this man. He has been *running away* ever since the war. That's what the drinking is about."

"It's his way of running away without having to even leave his chair," Sandoval offered. "The way it is with most drunks." He gazed to where the first light of dawn seeped up over the edge of the earth.

Sam asked the older bounty hunter, "Where do you know him from, Thorn?" He eased his stallion over closer. "What was all that about between you and him last night? I have a right to know."

"Indeed you do, Ranger," Thorn said, almost apologetically. He let go of a breath. "Tinnis Lucas was once a marine just like Mr. Sandoval and myself." He paused for a moment as if to allow the information to settle. Then he went on. "He must've known it was only a matter of time . . . that I would recognize him sooner or later."

"Lucas, a marine?" Sam said. "That's a hard one to believe." But even as he spoke, he recalled how expertly the drunken gambler had handled the lariat.

"I would not have believed it myself had I not seen it," said Thorn. "Not only was he a marine, he was one of the best. The corps was his heart and soul."

"He served under you, Captain?" Sam asked.

"No," said Thorn, "I was not an officer back then. My commission came later. But we served at the same post, in Charlestown Harbor. His name was not Tinnis Lucas then. It was Tinnis Mayes."

"What happened to him?" Sam asked. "Why'd he change his name?"

"The War of Secession is what *happened* to Tinnis Mayes, the same as it *happened* to many young marines at that time. We were given a choice of which side to fight for and Mayes choice the South."

"I see," said Sam. "So he was in the Confederate States Marine Corps."

"Yes," said Thorn. "But the CSMC never quite got its feet under itself. A few good men like Mayes were forced to be little more than ship and harbor guards." He stared ahead as if in grim contemplation. "But Mayes refused to settle for that. He became a blockade runner—a spy if you will. Eventually he became a special assassin for the Richmond Ring. After the war, members of the CSMC were welcomed back into the ranks. But not Mayes. He was treated with the same ranker as William Quantrill and other border guerillas. Secretary of War Edwin Stanton said 'his hands are too bloody.'"

Sandoval eased up beside the two and sat listening intently, even though the ranger knew he must be familiar with the captain's story.

"The day of President Lincoln's assassination," said Thorn, "before leaving for the theater, he was met at the White House by Missouri senator John Henderson, who brought two articles of pardon, one for Confederate spy Tinnis Mayes, and the other for confederate spy George Vaughn."

"I recall the pardon of George Vaughn," said Sam. "He was to be executed in two days. Signing his pardon was the last official act the president performed before his assassination."

"Yes," said Thorn. "Owing to the pressing nature of

Vaughn's case, and the fact that he'd been recruited into the Confederate Missouri State Guard cause by Martin Green, brother of U.S. senator James Green, the president signed his pardon on the spot, with an understanding between himself and the senator that he would sign Mayes' pardon the next day. Mayes, having no political well to draw from, was never pardoned."

Sam shook his head at the irony of it. "Politics and paperwork."

"Indeed," said Thorn. "It's been the bane of the corps from the beginning." He gave a bitter smile. "George Vaughn, the *mercenary spy*, went free. Mayes, the marine, while never prosecuted because of the common knowledge of Lincoln's intent to pardon him, was branded a killer and became an outcast. I can only presume that is why he changed his name."

Sam gave him a curious look. "Marines are trained to kill."

"Yes, as are all military men," said Thorn. "But there is a saying among the corps. 'Calling a young marine a killer will get you *saluted* . . . Calling an old marine a killer will get you *shot.*'" He gazed at Sam for understanding. "I, sir, am an *old marine.*"

"So, Mayes changed his name and became a drunk and consort of outlaws," Sam reflected.

"I don't excuse him for it," Thorn said. "His was a tough twist of fate, but it does not justify him turning to the company of men like Shear and his Black Valley Riders."

"What is it you want, then?" Sam asked.

"To give him room," said Thorn. "If he's standing

on the edge, I want him to fall in the right direction. He deserves the same chance as George Vaughn, and the more politically adept."

"He makes his own choices, Captain," said Sam, "he pays his own freight."

"He's a marine," Thorn countered. "As a fellow marine I am blood-bound to protect his flank."

"A *Confederate* marine," Sam pointed out.

"A marine nonetheless, Ranger," said Thorn.

Sandoval sat watching in silence. "It is an understanding that all marines share. The blood of *each* of us becomes the blood of us *all.*"

"There is another saying among the ranks, Ranger," Thorn said. "It's not something started by an act of Congress, or by any political movement. It's something we marines say among ourselves. It's *Semper fidelis.*"

"Always faithful," Sam translated. "I know what it means." He looked at Sandoval, who had spoken the words to him back in Minton Hill. Then he looked back to Thorn. "I'll go along with you on this, Captain. We'll give the gambler all the room he needs. But if he throws in with Shear and shows up looking down a gun sight at us, I want your word that he's dead."

"You have my word, Ranger Burrack," said the captain. He turned his horse back to the trail, the ranger and Sandoval right beside him.

In the morning sunlight, the gambler had pulled the horse off the wind-whipped valley floor. In a stand of sheltering white oak lining the bank of a thin runoff stream, he dropped from the saddle and plopped down on a rock. With his hands shaking he pulled the battered flask from inside his suit coat, unscrewed the cap and lifted it to his trembling lips.

"Holy God," he said aloud, taking the flask down and staring at it, "don't let me run out of rye." Pain pounded in his head beneath his sore and swollen scalp. He shook the flask upside down as if he didn't trust his findings. He stared at it grimly and shook his head as the truth finally sank in.

Why not . . . ? he thought to himself in a bitter tone of acceptance.

He let the empty flask fall from his fingertips and lay back on the rock, his arms spread wide like a man awaiting his crucifixion. He pictured Thorn's grim face, staring at him, staring through him, judging him severely. He thought about the squalor his life had become as he felt cold stark sobriety already beginning to take its toll.

What have I done . . . ?

The pain in both his head and his body grew more intense as the rye left his system. He closed his eyes against the sunlight and let himself drift, wishing he could fall asleep and never awaken. But he did awaken, and fast, when he heard a horse chuff nearby, followed by the sound of a rifle cocking.

"Well, well, if it's not the Tinman," said Mingo Sentanza, staring at him from fifteen feet away, his rifle in hand, aimed at the gambler's chest.

Well, hell, why not . . . ?

"Do you have any whiskey, Mingo?" Tinnis said first thing, rising and sitting slumped on the edge of the rock facing him.

"Huh-uh," said Sentanza in a somber voice.

"Well then, if you intend to shoot me, please do it this instant. Spare us both having to talk to each other," the gambler said.

"What's the matter, Tinman?" said Sentanza. "You look like you've slept in a barrel of rocks."

"That's putting it mildly," Tinnis said. He touched his shaved and stitched scalp cautiously. "I'm out of whiskey at a time when I need it the most." He sighed and added, "So, if you are going to shoot me, I'd just as soon we didn't talk—"

"Why are you riding my horse?" Sentanza asked bluntly, cutting him off.

"Why are you *not* riding him?" Tinnis asked in reply, looking Callahan's horse over.

"That was me back there with Dolan," Sentanza said with a jerk of his head. Noting that Tinnis wore no hat, he said, "Was that you I saw? You came walking out, but someone pulled you back?"

"It's likely," said the gambler, recalling himself stepping into sight earlier on the trail only to be yanked back into cover by the ranger.

"Is Callahan dead?" Sentanza asked.

"Yes, he is," said the gambler, "he took a sword through the heart. So, if you feel like you ought to go ahead and—"

"I don't care," said Sentanza. "I was ready to kill him myself."

"Oh . . . ?" The gambler stared at him.

Sentanza shrugged. "Anyway, I thought you were dead."

"Who told you that?" Tinnis asked him.

"Crazy Elmer Fisk," said Sentanza. "He didn't say it, but he made me think it, the way he talked."

"As you can see, I'm not dead," said the gambler. "You wouldn't happen to have any whiskey, would you?"

"You already asked me," said Sentanza. "I told you *no.*"

Damn it. . . . Tinnis let out a breath.

"Who were you riding with?" Sentanza asked.

"Which time?" said Tinnis.

"*This* time," said Sentanza. "The ones you brought into the valley."

"I rode up here with Crazy Elmer and two others. But I ended up with two bounty hunters and an Arizona Territory Ranger," he said without hesitation. "The one who killed Junior Lake and his gang."

"Whoa, *that* ranger?" said Sentanza. His hand drew tighter around his rifle. "Maybe I *will* shoot you after all."

"Be my guest, I hurt too bad to care," said Tinnis, spreading his arms wide. "The fact is, I had no choice but to bring them. They were just up here anyway. They found me stranded up a mountain pine after my horse walked off the high trail."

"Off of the high trail?" Sentanza said as if in disbelief. "No wonder Fisk thought you were dead. You are lucky to be alive."

"That's a matter of opinion," said the gambler, wincing from the pain in his head. "Anyway, the ranger and bounty men followed the trail up to where I'd fallen and rode right in. No way could I have led them. I didn't know the way myself."

"It's true I never saw you here before," said Sentanza, considering things.

Seeing the outlaw wasn't going to kill him, the gambler let out a painful breath. "Do you want your horse back?"

"Maybe later," Sentanza said. "Do you have your Colt Thunderer under your arm?"

"No, they took it from me," said Tinnis. He opened his left lapel and showed Sentanza the empty shoulder holster.

Sentanza considered it. The gambler would not have given up his gun unless he'd been a prisoner. "Are you headed for the cabin?" he asked.

"Yes, I am," the gambler said agreeably. "Where are you headed?"

"I am headed the same place," said Sentanza. He lowered the rifle but kept it in hand, his finger still on the trigger. "Why don't you get back on *my* horse and I will follow you there?"

The gambler knew he wasn't really asking.

"Good idea," Tinnis said, standing and reaching for his reins.

Chapter 12

It was afternoon when the gambler and Sentanza stepped down from the horses out in front of the empty cabin. Seeing that Shear and his men had pulled out, Sentanza turned around in the front doorway and gazed north along a distant jagged hill line. "I know where they are headed," he said over his shoulder to the gambler who had walked straight to a cupboard and opened both doors wide, searching for whiskey.

"Yeah . . . ?" Tinnis said absently. "And where might that be?" He stepped over to a shelf near the hearth and looked along a line of bottles and spices and herb jars.

"Hatchet Pass," Sentanza said. "Big Aces will leave some gunmen there to guard his escape while he takes the rest of the men on through Black Valley. Once he's out, they'll blow that pass with dynamite. If it don't kill the lawmen chasing him, it'll leave them staring at a rock wall."

"You don't say," said the gambler. He gave up on finding whiskey or anything else that might contain enough alcohol to quiet his pain and his jangled nerves. But what he did find was an eight-inch dagger lying beside the hearth. He grabbed it and sized it up in his hand as he turned and looked at Sentanza's unsuspecting back.

"It's a good thing for you that I am with you, Tinman," Sentanza said over his shoulder as Tinnis walked softly toward him with the dagger gripped in his fist.

"Really, and why is that?" Tinnis asked, approaching him quietly from behind.

"Because the gunmen that Big Aces leaves behind will have orders to kill any sonsabitches they don't recognize riding up the trail behind him."

Tinnis stopped in his tracks. "There'll be someone there who'd recognize me."

"There might be," said Sentanza, "but unless they know you carry a moon and star, they'll kill you anyway. That's the rules of the game."

"I see," said Tinnis. He sighed to himself and slid the dagger up the sleeve of his dusty black coat. "Then, lucky for me that you're with me. Lucky for you that you mentioned it." ·

"Oh, and why's that?" said Sentanza, turning, facing him.

"Pay me no mind, Mingo," said Tinnis. "Mine are the musings of a drunkard gone dry."

The two watered and grained their horses and rode on, following a trail of overturned dirt, broken brush, and rock scraped by ironclad hooves. In the long shadows of evening, they stopped at an entrance to a deep canyon, Sentanza having stopped first, then the gambler stopping and nudging his horse up beside him.

"What now?" Tinnis asked, looking all around the canyon edge lying before them.

"Now we wait," said Sentanza. "They've seen us. They know I'm one of them. They see that I'm doing everything just like I'm supposed to."

"What follows you on your trail, pilgrim?" a voice called out from the nearest jut of rock fifty feet above them.

Sentanza grinned at Tinnis and said quietly between them, "Here's the difference between you being with me or riding in alone, Tinman."

Tinnis sat in silence, knowing he had the bead of many rifle sights pinned to his chest.

"Only the light of the moon and the star," Sentanza called back to the rock and the darkening sky.

"So much for passwords," said Tinnis. He stared at Sentanza. "Now that I know it, what happens next?"

Sentanza's grin vanished. "Now we must kill you . . ." He let his words hang suspended for a moment. During that moment, the gambler's right hand slipped over close to his left coat sleeve, poised and ready. His eyes fixed on Sentanza's throat, the one inch of beard-stubble flesh between his chin and a dusty sweat-stained bandanna. That's where he'd put it, straight up from the sleeve across the throat . . . one strike, left to right, he instructed himself.

". . . or we must take you into the Black Valley Riders, eh?" Sentanza finished, his grin returning only a split second before the gambler made his move for the concealed dagger.

Tinnis felt himself ease down, relax, like a snake uncoiling. "That shouldn't take very long for me to decide."

"You don't decide. We do," said Sentanza as the clack of a single horse's hooves came toward them from the mouth of the canyon.

"Then let's hope all goes favorably," the gambler said. "The fact of the matter is, I always wondered when I'd be asked."

"Nobody ever asks you to join the Black Valley Riders," Sentanza said quietly between them. "You've got to be the one who asks to join us. I'm telling you this on the cuff."

"I'm obliged," said Tinnis, speaking barely above a whisper now as the rider came closer in the grainy evening light. "When should I ask?"

"You already did. Don't you remember asking me this morning when I found you on the rock?" He gave Tinnis a sly look.

"How foolish of me," Tinnis replied with the same look. "Of course I remember."

The single rider drew closer.

"Why are you doing this for me, Mingo?" Tinnis asked in a whisper, not recalling Sentanza to be one widely known for his generosity.

"It makes it easier for me to explain bringing you here," said Sentanza.

"Again, obliged," said Tinnis.

"Don't thank me," Sentanza whispered. "Just remember you owe me for it, Tinman."

"How could I ever forget?" said Tinnis. Raising his voice to the lone rider, he called out, "*Hola*, Dent Phillips. When did you show up? You weren't at the cabin when I left to stand lookout, or *were* you?"

"*Hola* yourself, Mingo," said the gunman, staring at

Tinnis as he spoke to Sentanza. "I was here at the pass, where Big Aces wanted me."

"I had no idea," said Sentanza.

"That's because he doesn't tell you everything," said Phillips. He shot Sentanza a look; then his eyes went back to the gambler. Only half recognizing him, he asked as his hand held his rifle ready and cocked and propped on his thigh, "You are Tinnis Lucas, aren't you?"

"Indeed I am, sir," said Tinnis with his Southern accent. "At your service." He gave a slight bow of his head, keeping both hands holding his reins chest high. "Might I trouble you for a drink?"

"I've got nothing for you to drink, Lucas," he said. He turned to Sentanza. "You best have a damn good reason for bringing him up here."

"I do," said Sentanza, his tone turning tight-lipped and guarded.

"Yeah? What is it?" Phillips asked.

"Is Big Aces still here?" Sentanza asked instead of replying.

"Yep," said Phillips, "he feels safe here. He's staying the night and pushing on come morning."

"Good," said Sentanza. "Big Aces will most likely be happy to *tell you* my reason, Dent, once *I've* told him."

"Are you packing anything, Lucas?" he asked the gambler, ignoring Sentanza's cross attitude.

"Nothing but what the Lord blessed me with at birth, sir," the gambler replied, opening his lapel slowly and showing him the empty holster.

"Good enough," Dent Phillips said. He looked back at Sentanza and asked, "Did you make sure your back trail was clear? We've got—"

"Who do you think fired those warning shots last night, Phillips?" Sentanza asked sharply, cutting the gunman off.

"No need to get your bark on, Mingo," said Phillips. "I'm just doing my job."

"Do it downwind from me," said Sentanza. He stared hard at the younger gunman. Tinnis sat staring, watching to see who would come out on top.

"All right . . . ," said Dent Phillips, finally backing down from any further words with Sentanza. "You two can ride on in. But there's going to be a couple of riflemen riding behind you."

Ten minutes down the trail into the canyon, the two riders turned onto a path winding around a tall chimney rock. Atop the natural pillar of stone, a gunman stepped into sight and looked down at both of them and the two riders following a few yards behind. Circling the towering rock, the gambler noted a long rope ladder eighty feet long hanging down to the ground.

They rode on, the gambler looking at every path in and out of a hillside maze of rock and crevice. "Here we are, Tinman," said Sentanza as they stopped their horses and looked down at an earth, plank and boulder cabin partly dug into the hillside below them.

Tinnis sat gazing back and forth at what he decided was a defense fort carved from rock. "As hideouts go, this one should hold its own," he remarked, looking the place over as they nudged the horses forward down an even thinner, steeper path.

At the bottom of the path they turned and stopped right in front of cabin where Shear sat smoking a thick cigar. On his right stood Elmer Fisk, on his left, Rudy Duckwald. The two paid no attention to Mingo Sentanza. Instead they stood staring with stunned expressions at the bare-headed gambler riding beside him.

Shear also stared at Sentanza, but only giving Tinnis a curt nod. The gambler returned the nod and sat in silence as Shear spoke to Sentanza.

"We heard the warning shots," he said. "Where's Dolan Callahan?"

"He's stone dead," said Sentanza. "According to Lucas here, the two bounty hunters and ranger tracking Fisk and these two killed him." He gestured his head toward Fisk and Duckwald, and at Epson, who sat nearby chewing tobacco and whittling. Epson had stopped whittling and chewing when he'd seen the gambler, still alive.

"We never led them here, Big Aces," Fisk offered, without taking his burning gaze off Sentanza.

"But they didn't kill you, Mingo," said Shear. "How come?"

"That was me who fired the warning shots," said Sentanza, ignoring the question.

Shear nodded. "Good job," he said. "Now, how come you're still alive and Callahan's not?"

"I was relieving myself in the brush," said Sentanza, lying when and where it benefited him. "I'd just started back when I heard a commotion. I snuck in and saw Callahan lying dead with a sword stuck through him from behind. There was nothing I could do for him. I had to get far enough away to fire some shots and warn you. So I hopped on a horse and lit out, be-

cause mine was too tired after riding back to lookout
last evening."

Shear seemed to dismiss Sentanza. He looked at the
gambler and said, "Tinnis Lucas, how are you?"

The gambler shrugged. "I've been better. I could use
a drink."

"Somebody get the gambler here a bottle," Shear
said to the gunmen standing around listening.

"Thank you, *Jesus!*" Tinnis whispered emotionally as
a bottle appeared as if out of nowhere and handed up
to him by Ted Lasko's gloved fist. Shear and the men
looked on as the gambler took an extra-long swig, then
a quick breath, followed by another long swig.

"Damn!" said Ted Lasko, staring up at the bottle
he'd handed him, seeing it was reduced to half its con-
tent and still not being returned to him. "Give it back,
Lucas. There's more in the cabin."

The gambler started to hand the bottle back. But
having second thoughts, he raised a finger, putting him
off, and said, "One second, Ted."

"Damn it to hell, Tinnis!" Lasko barked.

But the gambler took yet another drink. "Obliged,
Ted," Tinnis said sincerely. "I think you may have saved
my life." He held the almost empty bottle back down
to the angry gunman, feeling the warm glow of whiskey start to surge in his chest.

"Are you good now?" Shear asked.

"For now, yes, I believe I am," Tinnis said, settling
into a smooth, furry whiskey lull.

"All right," said Shear. He gestured his cigar toward
Elmer Fisk. "I've heard Elmer tell us what you said

happened in Minton Hill. Now I want to hear it again, from you." He grinned and stuck the thick cigar in his mouth. "After all, it's what I pay you for."

Shear's words chaffed Elmer Fisk, who thought of it as taking the story of drunk over his.

The gambler stared straight into Fisk's fiery eyes for a moment, then coolly turned back to Shear and told him everything that had happened in Minton Hill.

When he'd finished telling about the ranger and the two bounty hunters killing four Black Valley Riders, he stopped and sat staring once more at Elmer Fisk.

After a moment of stoic consideration, Shear let out a breath. "Well, life goes on. We'll just blow the hell out for these three and go on about our business." He looked back at the gambler. "Now, what is this Fisk tells me about you riding your horse off of the cliff out front of the valley entrance?"

The gambler stared at Fisk a moment longer, then said quietly, "It sounds about right to me. I was asleep one minute, flying down into a pine tree the next. Had it not been for the bounty hunters and the law dog, I'd still be up the tree."

"Then you brought them down on us?" Shear asked with a cold sinister look.

"No, I didn't bring them down on you," said Tinnis. "They walked in here following hoofprints that those three left clear as day."

"That's a damn lie!" said Fisk. "We cleared the trail, swept it off and everything, after the drunk here rode off it."

Tinnis sat staring, listening.

Finally Shear said, "What brought you up here looking for me in the first place, Lucas?"

Staring again at Fisk, the gambler said through his warm whiskey glow, "Crazy Elmer wouldn't pay me. He said I'd have to come to you to get my information money. So I did . . . or I tried to, before *I fell.*"

"What'd you call me, you son of a bitch?" Fisk said, stepping forward.

Tinnis sat calmly staring at him.

"Easy there, Elmer," said Brayton Shear with a dark chuckle. "Everybody calls you *Crazy* behind your back. Don't twist a knot in your cinch." He turned quarter-wise and looked at Fisk, his black-handled Dance Brothers pistol in hand. "Hell, even I call you *Crazy* when you ain't around."

Fisk seethed, but simmered and forced himself to calm down, still staring hard at Tinnis, who sat coolly staring back at him.

Shear turned back to the gambler. "So, you came all this way to get your money?" Then he glanced at Fisk and said, "Shame on you, Crazy Elmer," just to goad the angry gunman.

"That was a big part of it," said the gambler, letting out a breath, relaxing even more. The pain in his stitched scalp had dulled; his hands had stopped trembling. He'd grown less shaky overall.

"There's something else, Big Aces," Sentanza cut in on the Gambler's behalf. "Tinman here said he wants to join up with us—wants to be a Black Valley Rider himself."

"Oh, does he, now?" said Shear. He gave the gambler a faint smile as he appeared to give it some thought; the rest of the men stared in hushed silence. "A Black Valley Rider . . . ?" He studied Tinnis for a moment, then said, "Yeah, sure. Why not?"

The gambler stood staring, not sure what to say.

Shear stood up. "But you need to know something, Lucas. Once a Black Valley Rider, *al*ways a Black Valley Rider."

"I wouldn't have it any other way, sir," Tinnis said with a slight bow.

"Big Aces!" Fisk cut in. "You can't be serious."

"Why's that, Elmer?" said Shear, still looking at Tinnis. "We're riding out to pull off a big job. I've lost more men this week than I have in the past year."

"What about him proving himself? Like all the rest of us had to?" said Fisk.

"Don't worry, Elmer," said Shear. "Every Black Valley Rider has to prove himself. It's part of the deal." He gazed at the gambler. "What about it, Tinnis Lucas? Are you ready to prove yourself a Black Valley Rider?"

Chapter 13

The gambler's eyes swept back and forth among the faces of Shear's men. He looked up at the guards posted in the rock ledges above and surrounding them. A warm evening wind blew up dust devils amid the stone fortress, Tinnis felt the breeze lick at his shirt, his coat and his tender swollen scalp.

"I'm prepared to prove myself," he said to Brayton Shear. "What's my test?"

Shear nodded. "First things first. You're going to prove to me that you know how to lay that bottle down and leave it alone while we're working. Can you do that?"

The gambler swallowed a knot in his throat and forced something inside himself to accept the challenge. "Consider it done, sir," he said.

A silence set in, until Ted Lasko held up his nearly empty bottle and said, "Damn it! I wish to hell we'd've done this a few minutes sooner."

Laughter rippled across the men, except for Fisk and Duckwald, who stood staring sullenly. "What's the rest of his test?" Fisk blurted out through the laughter. "That can't be all of it."

Shear turned to him, this time with his hand on the big black-handled Dance Brothers pistol on his hip. "You do not want to keep questioning everything I say, Crazy Elmer," he said, his tone low and menacing. "Now either explain what you've got against Lucas here, or keep you mouth shut."

Fisk lowered his rifle in a show of peace. He stared in silence for a moment. Then he said, "All right, I'll tell you what I've got against him. I believe this drunken bastard blames me and Rudy and Epson for him going off the edge of the cliff."

"Well? Should he blame you?" said Shear.

"Hell no," said Fisk. "He should blame being wall-eyed drunk—too damn drunk to sit a horse bareback."

Turning to the gambler, Shear asked, "Well, do you, Lucas?"

"What? Blame him and Duckwald and Epson for me riding off that cliff?" said the gambler. "No." He shook his head, keeping his eyes on Fisk. "I don't blame the three of them for anything."

"He's lying," shouted Fisk, gesturing toward the gambler's cold, hard gaze. "Look at him! This bastard will stick me in the back the first chance he gets."

Shear chuckled at Fisk, then said to the gambler, "Are you going to stick him in the back first chance you get?"

"No," Tinnis said, coolly, still staring at Fisk.

"Make him give his word on it," Fisk cut in. "If he wants to be a Black Valley Rider, we need to know his word is good."

Shear took a patient breath and said to Tinnis, "Do you give me your word on it, Lucas?"

The gambler answered quietly, "I give you my word I will *not* stab Elmer Fisk in his back."

"There, Elmer, satisfied?" said Shear, his hand on the butt of his Dance Brothers again.

Fisk settled down and looked at Epson and Duckwald for their approval. The two only stared at him. "Yeah, I'm good with it," Fisk said, finally. "Maybe I got a little overwrought there for a minute."

"*Overwrought . . . ?*" Shear chuckled again. "Yeah, I'm thinking you might have."

Tinnis cut in, "Is *not* drinking and *not* stabbing Fisk in the back the only ways I have to prove myself, Big Aces?"

Shear spun toward him, the Dance Brothers pistol coming out of its holster, cocked and pointed at Tinnis' chin. "Nobody calls me Big Aces unless they carry a moon and star! Do you understand?"

The men around them backed a step and fell dead silent. The gambler looked back and forth slowly, then back into Shear's eyes, knowing he'd touched a raw nerve. "Yes, I understand."

Only the whir of warm wind cut through the tense silence. After a moment, Shear eased down and lowered his big pistol, uncocked and holstered it. "This is no drunken game, Lucas," he said. "This is serious business. A man who thinks otherwise is a dead man."

Fisk watched closely as Shear gave a gesture with his head that told Sentanza to get the gambler out of his sight. When Sentanza had done so and he and Tinnis turned and walked away toward a lean-to livery barn in the far corner of the rock fortress, Fisk leaned over to Duckwald and said, "Well, Rudy. I say this drunken whiskey sop won't last more than a week with the Black Valley Riders."

"Yeah?" said Duckwald with a dubious look. "You said he was *dead* back on the high trail."

Night had fallen by the time the ranger and the bounty hunters stepped into the empty cabin, their guns drawn and poised. They had traveled slowly and silently the last few miles, staying in the shadowy cover of scrub juniper and cottonwood trees strewn along the base of a short hill line.

"They're gone," said Sandoval.

"Just like we figured," the ranger said. He lowered the hammer on his big Colt and holstered it, his Winchester in his left hand.

Thorn walked across the floor and stood in a purple glow of moonlight through an open window frame. He looked out onto the yard surrounding the cabin and off across the land, along the jagged surrounding hills.

"Tinnis Mayes is with them by now," he said. "We'll need to keep a close lookout for any signs he leaves for us along the way."

Sandoval and the ranger exchanged glances. They had followed tracks to the rock where Tinnis and Sentanza had met up earlier in the day. Their hoofprints showed they had ridden off together. Instead of following Tinnis and the lookout guard, the three had veered away toward the cabin in hopes of catching Shear and his men before they left there. But that had not been the case.

"Captain," Sam said, "I don't want to see you putting too much faith in this gambler. He might have once been a good man. But that was a long time ago. We've both seen our share of good men turn bad, the same as we've seen bad men turn good."

"Yes, that's true," Thorn said thoughtfully. He turned and stared out from within the pale purple moonlight. "But how *much* faith is *too much* faith, when it comes to a man's honor and worth?"

"I won't try to address that question, Captain," said the ranger. "I have never commanded men, the way you have. I'm known as a loner and I prefer it that way. But I don't want you working with a blind spot for this man just because he once wore the same uniform—"

Thorn had heard something. He cut Sam off with a raised hand as he stepped quickly out of the moonlight and slipped his big horse pistol from its holster.

Sam and Sandoval had heard it too.

Boots running across the yard . . . ? Sam asked himself quickly.

Sandoval, standing nearest to the open door, spun around and slammed it shut in time to hear an arrow thump into it. War whoops resounded in the purple night amid pistol shots and arrows pelting the cabin both front and sides.

"That's not Shear's men, Captain," Sandoval said.

"No, it's the *Comadrejas*," Sam said. "They're after our horses. Cover me, Sandoval. I'm going up." He hurried to the rear door, and stood to one side as he threw it open, his rifle up and ready. Seeing that the warriors had not yet circled the cabin, he scrambled atop a rain barrel, swung up onto the roof and ran to the center, taking cover beside a thick stone chimney.

He took aim on a ragged warrior who'd just jumped atop Black Pot with the reins to the other two horses in hand. He nailed his heels to the big stallion's sides. The stallion neighed and bucked, but refused to go forward. He jerked the reins to the bounty hunter's horses, but the two stood stubbornly in place.

Wrong move . . . , the ranger said to himself. He pulled the trigger and watched the warrior fly from Black Pot's back and land facedown in the dirt.

As soon as the ranger had left the cabin, Sandoval threw the door shut and bolted it. At the front window Thorn had stooped onto one knee, and began firing steadily over the window ledge at the *Comadrejas* darting back and forth across the yard. On the other side of the cabin, Sandoval fired through a gun slot in a thick closed wooden window shutter.

Out front, two more dead *Comadrejas* had joined the one lying near the horses' hooves. The three horses whinnied and chuffed and reared slightly. But they only backed away a few feet, then held their ground, their reins dangling in the dirt. A hail of arrows and bullets nipped the chimney beside the ranger. Sam hunkered for a second, then came up firing.

A warrior ran toward the cabin with a lit torch in hand. A shot from Thorn's open window nailed him; he fell rolling in the dirt. The torch flew onto the porch and flared in a firebox piled full of dry, seasoned hearth kindling.

But in another second it was over as quickly as it had started. Sam stood and took long aim at a ragged warrior running full speed across the rocky ground. He squeezed the trigger and watched the man fall forward and roll in a swirl of dust.

"Captain, they're retreating," said Sandoval, holding his fire.

"Yes, I see they are, Sandy," said Thorn, standing and leaning back against the wall in the purple darkness. "Quick, put out the fire. . . ."

Sandoval hurried onto the porch, grabbed the blazing kindling box and hurled it off the porch into the dirt. He slapped fire from his arms as he stomped and kicked and extinguished the flames. When he'd finished he ran to the horses, gathered their reins and ran back inside the cabin with them.

Inside, he turned the horses loose, closed the door and bolted it, his shirtsleeves smoking and burned through in spots. Thorn had walked over to the back door, unbolted it and let the ranger in. He leaned back against a wall and gripped his upper shoulder where an arrow had lodged solidly beneath his collarbone.

Sam bolted the back door and looked at Thorn, as did Sandoval.

"I suppose there had to be one among them who could shoot straight," Thorn said. He offered a weak smile. "My only comfort is that he might be one of those lying dead in the dirt." He stepped over and slumped down into a chair with a sigh. "Sandy, you know what to do."

Sandoval walked to his horse and took down a canteen of water and walked to the hearth with it. Sam watched him reach stiffly for an empty pot to pour water into.

"Why don't you let me do that?" said Sam. "You

tend to your forearms." As he spoke he pulled a long knife from his boot well.

Sandoval allowed the ranger to take the canteen from his hands and take over the task of boiling some water in order to clean his knife blade.

"Obliged, Ranger," the young bounty hunter said. He unbuttoned his shirt and peeled it down off his scorched, reddened arms.

Sam saw peeled and blackened skin.

"I'll see if there's a tin of burn salve in my saddle-bags," he said, pouring the water and hanging the pot inside the hearth.

"No," said Sandoval. "Start the fire and boil the water. Take care of the captain first. I can wait."

The ranger wasn't going to argue. He quickly built a small fire beneath the pot of water. Capping the canteen, he carried it to Sandoval's horse and looped it around the saddle horn. He stepped over to his stallion and rummaged through his saddlebags and came out with a small tin jar of salve. Before taking a close look at Sandoval's burnt arms, he walked to the edge of the open window and gazed out and around in the purple darkness until he was satisfied the *Comadrejas* were gone for the night.

Behind him, Thorn said, "I hope you do your cutting quick, Ranger. We don't want to let these men get too far ahead of us."

"We're going to get both of you tended to," Sam said, turning away from the open window. "Then we'll get out of here. But we're only going far enough to lose Clato Charo and his warriors. Then we're going to have to sit down for the night and get some rest for us and our horses."

The captain started to protest, wanting to ride on through the night. But he saw Sandoval's pained face in the flicker of fire in the hearth and stopped himself.

"Yes, I believe you're right, Ranger. Some rest is in order for all of us. We'll get back on Shear's trail first thing come morning."

Chapter 14

At dawn, a boot toe reached out and nudged the gambler until he sat up beneath a ragged blanket on a pile of livery straw and looked all around in the silver-gray light. His first thought was of whiskey, feeling his dry mouth, the pain in his scalp, his aching body. But he put the thought of a drink aside, remembering his talk with Shear the night before. He had not taken a drink since then; he was determined not to.

"Wake up, Lucas, you whiskey-swilling dog," said Ted Lasko, still unhappy about Tinnis guzzling most of his booze the night before. He drew back his boot to kick the sleepy gambler again.

"Do not try that again, Ted Lasko, or I will ruin your day," Tinnis said flatly, raising a finger for emphasis. "I did not give my word that I wouldn't kill you."

"*Ha!*" Lasko scoffed under his breath, but he backed away. "I didn't kick you that hard, just enough to get you up. Big Aces said he wants you up on the cliffs atop the trail, *mas pronto*."

"Really?" Tinnis stood quickly to his feet, drawing

the blanket across his shoulders against the morning chill. "There," he said, "see how easy that was, even without the toe of your boot?"

"You can't blame me for still being mad, Lucas," said Lasko.

"Nor can you blame me for killing you," Tinnis said with a faint smile. "What does Shear want at this hour of the night?"

"It's not night," Lasko chuckled. "It's almost dawn out."

"*Almost* only counts in pitching horseshoes," Tinnis said, touching his healing stitched scalp.

"If it's dawn, it's almost daylight," said Lasko, belaboring the point.

"It is either dark out or light," Tinnis snapped, walking on ahead of him. "There is no 'almost' daylight any more than there's an—"

"You need a drink, gambler, I can see that," said Lasko, cutting him off with a dark chuckle. He reached inside his coat and jerked out a fresh bottle of rye. "Here you go. Help yourself."

Holy Mother of God!

Tinnis squeezed his eyes shut for a moment. His stitched scalp pounded with pain, but he summoned all the strength he could and said, "Obliged, but no, thanks, Lasko. I gave my word, remember?"

Lasko laughed and shook the bottle in his gloved hand, letting the gambler hear the sound of it sloshing around. "I say, what good is a man's word if he can't break it, then get right back to it?"

"Go to hell, Ted Lasko," said Tinnis. He walked on briskly.

In the same spot, in the same chair as the night before, Shear stood up with a fresh cigar in his mouth and said to Tinnis, "Good morning, Lucas. Have you had breakfast?"

"No," said the gambler.

"Good, take a ride with me," said Shear as if he hadn't heard his reply.

Tinnis gave an exasperated look at Lasko, who gestured for him to follow Shear to four horses that had been saddled and led out—among them the horse Tinnis had ridden in on. Behind Tinnis, Lasko and Tobias walked to the horses, their rifles in hand. The four climbed into their saddles and rode up a steep path to a high rim and stopped for a moment, staring out across the trails below.

"How'd you sleep, Lucas?" Shear asked.

"Good enough," the gambler replied.

"Have you drank any whiskey?" Shear followed up.

"Not a drop, sir," Tinnis replied.

Shear looked at Lasko for confirmation.

"He turned me down flat, Big Aces," Lasko answered with a half grin. "Said he *gave his word*."

"Hell, that's admirable," said Shear, looking the gambler up and down with pride. "I always thought you'd make a good moon-and-star Black Valley Rider, if you ever got your beak out of the barrel long enough to know the time of day." He laughed aloud.

Tinnis only managed a thin smile, his scalp still pounding, his hand starting to tremble, his nerves crying out for a long drink of rye.

"All right, then," said Shear. "I'm going to make this short and to the point. Ordinarily it would take you four or five good jobs to get your moon and star. But I've too much going on to wait. Are you ready to prove yourself to me, Tinnis Lucas, and take your place as a Black Valley Rider?"

"I am," said Tinnis in a serious tone.

"Then follow me to Hatchet Pass," said Shear.

The gambler turned his horse and rode behind Shear, toward the high lookout positions he and Sentanza had passed the evening before. Tinnis looked back over his shoulder at the two riflemen following close behind him.

They reined up twenty minutes later and stepped down on one of the high ridges overlooking the trail at the mouth of the narrow canyon. "How's your shooting eye, Lucas?" Shear asked. He drew a Winchester rifle with a long brass-trimmed scope mounted on it from his saddle boot and began jacking its bullets out onto the ground.

"I can usually hit whatever sticks its head up," the gambler said, still feeling the pain pound in his scalp without any whiskey to soothe it. "What do you have in mind?"

"The ranger and these so-called sailors, or bounty hunters, or whatever they are—"

"They're marines, Shear," the gambler said, correcting him.

"Yes, marines, then," said Shear. He grinned slyly as he stuck one bullet in the empty Winchester and levered it into the chamber. "Who is the leader?"

"I'd have to say Thorn is the man who carries the big stick," said the gambler.

"Oh, not the ranger?" said Shear.

"Not in this case," said Tinnis. "My money is on Thorn. He looks like he'd be in charge of anything he's got a hand in."

"All right, then," said Shear. He handed Tinnis the rifle and pushed the barrel toward the ground when the gambler let it drift up toward his chest.

"Sorry," said Tinnis.

Shear let it pass. "Anyway, they'll be riding up most any minute, the way I calculate. I want you to sink this bullet right into this man Thorn's heart for us."

"One shot?" Tinnis looked down at the rifle in his unsteady hands. "Don't you trust me with a loaded gun, Shear?"

"I trust you as far as one shot," Shear said, again with the same sly grin. "I'll trust a whole lot further once I know this sailor is lying dead in the dirt." He stared at Tinnis with narrowed suspicious eyes. "Is that a problem, killing him for me?"

"No problem at all," said Tinnis. "And is that my test? Killing the bounty hunter?"

"Yep," said Shear.

"Consider it done," said Tinnis.

"I do," said Shear. He took out a small silver quarter moon with a star dangling from its upper point. "That's why I'm giving you this right now." He reached out, opened the blanket still wrapped around Tinnis and pinned the small ornament on Tinnis' ragged coat lapel.

Tinnis locked his heels together military style and bowed slightly. "I will make you proud, Shear."

"Hey, I'm *Big Aces* to you from now on, Lucas," Shear said, reaching and patting the gambler's dusty shoulder. He stepped back. "Now I have to go."

"Go?" Tinnis looked surprised. "You're not going to be here when I do this?"

"No," said Shear. "I've got a big job waiting to be done. But I've got lookout men down there, and I'm leaving Lasko and Barnes to look after you—make sure you don't fall again." Again the sly grin.

"Obliged," Tinnis said wryly.

"I'll hear how it went as soon as you three catch up to us," said Shear. He started to turn away, but before he did, he wagged a thick finger in Tinnis' face. "Don't you let me down, Lucas. We're all counting on you."

"Yes, sir," said the gambler, drawing the blanket back around his shoulders. "I've got you covered."

The gambler and the two riflemen stood watching until Shear had mounted and turned his horse and rode back the way they'd come. Looking back over his shoulder, Shear said to himself under his breath, "He'll be lucky if he doesn't blow his foot off. . . ."

As soon as Shear was out of sight, Barnes led all three horses aside and tied their reins to a hitch rail set up beside the trail.

"Let's go, Tinnis," said Lasko, gesturing toward the lookout men standing on a rock shelf twenty yards down a steep path.

When two lookout men saw the gambler and the two riflemen step down onto the rock shelf, they moved to one side and gave them room to look around. Tinnis noted the Gatling gun sitting on its iron tripod frame aimed down at the trail below.

"My, but isn't this just the latest thing in fine armament?" he said, the Winchester cradled in the crook of his arm. To Lasko and Barnes he said, "Would you prefer if I used *this* and shoot all three of them when they show up?"

"You take care of the bounty hunter, Lucas," said Barnes. "Metcalf and Neely here will kill the other two quick enough."

The gambler smiled and shrugged. "I just thought I'd ask."

Metcalf, a big, burly gunman from Kansas, stepped over beside Tinnis and pointed out at a lower jutting cliff across the canyon. "Look down the scope over there and search until you see a round of dynamite." He paused and asked, "You have used a scope before, haven't you?"

"I have dabbled with it. It *has* been a while since I've even held a rifle, I'll admit," the gambler said, raising the scoped Winchester to his shoulder. He wouldn't mention that *yes*, he could use a scope, but his preference, his precision style of shooting had been with ladder sights, the gauging of wind, yardage adjustment—shooting with the naked eye. "But I shall try not to disappoint."

Lasko and Barnes gave each other a guarded grin, watching the gambler adjust the rifle into place and look down through the brass-trimmed scope. He searched the steep rocky hillside across the canyon from them until he saw the round of dynamite—eight sticks bound together—with a fuse leading off and disappearing into the rocks.

"Have you got it?" Metcalf asked.

"Got it," said Tinnis, his hand trembling a little, causing the scope to serve up an unsteady target.

"Good," said Metcalf. "Now you're seeing what's going to happen just as soon as you make your killing. We've got a man up there just itching to push a plunger and blow this canyon trail all to hell. He'll seal this canyon off. So if you miss, don't worry about it. Anybody down there is dead anyway. If the rocks don't kill them, we've got men down there who'll take care of them." He looked at Tinnis and added, "You'll find that Big Aces is always on top of his business."

Tinnis gave him a sincere look. "Thanks for telling me that. It makes me feel less *pressed.*" He gave Barnes and Lasko a dark look.

"Pressed . . . ?" Lasko chuckled. "You don't think Big Aces would actually put all his stock on a drunk like you making a shot like this, do you?"

"Damn, gambler," said Barnes, "take it easy. Like he told you, it's a test. He just wants to know that your heart is in it."

Tinnis ignored the two and asked Metcalf, "How long before you figure the ranger and the bounty hunters will show up?"

"If they found the empty cabin last night, they should have already been here by now," said Metcalf. "You three go back under the overhang, get yourselves some coffee. I'll let you know when they get here."

"Sounds good to us," said Lasko, already turning and walking past the Gatling gun toward the shadowy entrance to the cliff overhang. On the way there, he looked around at the gambler with a grin, then said to Tobias Barnes, "Just because this gambler gave his word not to drink doesn't mean we can't, does it?" He patted the whiskey bottle inside his coat.

"Not by any means," said Barnes. "There's nothing I like better than a good hard jolt of rye after breakfast coffee."

The gambler walked along between them cradling the Winchester. He looked back and forth at each of them and shook his stitched head. "Umm-um," he said with an air of disdain. "It's a good thing for the two of you that I'm *not* drinking."

"Yeah, why's that?" said Lasko.

Staring straight ahead as they walked, the gambler said coolly, "Because I would drink you two *children* under a rock, is why."

"You'd be the first one to ever do it," said Barnes defensively. "I was out drinking with teamsters and skinners when I was no more than twelve years old, and that's a God's-honest fact."

"Me too," said Lasko. "And that's also a God's-honest fact." He jerked the bottle out of his coat and examined it.

"Sure it is," Tinnis said critically. "You keep telling each other that."

"What're you saying, Lucas?" Lasko asked.

"I'm saying you two couldn't have made it through a Southern sewing party where I come from." He gestured toward the bottle in Lasko's hand. "That bottle will last the two of you for a week. "If I was drinking I'd pull the cork and kiss it good-bye."

"Yeah, but that's because you're a drunk, Lucas," said Barnes.

"Being a drunk's got nothing to do with it," said Tinnis. He gave a shrug. "Nothing against you fellows, but some of us can hold our whiskey and some of us can't." He walked under the cliff overhang, stooped down by a small fire and picked up an empty tin coffee cup. His hands trembled, but he kept them under control as he raised a battered coffeepot and poured. It took all his willpower to keep from grabbing the whiskey bottle, opening it and guzzling the fiery liquid until he felt its warm, furry glow overcome him.

Easy, fellow . . . , he cautioned himself.

While Tinnis filled the tin cup with coffee, he watched Lasko and Barnes set down a couple of rocks beside the fire. Lasko pulled the cork from the whiskey bottle and blew it away.

"I hate doing this in front of you, Lucas, you being a low-down drunk . . . needing a drink and all," said Lasko. He grinned and kissed the whiskey bottle the way he imagined the gambler had talked about doing. "Good-bye, old friend," he said to the rye, raising it to his lips.

Before he lowered the bottle, Barnes' hand was out, reaching for it.

Tinnis stared at the two and said, "It takes more than one long drink to even get my guts settled. After that the serious drinking begins."

"Yeah, well, here's to you, Lucas," Barnes said with a scoff. He tipped the whiskey bottle toward him. "Enjoy your coffee. . . ."

The gambler eased back, sat down on a rock and leaned back. He sipped his coffee, watching the two with a doubtful look on his face.

Chapter 15

Over a full hour had passed when Metcalf stepped under the cliff overhang and looked around. "Riders coming," he said to the gambler and the other two men. He spotted the empty whiskey bottle lying near the fire. "Damn . . . ," he whispered under his breath. "Are you fellows going to be able to do this?"

"We're coming!" said Lasko, trying to spring to his feet as if he were sober. Tinnis saw the man stagger a little before catching himself.

"It's about time they got here," said Barnes, wiping his face with both hands. He stood too, in the same faltering manner.

"I'm fine," Tinnis said to Metcalf. "Sharp-eyed and sober. What are we waiting for, gentlemen?" he said to the other two. He rose to his feet, the Winchester in hand, slung coffee grounds from the empty tin cup and set it upside down on a rock near the fire.

When the three arrived at the lookout post along the edge of the cliff, Metcalf handed a pair of binoculars to the gambler and said, "Look them over, Lucas. Tell me if they're the ones."

Tinnis leaned the Winchester against a short rock wall that stood in front of them and raised the binoculars to his eyes. The two bounty hunters and the ranger wobbled back and forth, then settled in the circling lens. "That's them all right," said Tinnis, moving the binoculars from one face to the next until he'd recognized each of them.

Barnes and Lasko stood close by his side, trying not to look too drunk. "Take your time, gambler," Lasko said in a thick voice, feeling he should say something.

"Nothing to worry about, gentlemen," Tinnis said, handing the binoculars back to Metcalf and picking up the scoped rifle. He kneeled down against the short rock and steadied his left arm on it. He raised the rifle butt to his shoulder and looked down the long scope.

As Tinnis prepared to make his shot, Metcalf looked at the other two with disgust. "What the hell got into you, Lasko?" he said in a harsh whisper, considerate of the gambler's concentration.

"There's not a damn thing wrong with me," Lasko replied in a gruff and less considerate voice.

"Me neither," said Barnes.

"Shhh," Tinnis said over his shoulder. "I've already told you, it's been a long time since I've held a rifle."

Lasko cursed under his breath. But both men settled down and watched.

On the trail below, Thorn rode at the head of the three riders, his broad chest held high—a perfect target, Tinnis told himself, watching in the circling lens.

Metcalf eyed Barnes and Lasko with disdain and stepped over closer to Tinnis. In a soothing whisper he said to the gambler, "Take it easy, Lucas. Remember what I told you—we're going to close this canyon anyway."

"Oh? Are you sure?" Tinnis said, as if he hadn't heard Metcalf say the same thing earlier.

"Oh yes, I'm sure," Metcalf said, in the same calming tone of voice.

"In that case . . . ," said Tinnis.

"What?" Metcalf asked, surprised, seeing the slightest shift in Tinnis' position.

"I've got it for you," the gambler said quickly. He settled into his shot.

"No, *wait!*" shouted Metcalf, seeing what was about to happen. But it was too late. He saw the gambler's trigger finger squeeze back, smooth and expertly.

"I got it," Tinnis said proudly.

"God Almighty!" shouted Lasko as the ringing shot turned into a heavy thunderous explosion. The whole valley and hillside beneath the cliff ledge seemed to lift in an upward thrust, then slam back down into place. Barnes tilted back against the rock wall and caught himself to keep from falling. Metcalf ducked down, taking cover beside Tinnis, seeing the high rise of dust, rock and debris billow above the down-sliding hillside.

"Jesus, what have you done, Lucas?" he shouted above the resounding blast.

"I blew up the valley, just like you told me to," the gambler said.

"No, you idiot!" screamed Metcalf. "I said *we're* going to blow the valley, not *you!*"

Tinnis' smile of satisfaction seemed to melt from his face. He stared at Metcalf for a moment, stunned, then said, "Oops."

"*Oops . . . ?*" said Metcalf. "How the hell can you make such a mistake? You knew what Shear wanted from you!"

"Don't raise your voice to me, sir," Tinnis said indignantly. "I'm a sobering drunk! I told you I haven't held a rifle for a long time—"

"That's no damn excuse," said Metcalf, cutting him off.

"I've been straddled with these two drinking right in front of me for the past hour . . . my nerves are jangled," said Lucas. "What do you expect? I thought you told me to blow up the canyon!"

Bits of broken green pine and chunks of dirt and small rock rained down on the ledge around them. Barnes and Lasko moved forward and hunkered down beside Metcalf and the gambler along the short rock wall.

"Damn it to hell, Lucas!" Lasko said, dust falling from his lowered hat brim. "Shear hears about this, he's going to go wild!"

"He's going to want to nail your nuts to a root cellar door, gambler," Barnes warned.

"I did what I thought Metcalf asked," Tinnis said, dust streaming on his bare head. "If I was doing wrong, you should have stopped me, Ted." He gave both Lasko and Barnes a condemning stare. "I'm sure one of you would have, had you not been drunk at the moment."

"Jesus, what have we done?" said Lasko, beginning

to realize the consequences of him and Barnes drinking when they were supposed to be in charge of the gambler.

Beside them, Metcalf fanned his hat and squinted into the heavy cloud of dust and debris. "The main thing is, don't lose your heads," he said. "I told him we were getting ready to close this canyon. Everybody down there is dead now anyway."

"You think so?" Lasko asked, venturing a drunken gaze into the thick dust cloud.

"Sure they are," said Metcalf. "It would've been better if they were thirty yards closer in. But they're dead, no way around it." He gave a thin smile as he looked around at the others in the falling dust and debris. "All you've got to do is get your story straight and stick to it. Who's going to say otherwise?"

Barnes and Lasko turned their hard stares to the gambler.

"Not me," said Lucas. "I'm the one trying to get in the gang, remember?" Dust gathered on the shaved area of his stitched-down scalp. "Whatever lie you tell, I'll go along with it. I do hope you'll mention me *favorably*, of course."

The two gunmen looked at each other. "What else can we do?" Barnes said to Lasko with a shrug.

"What else? I'll show you what else!" Lasko turned wild-eyed. He jerked his dust-covered Colt from his holster and pointed it toward Tinnis.

"Now, that's *real* smart," Tinnis said with quiet sarcasm. He shook his dust-covered head. "And to think, you're the one who brought along the bottle just to entice me, as I stumbled ever further along my rocky road to sobriety."

"Put that damn six-shooter away, Lasko," Metcalf demanded, reaching out and shoving the Colt's barrel away from Tinnis' chest. "How are you going to explain killing him to Big Aces?"

Lasko bit his lower lip in frustration. Finally he said, "Damn it to hell!" and put his Colt away.

"That's more like it," said Metcalf. "Let's fan our way over and make sure the canyon's sealed down. At least we'll get something right out of all this mess."

"You do that, Metcalf," said Lasko, "if you've got a mind to." He looked at Barnes for support. "The three of us are getting out of here. I'm not missing out on this big job if I can help it."

"And nor will I," said Tinnis with a dust-streaked grin. He fingered the quarter moon and star Shear had pinned on his chest. "Now that I am a member of the Black Valley fold."

The ranger and the bounty hunters had felt the sudden rumble and thrust of the explosion above the trail in front of them. But before the fiery blast had reached its highest level, and before the dense canyon wall cracked like thick glass and began falling, they turned their horses and raced away.

With the heat and the dust and debris gaining on them, chasing them, it appeared, they cut around a sharp turn in the trail and veered in close to the sheltering hillside. They watched the blast sweep past them along their trail like some angry hoard in their pursuit.

As the dust found them and closed around them, the three watched boulders larger than houses roll and toss and rumble to a sliding halt, filling the trail and the narrow canyon floor.

"Are you two all right?" Sandoval asked, rocks and broken pine limbs still bouncing down and coming to a heavy landing on the rocky ground outside their hill-side sanctuary.

"I'm all right," Sam said, stooping, inspecting his stallion's forelegs.

"As am I," said Thorn. Taking off his hat, he fanned it back and forth, and said, "Well, at least we know they're here."

"Yep," said Sam. "And I expect we'll be hearing from some of them any minute." Standing, he drew his Winchester from his saddle boot and levered a round into the chamber.

"Right you are," said Thorn, picking up on what Sam had said. "Shear wouldn't blow this canyon unless he had some men down on this lower side to make sure we're all dead."

"I wonder why they didn't wait just one minute longer before igniting the blast?" Sandoval said, dusting chips of rock and small splinters from the front of his shirt. "It would've caught us riding right under the blast area. We *would have* all been dead."

"I heard a rifle shot before the blast," Sam said, already trying to see through the thick cloud of settling dust. "I'm wondering if somebody made a mistake and shot the dynamite instead of waiting and using the plunger."

"Are you thinking Tinnis Mayes might be our benefactor, Ranger?" Thorn asked. He grinned. "Don't tell me you're about to give Mayes reconsideration."

"He's growing on me," Sam said. "If he pulled us out of this blast, I'm liking him better every minute."

"Here they come," Sandoval said, rifle in hand.

Through the thick cloud of swirling, settling dust, the three saw the grainy outline of four riders stepping their horses cautiously onto the rock-and-pine-strewn trail.

At the head of the riders, a gunman named Bart Quill said to the three men flanking him, "I can't see squat. All of yas spread out, so one bullet doesn't wind up killing the lot of us."

Even as the other three eased their horses away, one of them, a man named Hugh Jasper, said low under his breath, "What the hell did Metcalf mean blowing this up so soon? I was off the site using the jake. Next thing I knew I was scrambling for my saddle, one hand holding up my britches."

"Don't ask me, Jasper," said Quill. "I just work here like the rest of yas."

Jasper eased farther away, searching squint-eyed through the thick dust.

The other two men, Irv Stokes and Jimmy Creed, rode a little ways in opposite directions, then searched back toward each other until they caught each other by surprise. Creed almost fired a shot at a lurking figure in front of him. But he caught himself and said, "Damn it, Jimmy, let me know something out there."

"I'm just as surprised as you are, ol' buddy," said Creed. "Maybe we ought to all be sticking together after all—"

His words fell short as a bullet from Sandoval's rifle punched a hole in his left side and came ripping out his right side, leaving a fist-sized exit wound in its bloody wake. He let out a loud grunt and spilled to the ground beside his horse.

"Was that you, Jimmy?" Stokes asked, dropping quickly from his saddle, crouched, his Colt in hand, looking all around.

Hearing no reply from Creed, he jerked his horse along by its reins toward the cover of a downed and broken pine lying in a pile of rock and broken limbs. In the settling dust he saw the other two gunmen had dropped from their horses and managed to take cover out of sight.

"Good work, Sandy," Thorn said quietly. "One down, three to go?" he asked the ranger.

"That's what I counted," Sam replied. "They've taken cover now."

"We can't afford to leave them dogging us on the trail," Sandoval said.

Thorn gave the ranger a questioning look. "Shall we spread out and have after them, Ranger?"

"I'm with you, Captain," said Sam, surveying the settling dust as the outline of boulders, tree lines and the littered trail came back into sight.

Chapter 16

From atop the cliff, Raymond Metcalf and Call Neely couldn't clearly see the gunfight for the thick cloud of dust still looming above the sealed-off canyon trail. But what they heard was enough to make them nervous, not knowing if it was their men or the ranger and the bounty hunters who were getting the upper hand.

"What're we going to do, Metcalf?" Neely asked, seeing only flashes of rifle fire back and forth through the thick dust.

"We can't take a chance," said Metcalf. He turned and walked to where the Gatling gun sat with its barrel tipped down in front. "We have to start shooting anything moving down there. If our men don't get out of the way, that's too bad for them. We can't risk letting these three get up here past us and onto Big Aces' trail. He'd kill us for it."

"Now you're talking!" said Neely. He ran under the cliff overhang and came back dragging a wooden crate filled with loaded ammunition clips. "Which are you going to do, feed or shoot?"

"I'll do the shooting," said Metcalf. "Get me loaded up good. I want to really chop this canyon trail all to pieces. We can't let these three get up out of there alive." He jerked on a pair of cavalry-style gloves as he stepped around behind the big mounted gun and raised its barrel a few inches.

"What do you want us to do, Ray?" one of the other two trail guards, a man named James Addison, asked Metcalf.

"You and Pembroke get the wagon horses hitched and ready, Jim. As soon as we see what's left down there, we're cutting out of here."

"What about Delbert?" the trail guard asked, gesturing a nod across the dusty canyon.

"He was told to get away from here as soon as he shoved the plunger," said Metcalf. "I expect he's smart enough to see that his job was canceled."

On the rocky trail below, Sam and Sandoval had dropped flat onto their bellies as two of the riflemen had targeted their muzzle flashes in the looming dust and unleashed a hail of rifle fire on them. But thirty yards away, Thorn had dropped behind the cover of a large broken rock and began returning fire on their behalf.

While Thorn kept the riflemen busy, Sandoval rolled away in one direction, the ranger in another, each mindful of the other's position, lest they fire on each other. When they both suddenly began firing again, Irv Stokes took bullets in his chest and side simultaneously and fell to the ground, dead. Seeing Stokes go down, Bart Quill backed away. He stumbled in the blinding dust until his hands found his saddle horn; then he swung up into his saddle to ride away.

Yet before he could bat his heels to the horse's sides, Thorn spotted his grainy outline and fired. The impact of the shot took both Quill and his horse to the ground. "Two down, two to go...," the older bounty hunter murmured to himself, levering another round into his rifle chamber.

Through the thick dust, Sam and Sandoval saw the horse and rider fall. As each of them rose from their positions into a crouch and moved away in the same direction, the Gatling gun began to throw down a blast of bullets from high above them, causing them to drop back onto their bellies as bullets riddled the rocky ground.

Sam heard one of the two remaining riflemen let out a scream as three of the big gun's rounds stitched across his chest. Even as the Gatling gun continued to pound out blast after blast from the cliff high above them, Sandoval came crawling in beside the ranger, his bandanna pulled up against the swirling dust.

"Come on, they're shooting blind," the younger bounty hunter said, as if a bullet needed eyes in order to kill them. But as he crawled away, Sam followed.

"Where are you headed?" he asked, crawling up beside Sandoval.

"To higher ground," Sandoval said beneath the repetition of the big gun. "That's where we'll find the captain, if he can get there."

The big mounted gun began to settle into a firing pattern back and froth, left to right across the dust-choked canyon trail. Moving in the opposite direction, the two crawlers made it to the base of the hillside and collapsed, knowing they were at an angle the gun couldn't reach.

After a moment of coughing and fanning their hats, Sandoval shook the ranger's shirtsleeve. "Look at this." As he spoke he raised his hat and waved it once slowly.

Along the base of the hillside, Thorn came toward them, crouched, but moving quickly, leading their animals at a trot behind him.

As the older bounty hunter spotted them and came to a halt beside Sandoval, the younger man turned to the ranger and said, "I told you he'd head for the higher ground."

Above them the Gatling gun continued its repetitious firing, but the three heard its bullets striking and ricocheting off rock fifty yards from them. "The fourth man is either dead or afraid to stick his head up," said Thorn. He handed the other two the reins to their horses. "This is a good time to ride out of here."

"Our only way to go is up," Sam said, standing in a crouch and taking the reins to his stallion.

"Yes, onward and upward," said Thorn. He added with a thin smile on his dust-streaked face, "Now that we know they have a Gatling gun, I can't resist taking it from them. What say you, Ranger Burrack?"

"It couldn't hurt to have one where we're headed," the ranger replied. "But these men will have the Gatling gun loaded and gone before we get there."

"Do you know any shortcuts?" Sandoval asked.

"No," said Sam. "By the time we follow a few dead trails and have to turn back, we'd be better off riding all the way around this canyon to begin with."

"That could take a day or two," said Thorn. "Shear won't be there."

"He's not there now," Sam said. "He was gone before the first shots were fired. This is nothing new for him. Brayton Shear knew the kind of hideout he had here when he set up this place. But that's the hand we're dealt."

"There is no chance of us having the element of surprise on this man," Sandoval commented.

"Not so, Sandy," said Thorn. "What will catch Big Aces Shear by surprise is the fact that we've gotten past all the defenses he left behind himself, and are still standing, looking down his throat."

Sandoval considered it, then said, "Yes, to a man like this, us getting there alive will be the last thing he'll expect."

Sam nodded his agreement. "I like the way you think, gentlemen," he said. Gesturing toward the high cliff, he said, "This Gatling crew knows that if we're alive we'll be coming for their gun. But we won't be. Instead, we'll swing around them and be waiting for them. Let them run into us for a change. Then we'll be dogging Shear with his own gun. That will make him realize he has to stop and fight us."

Leading his stallion, Sam walked away along the base of the protective hillside, the Gatling gun still firing relentlessly above them. Thorn and Sandoval gave each other an approving nod and followed close behind him.

Atop the high ridge, Metcalf and Neely sat staring down, all around the looming dust still settling in the canyon floor. Addison and Pembroke had hitched the wagon horses to the gun wagon and had stacked their supplies and water casts in the wagon bed. They set the wagon brakes and walked down to the edge of the cliff, where Metcalf sat with one gloved hand resting on the gun's iron crank, his other hand on the wooden handles. Beside him, Neely sat staring down, empty ammunition clips at his feet.

"We're all hitched and packed," said Addison.

"Good," Metcalf said flatly, without taking his eyes away from the swirling dust.

Addison and Pembroke looked at each other.

"What I'm saying is, we're ready to get the hell out of here," Addison said.

"We're not," Metcalf said in a clipped tone. "So make yourself at home until I say otherwise." He hadn't looked up from the dusty canyon.

Beside him, Neely looked down at a watch in his gloved palm and said, "Ray, it has been two hours since we've heard a shot."

"Can you see anything down there yet?" Metcalf asked, shooting him a quick glance, then turning his eyes back to the canyon floor.

"Not much," said Neely. "But if there's nobody fighting, I say it's over."

"I want to see who's lying down there before we cut out of here," said Metcalf. "If I tell Big Aces these jakes are dead, I want to know that they *are* dead."

"Damn," said Neely, "it could take all day for this dust to settle."

"Have you got plans?" Metcalf snapped.

"No plans," Neely said. He shrugged. Now the three of them looked at each other.

"Go boil a pot of coffee," said Metcalf over his shoulder to Addison and Pembroke. "We'll have some.

If this dust hasn't settled by the time we've finished the pot, we'll pull out of here anyway. Fair enough?"

"Suits us," said Addison on his and Pembroke's behalf. The two walked away toward the wagon.

"Damn," said Pembroke between the two of them, "I just packed everything away."

"Then unpack it," Addison said, sounding testy. "What do you want from me? I can't make the sumbitch leave until he's damn good and ready. We could be here for supper, for all I know." The two walked on. . . .

An hour later, after two cups of strong hot coffee, Metcalf stood up, rubbed his eyes and slung coffee grounds from his tin cup. "Hell, this dust ain't never going to clear out of here."

Neely stood up beside him and sighed. "A hundred years from now, they'll be saying, 'Why is this canyon always full of dust?'" He chuckled to himself and shook his head.

"All right," said Metcalf, "let's get out of here. If the bounty men and the ranger are alive, they'll be coming for us."

"But we won't be here," said Neely, walking over and loosening the tall ammunition clip from the Gatling gun in order to carry it to the wagon.

On a steep winding path reaching upward toward the main trail, Sandoval stopped his horse and held up a gloved hand, cautioning the ranger and Thorn to stop five yards behind him.

"What's this . . . ?" Thorn whispered, he and the ranger seeing the single rider across a narrow gorge

from them, his horse climbing upward along a path
running parallel to theirs.

"I'm betting it's one of their men," Sam said quietly,
watching the rider continue until he rounded a jagged
turn and disappeared from sight. The two looked
down the steep trail behind the rider, noting the widen-
ing gorge.

"He had to be on the other side of the canyon when
the explosion went off," said Thorn.

"Yep," Sam said, the two pushing their animals forward now that the rider was gone. "That means the
trail he's on must lead to the top quicker than this
one."

"This could be a good piece of luck for us," said
Thorn to both the ranger and Sandoval as the younger
man rode back and slid to a halt to meet them. Gesturing toward the narrowing gorge ahead of them, Thorn
said, "As soon as we can cross, we'll cut our time in
half." He tapped his horse forward with the heels of his
knee-high boots. Sam and Sandoval followed.

Two hundred yards farther up the narrow path, the
gorge between the two trails turned into a rough,
brush-filled gully. The three men dropped from their
horses and led them across spilled and broken boulders left over from ancient landslides. On the other
side, Sandoval looked down at the rider's hoofprints in
the dirt.

"Here's some more luck, Captain," he said. "His
horse has thrown a shoe."

The three studied the prints for a moment.

Sam reached over and slipped his rifle down into its
boot. Drawing his Colt from his holster and checking it,

he said, "Three sets of hooves are too easy to hear. Give me a ten-minute head start, then catch up to me."

"What makes you so sure, Ranger?" Sandoval asked.

"He's not sure, Sandy," said Thorn, speaking for the ranger. "But he figures it's worth the try." He looked at Sam. "Ten minutes, Ranger. Good luck."

"Obliged," Sam said. He stepped up into his saddle and rode away at a quick, careful clip.

Before ten minutes were up, Sam rode around a turn in the steep trail and came upon an abandoned horse, limping and chuffing under its breath. "Easy, there," he said to the limping animal. He stepped down, loosened the horse's saddle and let it fall to the dirt, noting the empty rifle boot.

Raising the horse's front foreleg, he examined the tender shoeless hoof. *Stone bruise . . .* , he decided, lowering the hoof gently. The horse would be okay if he could stay alive for a few days of convalescence here in the wild, desolate terrain.

Back in his saddle, the ranger rode on at a walk, knowing the gunman couldn't have gotten much farther along on foot climbing the steep path.

Less than a hundred yards ahead, he heard the man's gasping breath and then he saw him step into the middle of the trail, hatless, his empty hands held high, sweat pouring down both cheeks. Over at the edge of the trail, Sam saw the man's rifle leaning against a rock. On the ground beside it lay the man's rolled-up gun belt.

"All right . . . don't shoot," the man said, his breath heaving in his chest. "I'm . . . not used to . . . climbing like this. I give up. Whew, this could kill a man."

"Who are you, mister?" Sam asked.

"I'm . . . Delbert Himes," the man wheezed.

Sam studied him for a moment, noting the moon and star hanging from his watch pocket and a watch fob. His big Colt in hand, Sam nudged Black Pot a step closer and said quietly, "Does this trail run up to the gun position?"

"Yes . . . it does," the man said. "But it's a . . . hell of a climb . . . on foot."

"How far?" Sam asked.

"Eight . . . nine miles at . . . the most," the gunman said, his breath still labored. "Was that you . . . set off the charge?"

"No," said Sam. "It wasn't us. It must have been one of your own."

"Huh-uh." The man shook his head. "That was my job sealing . . . off the canyon. Somebody was . . . supposed to shoot one of you . . . Then I'd blow the charge."

"It didn't work out that way," Sam said.

"I'll . . . be damned," the man said, looking disappointed.

"Turn around, mister," Sam said.

The panting man looking surprised. "What . . . for?" he said. "Can't you see that . . . I'm done in?"

"It would make me feel better," Sam said, gesturing with the barrel of his Colt. "It lets me know right off how well we're going to get along."

"Damn it. . . ." The man stalled for a second, the look of a trapped animal coming over his sweaty face. Then he lowered his hands quickly, stuck his right hand behind his back as he let out a yell.

The ranger's Colt bucked once in his hand just as

the gunman snatched a big Smith & Wesson pistol from his belt behind his back and swung it around toward him. As the shot resounded back along the trail, the man hit the ground and lay dead, his blank eyes staring up at the sky.

Back where the two bounty hunters sat waiting on the trail before following the ranger, Thorn said, "Time's up. Let's go."

When they reached the Ranger, he was sipping water from his canteen and standing beside Black Pot, who was sipping from a stream. He had dragged the gunman's body to the edge of the trail, picked up the rifle, unloaded it and pitched it out over a deep ravine. He did the same with the big Smith & Wesson as the two bounty hunters arrived.

Sam waited until they rode over to him, then said, "He told me it was his job to blow the canyon walls. Said somebody was supposed to shoot one of us. Then he was supposed to set off the blast."

"Somebody . . . ?" said Thorn. "He means Tinnis Mayes."

"Could be," said Sam. "If he was supposed to shoot one of us, Shear is going to be mighty disappointed." He shook his head, thinking about it, then said, "Mayes did some pretty good shooting, for a drunk."

"I would expect no less of him, drunk or sober, Ranger," Thorn said with pride. "I know where he learned it."

"Nevertheless, he'll have to answer for it when Shear finds out," said Sandoval.

"Then let us get there forthwith," said Thorn. "If

Mayes did all this to save our lives, we can do no less for him in return."

Hearing Thorn, Sandoval turned his horse and rode on ahead of them scouting the steep trail.

Sam wondered if the gambler really had done all this to save anybody's life, or if he had some other motive in mind. But this was something between Thorn and the gambler to reckon with, he thought. When Thorn turned his horse back to the trail, Sam swung up atop his stallion and fell in beside him. The three rode on.

PART 3

PART 3

Chapter 17

————

Nuevo Oro, New Mexico Territory

Big Aces Shear stared at the three riders until they drew close enough for him to recognize them. When he saw it was the gambler, Lasko and Barnes, he gave a faint smile. Beside him sat Mingo Sentanza, Crazy Elmer Fisk, Rudy Duckwald and George Epson. The rest of the men sat gathered in the dirt street, roasting a calf on an open spit in front of an adobe hotel and brothel in the lawless rail town now called New Gold Siding.

"Look who's coming here," said Shear, rising from his wooden chair in the midst of the four men. "Right on time too."

Up the street, a crew of railroad workers loaded firewood onto two large-frame buckboard wagons. On a third large-frame buckboard sat a large item covered by canvas and held in place by drawn steel chains. Six armed guards stood stationed in a circle around the third buckboard. The number of guards had doubled when Shear and his men rode in three hours earlier.

Beside Shear, Sentanza said, "Tomorrow is the day all dogs get fed."

"Fed indeed," said Shear, staring out at the three newly arrived riders as they entered town and turned their horses toward the iron hitch rail. Turning his eyes to the street, Shear said to Ben Longley, "Ben, ride on out and make sure everything's going good with our road crew."

"On my way, boss," said Longley, standing, throwing down a rib bone he'd been gnawing on. He wiped his hands on his leather chaps and hurried to another hitch rail a few feet up the dirt street.

"I love this time, right before pulling off a big job," said Shear to Sentanza. He took a deep breath and let it out. "Everybody is pepped up, willing and eager to do their part." He grinned and looked at Sentanza and added, "Ready to kill any son of a bitch that gets in our way."

"We've got the town nervous, that's for damned certain," Sentanza said, gazing off up the street at the armed guards circling around the buckboard.

"Yes," said Shear as the three riders stepped down in front of him, "if that buckboard wasn't so cleverly disguised with canvas, a fellow might suspect there's a safe hidden underneath it."

Shear laughed; the men standing around laughed along with him.

"I'm glad we caught you in a good mood, Big Aces," said Lasko. Barnes and the gambler stood right behind him tying the horses' reins to the hitch rail.

Shear's smile fell away, replaced by the darkness of a thunderstorm. "Why are you *glad* you caught me in a

good mood, Lasko?" he demanded. "What happened
back there? What went wrong?" His hand went to the
black-handled Remington on his hip.

"Whoa, nothing happened!" said Lasko, freezing up
for a second in fear.

"Leastwise nothing went *wrong*, Big Aces," Tinnis
cut in, using the leader's name now that he was one
of the Black Valley Riders. "On the contrary, everything
went smooth as Chinese silk." He gave a wide, dust-
streaked smile. "I made the shot of my wicked life, and
we left everybody lying under a canyon full of rocks."
He swept a hand theatrically and gave a slight bow at
the waist. "How much sweeter can life get than that,
sir?"

Shear stared at him, then broke out in a smile and
said to Lasko, "There, why couldn't you have told me
that way, instead of making me near blow your head
off?"

"Sorry, Big Aces," said Lasko with a whipped look
on his lowered face.

"Is that how things went . . . just like the gambler
says?" Shear asked.

"Pretty much, it is," Barnes cut in, not wanting
Lasko to say anything that might start trouble for them.
"The ranger and the bounty hunters are dead. The can-
yon is sealed off." He shrugged. "End of story."

"Damn, that's good news," said Shear. He turned to
Tinnis. "No whiskey beforehand, or after?"

"Not one drop, Big Aces," said the gambler, beam-
ing, his head still pounding and his body aching for a
long, hard shot of rye.

Shear looked at Barnes and Lasko.

"It's the truth, Big Aces," said Lasko. "He never drank a drop."

"I vouch for him on it," said Barnes. "He's stayed stone sober all day."

"Good man," said Shear to the gambler. "No more crumbs from the table for you, my friend. You're one of us now." Reaching behind his back, Shear took a double-action Colt from his belt and held it out to the gambler. "This isn't nickel-plated like yours was. But I hope it'll make you feel at home."

"My goodness . . . ," said Tinnis, looking genuinely moved by Shear's gift, and the way in which Shear had presented it to him. It had been a long time since the gambler had felt himself a part of anything except the trash the bar swampers swept out of the saloons after a hard night of drinking.

"I'm most obliged, Big Aces," Tinnis said in a quiet tone.

"Aw, hell, it's nothing," said Shear, waving the matter aside. "I'm sick of looking at that empty shoulder rig of yours. Stick the gun in it and shoot it in good health, now that you've decided to be a killer instead of a damn drunk."

Tinnis looked all around at the others with a smile, holding the gun in a way to show it to them.

"Show us your stuff, Lucas," said one of the men at the fire, a cup of coffee in one hand, a slab of roasted calf in his other.

"Watch closely," said Tinnis, "but don't let it blind you."

The men watched as he twirled the gun into a blur on his trigger finger, flipped it shoulder high, cocked his hip and caught the gun in his lowered palm as if catching it in his holster.

"Whoo-iee," said Longley, slapping his hands, goading him on.

Tinnis flipped the Colt up, snatched it out of the air with his other hand, twirled it and tossed in back and forth as it spun. As he worked the gun expertly, the men whistled and cheered. He tossed the gun back and forth, once, twice—but on the third time, he fumbled and almost dropped it to the dirt.

"All right, that's enough for one night," he said jokingly. "Come see me a month from now when the demons have ceased to claw on my brain."

Behind Shear and off to one side, Fisk leaned over and whispered to Duckwald, "I'll claw his brain. . . ."

Shear stared off at the guards around the buckboard wagons. "All right, everybody," he said in a lowered voice, "they've got a good idea who we are and what we're doing here. Be on top of your game in the morning. We're following them out of here to the Skull Rock trestle."

Tinnis shoved his new Colt down into his shoulder harness and closed his lapel. He glanced past Elmer Fisk, but pretended not to see the harsh angry stare Fisk directed back at him.

Late in the night, the hotel had fallen silent. Only a few oil pots sat burning themselves out along the empty street. The only signs of life in the far end of town were the six railroad guards still posted in a wide circle surrounding the heavily loaded buckboard. From the front of the hotel to the other end of town, the only sign of

life was Crazy Elmer Fisk walking back and forth, twenty
yards in each direction. Each time he stopped in front
of the adobe hotel, he stared over at the gambler, who
lay leaned back against the front of the hotel with a
ragged blanket over him.

Feigning sleep, the gambler kept watch on Fisk for
a full hour. At the other end of the boardwalk, Dave
Pickens sat tossing a pocketknife into the walk plank
in languid repetition. Finally, the slow steady thumping sound of the knife blade stopped and Tinnis knew
Pickens had at last lain back and fallen asleep.

Thank God. . . .

Gazing through lowered lids, Tinnis waited until
Fisk made his next pass, his cradled rifle in arm, and
headed back away from the hotel. Then the gambler
arose silently, flipped his blanket aside and moved as
silently as a dark spirit around the corner of the hotel
and into a long alleyway behind it.

At the loaded buckboard, one of the railroad guards,
a Nebraskan Mormon named Oran Wadley, said to the
closest guard to his left, "*Psst . . .* Riggins. Did you see
something move down there?" As he spoke he stepped
sideways, keeping his eyes on the boardwalk full of sleep-
ing gunmen.

"No," whispered a Kansas rail detective named Lionel
Riggins. He turned more attentive to the dark adobe
hotel flickering in the dim glow of oil-pot flames. "But
if you see it again, tell me. I've been expecting something out of this bunch of trash ever since they started
gathering in here."

"Yeah, I know," whispered Wadley. "It's like somebody tipped them off, what it is we're doing here."

"Oh? Do you think so?" Riggins whispered with a twist of sarcasm in his voice.

Wadley ignored the sarcasm, and asked, "Do you think they can tell we've got a safe under the canvas?"

"Jesus, Wadley," said Riggins. "My *horse* can tell we've got a safe under here."

"Well . . . I best get back to my spot, keep an eye on things," Wadley said, wanting no more conversation with the prickly Kansan.

"Good idea," said Riggins.

On the dark street, Fisk walked out of the glow of the last oil pot and continued at a steady pace. At the dark edge of town, he tuned and started walking back. As he passed close to a stack of empty wooden shipping crates out in front of the soon-to-open mercantile store, he did not see the dark figure swing around in front of him until he felt a wiry hand clamp over his lips and muffle his voice.

"So long, *Crazy*," the gambler whispered only inches from his ear.

Fisk felt a cold, sharp, blinding pain run deep into his chest. The severity of it forced him up onto his tiptoes. He remained there for a moment as if suspended in air, impaled, up to the hilt of the dagger the gambler had thrust upward into his heart. Then he relaxed into the gambler's arms.

From the buckboards, Oran Wadley called out to Lionel Riggins again, "*Pssst*, I think I saw something else, farther down the street."

"Quit making that sound, Wadley," said Riggins. "It makes you sound simpleminded."

"You said to tell you if I saw anything else," Wadley said.

"Okay, you've told me. Now shut up," said Riggins.

Hearing the two, another guard named Chester Gerst chuckled under his breath. He shook his head and said to the other guards, "Keep me covered. I'll walk down and take a look." He adjusted a faded black sombrero atop his head.

At the dark end of the street, Tinnis saw the long-haired, thick-bearded rifleman coming toward him, walking in and out of the glow of flickering oil pots. As the man drew closer, the gambler quietly and quickly pulled down two wooden crates, dragged Fisk's body in between them and restacked them back in front of him. With the crates back in place, he rubbed a boot back and forth over the dirt to hide his footprints, then backed away into the alley as the rifleman walked up and looked all around in the darkness.

"Who's there?" Gerst asked toward the pitch-black alleyway, hearing the slightest sound of what he thought to be footsteps on the hard-packed ground. After listening intently for a moment, he shrugged and walked back toward the buckboards. Out in front of the hotel, he saw a figure on the boardwalk adjust a blanket over himself and turn onto his side.

"See anything?" Wadley asked just as soon as Gerst walked back to the buckboards.

"Not a thing," Gerst replied. He took off his battered hat and ran his hand back along his shoulder-length hair.

"Maybe I was mistaken," said Wadley.

"Maybe you were," Gerst said in a harsh tone, a grim look on his bearded face.

From the darkened hotel window overlooking the empty street, Shear stood naked, save for a pair of high-reaching black socks. He had not seen Fisk disappear from walking guard, nor had he seen the gambler go about his gruesome handiwork. All he had arrived at the window in time to see was the lone bearded rifleman walking down to the far end of town, and back.

"What's the matter, Mr. Shear. Can't you sleep?" asked a naked young whore lying on the bed behind him.

"Don't want to sleep, Louise," said Shear over his shoulder.

"In that case, you just bring yourself right back over here," said the woman. "We can stay awake together *all night* if you want to."

Shear gazed down at the empty street for a moment longer, then grinned to himself, turned and walked back to the rumpled bed. "Why not?" he said.

The naked woman wrapped her arms and legs around him as he lowered himself onto her. "I know you are on your way somewhere to do important business," she said. "But when you return, you must allow all of your men to stay inside and visit the doves."

"Yeah, I will do that, on the way back," said Shear, his voice muffled by her large, firm breasts.

"Tell me, what is this business you and your men are going to do?" she asked, drawing slow circles on his thick chest with her fingertip.

"Shut up, Louise," Shear said, "and do what you're best at."

Chapter 18

An hour before dawn the riflemen had changed guards at the buckboards. Shear's men had already begun to slowly rise along the boardwalk and form around the blackened fire site in the middle of the street. Ballard Swean scratched his disheveled head and looked up from preparing to boil coffee.

"Where's Fisk?" he asked.

"That's what I was asking myself," said Dent Phillips. "He was prowling the streets like a bobcat when I bedded down. Said he'd stand guard all night, like he often does."

"Crazy bastard," said Swean. He looked back and forth, then added, "But it ain't like him to not come sniffing around for coffee, first thing."

Tinnis sat up from against the front of the adobe building and wiped his eyes with his knuckles and looked all around.

Having heard the conversation on his way to the front door, Shear stood in the open doorway and looked back and forth, his hands on his hips. "I don't like this," he said with suspicion, turning his eyes to the wagon guard at the far end of the street.

Rudy Duckwald stood and walked closer to the gambler and looked down at him. To Shear, he said, "Why don't you ask this sneaking gambler where Fisk is?"

"Rudy, I appreciate neither your implication nor your attitude," said Tinnis, standing as he spoke and picking up his suit coat from the planks beside him.

"Yeah?" the big gunman snarled. "Maybe you'd like to do something about it."

"No, sir, not before breakfast," said Tinnis, slipping on his coat and straightening it down the front. "I would bring myself bad luck killing an idiot on an empty stomach."

Duckwald's eyes filled with rage. "I'll blow your brains out—"

"Rudy! Get your bark off!" Shear shouted, seeing the gunman's big hand ready to go for his pistol, Tinnis seeming to not take Duckwald's threat seriously. "We're looking for Fisk, remember?"

"Elmer's probably gone to the jake," Calvin Kerr cut in. "He spends more time sitting in a jake than any man I ever seen." He gave a shrug. "I don't know what he does in there."

Duckwald had settled down, but he hadn't let go of his accusations. "I say this gambler has done something to him."

"Shut up, Rudy," said Shear. "Tinnis Lucas is one of us now. He gets the same respect as the rest of us."

Duckwald stared hard at the gambler; the gambler didn't back an inch.

"Sentanza," said Shear, "go check some of the jakes

along the alleyways. If he's in one, tell him to get himself out here. We've got a busy day coming. I want everybody sticking close together."

Sentanza left with his rifle cradled in the crook of his
arm. He swatted at buzzing flies as he searched along
the alleyway, one outhouse after another. Other men
went off searching the livery barn, a bathhouse and the
town dump. Ten minutes later when Sentanza was finished in the long alleyway, he walked back with his hat
hanging from his hand.

"I checked them all," he said. "Fisk ain't back there."
Sunlight had crept over the edge of the horizon and
spread slantwise along the dirt street.

Shear only nodded and looked off along the street at
the buckboards. "Never trust a railroader," he said to
no one in particular.

"What?" Sentanza asked.

But before Shear could say anything else, Dent Phillips called out loudly from the soon-to-be mercantile
store.

"Big Aces, down here! It's Crazy Elmer! He's deader
than hell."

The guards around the buckboards heard Phillips
call out to Shear. They looked at one another uncomfortably as Shear's gunmen gathered in front of the
mercantile where Phillips had pulled out the shipping
crates hiding Fisk's body.

"Everybody hold tight," the leader of the buckboard
guards said with determination. "We might have our
hands full any minute here." He said to the nearest
guard, Tom Marlin, "Tommy, run in and tell Mr. Brewer
what's going on out here."

On the street, the gambler walked toward the mercantile store at an easy pace, a couple of the other men hurrying past him on his way. When he arrived at the spot where the two crates had been pulled away, he looked down innocently at the body of Elmer Fisk. A broad patch of blood had blackened on the hole in Fisk's chest. The dead outlaw's eyes were open, staring straight ahead in surprise.

"He's stabbed through the heart!" said Duckwald, he and his brother-in-law, George Epson, having been the first two to arrive as soon as Phillips had announced his grizzly discovery.

Shear looked at Fisk's gun still in its holster. "He was taken unawares. That's for sure," he said. "Fisk would have fought like a panther otherwise. He half turned and stared coldly at the buckboard guards. They stood curiously staring back from the far end of town.

"Here's the son of a bitch who killed him," said Duckwald. He stared at the gambler. "I'd bet my life on it."

"Careful, Rudy," said Tinnis, with no joking manner to either his tone or his expression. "You may be doing *just* that." His coat lapel lay open, the Colt Thunderer Shear had given him in clear view.

"Rudy, you've got to stop accusing Lucas," Shear said in a gruff voice.

"He killed him, Big Aces," said Duckwald with conviction.

"For God's sake," said Shear in a disgusted tone. He stared at the gambler. "For once and for all, Tinnis, did you kill Elmer?"

"Of course I killed him," the gambler said, staring at

Duckwald. He pulled the dagger from inside his shirt and held it up. "Here's the knife I killed him with. I've been waiting for my chance to kill him ever since he ran me off the cliff."

"See, I told you he killed him," said Duckwald. "He knew what Elmer did to him."

"Fisk ran him off the cliff?" Shear said with a dark, curious look on his face.

"No!" said Duckwald, getting rattled. "I mean, *yes*! I mean, hell, I don't know, but Lucas must've thought he did. That's all that mattered to him. You heard him. He killed Elmer."

"All I heard was him making an ass out of you," said Shear. His black-handled Remington streaked up from his holster, cocked and aimed at the big gunman's face. "Get out of my sight, Rudy, before I shoot your eyes out."

Duckwald backed away, Epson right beside him. When the two were gone, Shear turned back to the gambler, who still held the dagger in hand.

"Obliged, Big Aces," Tinnis said quietly.

"Put the pigsticker away, Lucas," said Shear. To the men, he said, "I know for a fact that Lucas didn't kill Fisk. I saw one of them guards walking away from here in the night."

The men grumble and milled and gave hard looks toward the buckboard guards.

"Don't worry about them right now," Shear said to them under his breath. "They'll all get what's coming to them before this day is over." He looked back at the gambler and asked, "Why'd you say you killed him, Lucas, when you *didn't*?"

The gambler didn't answer. He slipped the dagger back inside his sleeve and looked away toward a distant mountain range.

The rest of the men stood staring, not knowing what to make of the matter.

"Even if you had, I'd have to say he deserved it, running you and your horse off the cliff like that." He looked at the other men for support; they nodded in agreement.

"I always said Crazy Elmer was crazy," Phillips said sincerely.

"Well, hell, Dent, we all did," Shear said, spreading his hands patiently. He said to the rest of the men, "Get fed, get ready." He gave a secret thumb toward the buckboards and the guards surrounding them. "These jakes won't know what hit them."

Tinnis Mayes smiled to himself and pulled his coat closed over the Colt Thunderer holstered under his arm.

Before the sun had reached its midmorning level in the wide blue sky, the three buckboards had rolled out of New Gold Siding, headed east into a long stretch of deep-cut hills reaching toward the Sangre de Cristo Mountains. Ten railroad security riders flanked the buckboard wagons, five on either side. In addition to the security riders, a crew of five rail hands sat in the bed of the lead wagon, atop a tall load of firewood. A shotgun rider sat beside the driver of the middle wagon, the one carrying the big heavy safe covered with tied-down sheets of canvas.

"There they are, men, right below us," said Shear, "just like plums ripe for the picking." He looked down at the three-wagon procession from a ridge above a sandy flatlands dotted with creosote, cactus and mesquite. Along the other side of the pass, four more of his men rode along at the same fast, steady clip.

Riding parallel to the wagons below, Shear looked from face to face of the railroad men until he spotted Chester Gerst, the shoulder-length hair, the thick beard, the faded sombrero—the partly shadowed face of the man he'd seen on the street the night before.

Behind Shear, Swean got excited and said, "Hot damn! When, Big Aces, *when*?"

"As soon as we can get ahead of them and catch them in a cross fire," said Shear. He batted his heels harder to his horse's sides. "Just remember, the second guard on the left is all mine . . . the man with the black sombrero." He pushed his horse harder, veering away from the edge of the ridge just enough to stay out of sight for the time being.

"Is that the snake who killed Elmer Fisk?" Swean asked, gigging his horse right behind him, along with the others.

Shear didn't answer.

Riding side by side, Tinnis and Sentanza looked at each other. The gambler saw the question in Sentanza's dark eyes, but he refused to reveal the truth to him.

Sentanza finally leaned over a little and said beneath the sound of the horses' hooves, "If a man did to me what Crazy Elmer Fisk did to you, he could never turn his back on me. I would kill him any way I could, even if I had to mash his head with a rock." He stared at the gambler as if expecting a reply.

But Tinnis had admitted the killing to Shear and Shear

had turned it down. He only returned Sentanza's stare. "I have no more to say on the matter, Mingo," he said sidelong.

"You and I could be pals, amigos, Lucas," Sentanza whispered, smiling. "I cover your back, you cover mine, eh?"

"The way you covered Callahan's back?" said Lucas.

"That was an unfortunate thing," said Sentanza. "I wish it had gone differently."

"I bet Callahan does too," said the gambler. He jerked his horse's reins and pulled the animal away from Sentanza a little. But the persistent Sentanza pulled his horse right alongside him.

"When this is over we will all split up and go our own way to lie low for a while," he said. "You would do well to stick with me. I am going to Mexico. I have many friends there. They would welcome you, if you are with me."

"Obliged," said Tinnis, "I'll keep it in mind." They pounded on in unison, keeping up with the rest of the riders.

"Good," said Sentanza. "You must be careful carrying a large amount of money in this wild, lawless land."

"Sound advice," said Lucas. He keep his horse moving quickly along the rock trail, knowing if he ever went anywhere with Mingo Sentanza, he would not even expect to ever come back alive.

In the shotgun rider's seat in the second wagon sat an older railroad man known as Papa Dorsey. He sat in silence with his shotgun across his lap. He looked up and all around as the wagon entered a pass into the hillside that had been blasted and carved out two years earlier to allow wagons and crews to reach a new high trestle over Skull Rock Canyon.

Once the wagon had followed the lead wagon deeper into the pass, Dorsey eased the tip of the shotgun barrel over into the driver's side.

"From here on, Mason, you'll still be doing the driving, but I'll be giving you the directions," he said in a lowered voice.

"What?" said the driver, a younger man named Mason Edwards. He gave Dorsey a bemused grin and tried to scoot away from the tip of the gun barrel.

"Don't try pulling away from me," Dorsey said in the same low, even voice. "One more mistake like that and I'll blow you in half."

"Papa?" said Edwards. "What is—"

"Shut up and pay attention. Do like I tell you if you want to stay alive," said Dorsey, jamming the barrel into the young teamster's ribs to make his point. Dorsey stared straight ahead, to keep from drawing any attention from the guards. But above them he had already caught the first glimpse of Shear and his men spreading out in front of them along both sides of the trail.

The young teamster drove along with a worried look frozen on his face. But only a few seconds later both edges of the cliffs above them began to erupt in gunfire, much of it concentrated on the wagon in front of them.

"Go!" Papa Dorsey shouted in the driver's ear.

In front of them the driver of the first wagon flew off his seat and fell to the rocky ground as a bullet tore through him and left a bloody mist in the air. The shotgun rider tried to grab the traces, but the wagon had already begun to veer to the right side of the trail.

"Get around it!" Papa Dorsey shouted above the heavy gunfire and screaming bullets. On either side of them, the armed guards' horses reared and whinnied wildly. The guards struggled to get the animals under control, but the rifle fire took both man and animal to the ground.

The young teamster did as he was told, rather than be chopped down like the others. He slapped the traces to the wagon horses' backs and sent the heavily loaded wagon around the first wagonload of firewood that had gone up one side and turned over in the rocks beside the narrow trail.

"Dorsey, help me!" the shotgun rider from the first wagon shouted as the second wagon went by. But as he grabbed for the wagon, Dorsey lifted a Colt from his holster and shot the man backward without taking the shotgun off the young teamster.

Dorsey shouted above the melee to the young teamster at his side, "You're doing real good, Mason boy! Don't stop now."

Chapter 19

———

It was midmorning when the ranger and the bounty hunters rolled on toward Nuevo Oro. Sandoval drove the wagon they had taken from Ray Metcalf and the other three gunmen on their way to catch up with Shear and his men. The ranger sat on the wooden seat beside him. Thorn sat in the wagon bed, his gloved hand resting on the Gatling gun, his head slightly bowed in sleep. Sam looked back at Thorn, then to his left at Sandoval as he recalled the running gun battle the evening before.

The three had cut their ride short by using the steep trail the ranger had learned about from the man he left lying dead on the hillside. By the time they'd caught up with Metcalf and his three cohorts, the wagon had traveled halfway across a stretch of flatlands on a thick carpet of sand, broken by land-stuck rock and boulders and strewn with saguaro cactus and mesquite.

When they'd swung wide around the wagon and cut the men off, the Gatling gun had held them pinned to the ground for half hour before they'd split up and attacked from three directions at once. When the fight was finished, and three of the gunmen lay sprawled dead along the wagon tracks in the sand, Thorn stood with his knee-high boot clamped down on Metcalf's chest.

"Never fire a Gatling gun at a marine and expect him not to take it away from you," Thorn said, his left hand resting on the hilt of his Mameluke sword. He held his big horse pistol pointed at Metcalf's forehead.

"A—a what?" Metcalf asked haltingly. He lay wounded, bleeding in the hot sand, one leg cocked at the knee. He stared up as if confused. Yet as Thorn took his boot from Metcalf's chest, lowered his horse pistol and shoved it into his holster, the gunman's hand inched toward his raised boot well.

"Never mind," said Thorn. He half turned and looked out across a thick swirl of wind and sand.

"Look out, Captain—" Sam shouted, seeing Metcalf sit up quickly, his hand coming out of his boot well holding a small hideout pistol. But before Sam's words got out of his mouth, even as his big Colt came up from his holster, he heard a sharp rush of wind whistle through the air.

Metcalf's hideout gun swung away and fired wildly as Sandoval's fourteen-inch sword sliced through his chest, stopping at its hilt with a jarring impact.

Sam's Colt was out now, and so was Thorn's horse pistol. But neither of them fired; they didn't need to. Instead they stood staring at Metcalf as he fell backward to the ground. The point of the sword blade behind him stopped on a broad flat rock and slid back up, the hilt rising out of his chest as if drawn by some unseen hand.

Lowering his pistol again, this time closing the holster flap over it when he put it away, Thorn said in a proud but matter-of-fact voice, "Keep up the good work, Sandy."

"Aye, aye, Captain," Sandoval had said, walking over and retrieving his bloody sword. . . .

Sam pictured it now in his mind as they rolled along in the gun wagon, their horses' reins tied to the tailgate.

These two were fighting men, Sam thought to himself.

They were without doubt among the best he'd ever seen. Even here in these lawless badlands, the two had handled everything the land and its inhabitants had thrown at them.

Yet Thorn had made a mistake taking his eyes off Metcalf. Even though it had only been for a second, the ranger knew all too well how quickly a second became an eternity in this unforgiving terrain. Looking away for only a second had nearly cost the battle-seasoned old captain his life.

Had Thorn seen it . . . ? Sam asked himself. Sandoval had seen it, he was certain. At any rate, it wasn't his place to mention it, Sam told himself, watching the dusty trail ahead of them.

But as they rode on, as if he'd heard the ranger's thoughts, the bounty hunter looked back over his shoulder at Thorn dozing.

"The captain is tired," he said quietly, with a thin smile.

"So am I," Sam said, showing courtesy.

"And I too," Sandoval agreed. "But I have watched my father closely this trip. He is more tired than I have ever seen him."

His father . . . ? Sam noted that it was the first time he'd heard the younger bounty hunter call Thorn his father. He weighed and considered his words before saying them.

"Why bounty hunting?" he finally asked as the wagon rolled along, the rooftops of Nuevo Oro rising up through the wavering heat and swirling sand before them.

"Why not bounty hunting?" Sandoval replied, staring ahead.

The ranger let it drop. He had stuck his nose where it didn't belong. Now he needed to back away.

But after a pause, the bounty hunter said, "When a man spends most of his years in battle, it's hard to find another way of life . . . one that suits his nature." He paused for a moment, then said, "My father has *lived* as a warrior. I believe he would prefer to *die* as a warrior. Does that make sense to you?"

"It doesn't have to make sense to me," Sam replied. "It only has to make sense to the captain . . . and to you, since you're the one having to reckon with it."

Sandoval only nodded, and put the matter aside as they drew closer to the town.

When the gun wagon rode onto the main street of Nuevo Oro, stirring up fresh dust, townsmen ventured out of their shops and houses for a better look. At the sight of the Gatling gun, and the badge on the ranger's chest, they hurried over to the hitch rail out in front of the adobe hotel.

"Welcome to New Gold, Ranger, or Nuevo Oro as it was called," a man said. He jerked his hat from his bald head just as the wagon came to a halt. "I'm Fenton Wright." He added with relief, "It is danged good to see some law riding in here!" He looked at the badge on Sam's chest and big Gatling gun beneath Thorn's gloved hand. Thorn was awake now and sitting tall.

"I'm Ranger Sam Burrack," said Sam. "This is Cadden Thorn and Dee Sandoval."

"All three of you rangers, are yas?" Wright asked, as other townsmen gathered around them.

"No," said Sam, "but we're working together, tracking the same men."

"Well, that's good enough for us," said Wright. "We all feel better just seeing yas."

"Why?" said Sam. "What's happened here?" He looked all around, already satisfied that Shear and his men had been here and gone. He saw the large charred circle of ground where the men had roasted the calf.

"There was a man killed here last night," the townsman said. "He was with a gang of desperate-looking gunmen, the ones you're tracking, like as not."

Sam, Sandoval and Thorn swung down from the wagon as a man in a leather apron stepped forward from among the other townsmen. "Want all these horses watered and tended?" he asked, reaching out as if to step into the wagon.

Sandoval stopped him. "This wagon doesn't leave my sight. Bring four fresh wagon horses if you've got them. We'll swap them out. Water these other horses with buckets, right here while they're resting." He fished a gold coin from his vest pocket and flipped it to the livery hostler.

"You've got it coming, mister," said the hostler. He hurried away to get four fresh wagon horses.

"Where is this man who was killed?" the ranger asked Fenton Wright.

"He's cooling in a root cellar out back of here," said Wright. "Want to see him? I'll take yas to him."

"Yes, obliged," Sam said. "On the way you can tell us everything."

"Are you in a hurry?" Wright asked. "Because if you *are* I can talk pretty danged fast. I am, among other things, a professional auctioneer, or *augere*, if you will."

"*Fast* suits us," said Sam.

Sandoval stayed with the gun wagon, his rifle in hand. By the time Sam and Thorn had reached the root cellar, Wright had given them the full story, about the railroad men with what appeared to be a large safe in one of their firewood wagons. He told them about the body they were going to see and how someone had hidden it among some wooden crates. He finished talking as he reached down and pulled the root cellar door open.

"Did one of the riders wear a black swallow-tailed suit coat and have stitches in his head?" Thorn asked.

"Yes, that is correct," said Wright, sounding a bit winded from rattling on nonstop in a steady singsong voice.

Inside the shadowy root cellar, Sam pulled a ragged sheet back off Fisk's dead bloodless face.

"Crazy Elmer Fisk," Sam said, recognizing the dead outlaw. He looked closely at the dagger wound in the pale bare chest.

Thorn looked at the body knowingly.

Seeing his expression, Sam said, "Tinnis Mayes?"

"Could be," said Thorn. "Whoever did it knew how to do it right. No bruises from a struggle, just one quick stick in the right place. This man went down fast and never made a whimper."

Sam studied Fisk's wound for a moment. Dropping the sheet back over the corpse, he turned and walked out the cellar door. Thorn walked beside him.

"We'll carve him a plank if you'll tell us what name to put on it," said Wright. "Everybody was a little shy to approach his pals, if you know what I mean."

"His name was Elmer Fisk," Sam said. "How long ago did these men leave?"

"It was early this morning, right after daylight, give or take," said Wright. "They left a few minutes behind the firewood wagons. Do you think they were trailing the wagons? It looked to me like the railroad guards acted awfully suspicious of them."

Sam and the bounty hunter shook their heads and walked on. "I know you don't agree, Ranger," Thorn said, "but I feel good knowing Mayes is still in there, keeping these killers at arm's length."

"With all respect, Captain, you're right—I don't agree," said Sam. "The farther he goes with these men, the worse he looks to me."

"And the better he looks to me," Thorn said with a thin smile. "Don't forget, Ranger. I know this man."

"Sorry, Captain, but no, you don't," said Sam. "You knew him a *long time ago* and a *long way from here*." He looked at Thorn. "This country can twist a man until he doesn't even know himself."

"Not Tinnis Mayes," said Thorn. "I still have faith in him." He gave the ranger another thin smile beneath his gray, straight mustache. "We'll find him. I'll prove it to you."

"I hope you're right, Captain," said Sam. "And I hope we find him alive. But those two hopes are at long odds with each other. If his hands *are* still clean, he can't keep them that way long with this bunch. If he does they'll kill him."

From a rock-protected position atop the cliffs, Sentanza and the gambler looked down at the one-sided battle raging below. "Whoo-*ieee!*" said Sentanza, levering a round into his rifle chamber and raising the butt to his shoulder. "This is the kind of action I always dream of!" He fired repeatedly into the men and horses below.

The gambler only stared down in grim observation, his fists gripped tight at his side, knowing he was powerless to do anything to stop the slaughter. On the lower rock trail, the first wagon lay on its side, the load of firewood having spilled over onto the ground. The four horses pulling the load had broken free and now ran back and forth wildly as bullets punched and nipped at them.

After his fourth shot, Sentanza turned to Tinnis and

said, "What's the matter, my friend? Don't you want some of this?"

"It's not my style," said the gambler without looking up from the bloody carnage.

"What?" Sentanza asked, unable to hear him clearly above the den of gunfire.

"I'm out of range," Tinnis said, changing his reply to something more acceptable to a man like Sentanza. He patted the double-action Colt under his arm. "I don't have a gun that'll reach that far."

"So?" said Sentanza. "Find a closer target. Shoot whoever you want to shoot, eh?"

He gestured with his gun barrel toward some of the wounded guards who had abandoned their fallen horses and began climbing frantically up the rock walls seeking any cover they could find.

"Good idea, Mingo," Tinnis replied amid the fierce shooting. He pulled the Colt from his holster.

"Always listen to me, *mi amigo!*" Sentanza said with a wide, excited grin. He tapped a finger on his forehead. "I know about these things—"

His words cut short as the Colt Thunderer bucked twice in the gambler's hand and two bullets ripped through his chest. The impact knocked him backward onto the outermost edge of the cliff, where he tittered back and forth, his rifle flying from his hands and clattering down the rock wall.

"I didn't mean . . . for you . . . to shoot *me!*" he cried out, stunned, in disbelief.

Whoever I want to . . .

Tinnis watched him fall off the edge and bounce and

slide, then bounce some more, brokenly, for a hundred feet, until he splattered in every direction on the stony bottom trail. "So long, Mingo . . . ," he said, expressionless.

When Sentanza had landed, Tinnis let out a breath, turned and walked up the steep rock incline to the place where they'd left their horses. He swung up onto his saddle and rode away, with no more direction in mind than the day he'd suddenly ridden away from the ranger and the two bounty hunters. Except this time he was sober, he reminded himself—sober enough to realize that he had no idea where he was going . . . or why.

He rode along the edge to the spot where he'd seen Dent Phillips and Calvin Kerr firing mercilessly down onto the railroad men. Leaving his horse on the trail, he slipped down from his saddle and walked calmly down over the rocks until he stood staring at the two men from behind.

"Phillips, Kerr! Back here!" he shouted above the melee.

As the two men turned facing him, he began pulling the trigger on the double-action Colt.

Kerr flew backward off the cliff with a yell as a bullet slammed into his chest. But Phillips didn't go down as easily. He got off a shot with his rifle just as the gambler's bullet hit him high in his shoulder and spun him around. It took another shot to send him flying out off the rocky edge.

But the bullet from Phillips' rifle had nailed the gambler in his side and bowed him at the waist. He

staggered backward and dropped down onto a rock.
Then he toppled off the rock onto the hard ground.

*What the hell were you thinking, Tinnis Mayes, pulling a
stunt like that . . . ?*

He stared up for a moment, clutching his side, watching the blue sky toss and swirl, then turn black above
him.

Chapter 20

———

Skull Rock Canyon, New Mexico Territory

On the rear platform of the train's caboose, two rifle-men stood looking off into the line of hills rising up in the Sangre de Cristo Mountain Range. It had been well over an hour since they'd heard the last of the sporadic gunfire resound in the distance, yet that fact offered them no solace. In fact, the lapse of time only made them even more wary, more apprehensive—more expectant of trouble coming their way.

"What are we doing here? None of this makes sense to me," one guard said to the other, an older man who wore a thick red beard, a permanent tobacco stain down one edge of his mouth.

"Really?" said the older guard. He grinned and spat off the side of the platform onto a bed of gravel lining the tracks. "Say *railroad*," he instructed the younger guard.

"Railroad . . . ?" the younger guard said, complying with him.

"See, once you say *railroad*," the older guard advised, "you can grab *making sense* by its tail and throw it right out the window."

"Is that all you've learned, fifteen years with the railroads?" the younger man asked, going back to scanning the hills, the open trails leading upward out of sight.

"It's all you *need* to learn, carrying a gun for these people. They didn't hire us 'cause we're smart." The red-bearded guard gestured at the rifle in his hands. "They figure if we were smart enough to understand anything at all, we'd be too smart to work for them." He spat again and chuckled. "That's why if you get *too smart* they'll fire you, or leastwise jerk your gun out of your hand and stick a pencil in it. They do not want a man armed and smart, *huh-uh.*" He shook his head.

"Damn railroad," the young guard said. He paused, then said, "Think about this. We're sitting dead-still here, exposed, in ambush country, waiting for a safe, so we can put gold in it that we've already got locked inside a rail car with armed guards sitting on it."

The older grinned knowingly. "That one, I know the answer to."

"Yeah, why?" asked the young guard.

"Because the *generalissimo* Ceballos wants his gold delivered to him in a safe. What the *generalissimo* wants, he gets these days."

The young guard shook his head. "They've had three presidents in the past year. Mr. Hargrove must figure that General Ceballos is next."

"It's no wild guess on Hargrove's part," said the older guard. "This gold might just be the thing that cinches the deal."

The guard gave a sigh. "Imagine having enough money to make a man president."

"Imagine what making him president will do for Hargrove and his railroads," said the older guard. He spat and added, "Hell, he might give us goose every Christmas."

"I wouldn't count on it," said the young guard. The only goose he'd give us is his big thumb up our—"

An arrow thumped into the caboose beside his head. "Jesus H. Johnson . . . ! *Comadrejas!*" shouted the older guard as more arrows whistled past them and thumped into the train. He threw his Winchester to his shoulder and began levering shot after shot at the horde of whooping, yelling warriors riding down on them, following the rails down out of the canyon behind them.

"Man, we are dead!" shouted the young guard.

"Shut up and shoot something!" shouted the older guard, still levering out rounds.

From along both sides of the train, guards leaned out the window and began firing. Clato Charo, the leader of the *Comadrejas*, waved a recently acquired Spencer rifle above his head and divided his riders, sending half along one side of the sitting train, and half down the other.

The older guard slung open the door of the caboose, shoved the younger man inside and slammed the door as a bullet tore through it and showered them with splinters. "Take the window!" he shouted, gesturing the young guard to a rear window on one side of the door while he took the other one.

As the two guards fired repeatedly and other guards inside the train continued to fight from the open train windows, the front door of the caboose swung open and shut and a former trail scout turned railroad guard stood with his rifle in hand. He gave a thin cavalier smile. "I thought you men might need a hand back here."

"Not if you just come to grin and talk!" shouted the older guard.

"Oh, I come to fight," said the buckskinned man. As he spoke he took his time pulling on a pair of gauntlet gloves with Indian bead braiding on their cuffs. His yellow hair hung to his shoulders, William Cody–style. "That's Clato Charo's *Comadrejas* out there. They're not the best fighters, these Desert Weasels, you know?"

"I don't give a damn if it's Marco Polo. They're trying to kill us! Start shooting!"

"I will, but first I'm going to try talking to them," said the former scout. He walked to the door and grabbed the handle. "Hold your fire," he added coolly, leaning his rifle against the wall.

"Don't open that door—" the older guard shouted. But he was too late.

The buckskinned man threw the door open wide and stood in the open doorway, his left arm raised high in a fist, a show of peace he'd learned years ago on the high mountain range.

"My brothers!" he called out in a loud voice.

Three arrows laced across his chest; two bullets ripped through his belly. A third bullet nailed him squarely in his forehead and sent blood and brain matter splattering all over both guards as they ducked away to avoid it. The buckskinned man flew backward the length of the caboose and fell dead against the front door.

"The most ignorant son of a bitch I ever seen!" said the older guard, wiping a streak of blood from his face as he jumped over to slam the door. "Nobody can talk to *Comadrejas* . . . all you can do is kill them."

But as he closed the rear door, he caught sight of two loaded wagons and a number of riders coming along the track beyond the raging warriors, charging them from behind with a barrage of rifle fire. In the front wagon he recognized Papa Dorsey's white beard. Slamming the door, he leaned back against it with a sigh of relief.

"Boy, our bacon just got saved," he said.

Rolling along in the front wagon, Brayton Shear spread a wide smile and chuckled aloud. As the *Comadrejas* broke away into a hasty retreat, not even firing back over their shoulders, Shear looked at Ted Lasko, who drove the wagon.

"Sometimes, Lady Luck just jumps up and slaps you cockeyed," he said, his big black-handled Remington smoking in his hand.

"Yeah," said Lasko. "I thought maybe and you and Charo planned it this way."

"You can't deal with *Comadrejas*," Papa Dorsey cut in, standing in the wagon behind the seat.

"But this could not have worked out better if we *had* planned it," Shear said. He stood up and waved his hat back and forth at the train, where cheers and shouting and waving hats came out of the open windows.

As Lasko rolled up beside the express car, two riflemen and a tall man in a pin-striped suit ran back to meet them. "Goodness gracious, sir! You must surely be angels!" the man in the suit said. He jerked off a black derby dress hat to reveal hair neatly parted down the middle. His brown mustache was heavily waxed and sharply pointed.

"Angels . . . ? No, sir," Shear said modestly. "Just *good* men doing what *good* men do." He touched his hat brim toward the man and said, "You must Mr. Oaks?"

"Indeed I am, but not to you, sir," the man said, bubbling over with gratitude. "Call me Ronald, I must insist."

"Well, *Ronald*," said Shear, emphasizing the man's first name almost playfully, "I'm Byron Braynard, security chief for your very employer, the Great Western Frontiers Railway. You can call me Chief." He'd seen the name on an identification card inside a dead man's wallet after they'd ambushed the wagons.

"Bless you, bless you, sir," said Oaks, appearing ready to bounce on his tiptoes with joy.

Shear gestured toward the second wagon pulled up behind him, and the armed riders surrounding it. "As you can see, we have brought the safe, all the way from St. Louis, as requested."

Along the side of the train, two riflemen pulled the body of one of their own from where it lay hanging out the open window, its arms dangling toward the ground, bleeding down the side of the passenger car.

"If you'll open the express car door, Ronald," Shear said, "we'll get under way. I don't mind saying, this is a most dangerous spot. I look all around and see the potential for terrible consequence." His eyes slid over his own men as he spoke. He almost smiled.

"Yes, right you are, Chief Braynard," said Oaks. He

hurried over to the large thick express car and gave a series of knocks. At the sound of a steel bolt sliding back inside the door, Oaks grinned at Shear and said, "Had I not given that rapping sequence, the door would still have opened, but when it opened you would not have liked the welcome."

"Now, that is darn good thinking, Ronald," said Shear. He looked down at Lasko and said, "Write that down first chance you get. These are the kinds of ideas I want to be hearing from *my* men."

Along the side of the train, riflemen had stepped down and began to gather around the wagons. As the big door slid open, Oaks said to the riflemen, "Don't crowd Chief Braynard and his men."

"Chief Braynard . . . ?" said the older rifleman from the caboose. He squinted hard at Shear.

"That's quite all right, Ronald," said Shear. "The more the merrier."

"I only hope someone is left to keep an eye out for those heathen *Comadrejas*," Oaks called out.

Shear said, "Whoa! My goodness!" as the door opened and he found himself staring down the barrel of another Gatling gun, just like the one he himself had set up at Hatchet Pass. "I dare pity those *Comadrejas* had their attack been successful."

Seeing Oaks and the rest of the men gathered around the wagon, the man behind the Gatling gun turned loose of the handles and stood. Beside him his loader grinned and took his hat toward Shear and Oaks.

"Chief Braynard . . . ?" the older guard repeated, looking all around at the other riflemen around him. "Hell, he ain't Braynard—"

"Of course he's Chief Braynard, you old fool," Papa Dorsey snapped at the older guard. "Didn't you hear him introduce himself?"

"I've known *Big Balls* Byron Braynard fifteen years, and by God this—"

One shot from Dorsey's Colt stopped him cold. The bullet hurled him and flipped him so quickly that one of his boots spun up in the air. He lay stretched out dead, a naked toe shining through a hole in his sock.

"My God," Oaks gasped.

But even as he did so, Lasko sprang up from the wagon seat and put a bullet in the man standing behind the Gatling gun. He fell forward onto the gun and lay there, his arms dangling.

On the ground, Swean stood with his rifle pointed and cocked at the second man in the express car. "Hands high, loader!" he said.

The loader did as he was told. All along the train Shear's men had the railroad men covered.

"Now jump down," Shear said to him.

As the loader jumped to the ground, Swean jerked his sidearm from his holster and pitched it away. "Go stand over there by your railroad pals," he ordered him.

"Skin them all down, men," Shear called out to his riflemen.

"You jakes heard him," said Dave Pickens, gesturing with his cocked Colt, "put your iron in the dirt or we start chopping yas down!"

Shear called out to the open windows, "Anybody left in there?"

A couple of heads came out the windows, hands first, raised and empty. Shear grinned and jumped to the ground beside Oaks.

"That's what I like to see," he said, "willing participants . . . everybody doing their part to see to it nobody else has to die." He turned back to Oaks with a dark laugh and smacked him across the jaw with the big Remington. Oaks flew sidelong, but Shear caught him by the shoulder and jerked him back into place.

"Plea-please, sir, no more . . . ," said Oaks, blood running from a gash the Remington's front sight made on his cheek.

"All right, *Ronald*," Shear said, "what do you think of us *angels* now?" He shook him and said close to his ear, "Now you tell everybody here to not do anything stupid. If they do I'll stick this gun straight down your neck and pull the trigger."

"Any-anything you say, sir," said Oaks.

"That's real good, *Ronald*. Now you talk to them, tell them how it is." He gave a dark grin, looking at the Gatling gun, then at the firewood wagon. "Have them get this wagon unloaded. You can even keep the firewood."

While Oaks explained to the men that to resist would cost them their lives, Shear's men hurriedly searched the railroad men, collecting their weapons, tossing them in big burlap feed sacks.

"What if we get set upon again by that bunch of Desert Weasels?" a guard asked Longley, knowing once the firewood was unloaded the Gatling gun was going onto the wagon.

"Run like hell, I guess," Longley said, shrugging, snatching the man's rifle from his hand. Beside him Papa Dorsey laughed and slapped his leg.

"Dorsey, how can you do this to us?" the railroad man asked. "You've been with us every day for all these years."

"Hell," Dorsey laughed even louder, "you just answered your own question."

When the firewood was unloaded and the railroad men were back in a line, Shear had his men pass the big gun down and set it up. Then he waved the second wagon forward—the one carrying the big safe. As soon as the canvas was loosened and thrown off, the men loosened the chains holding the big safe upright and tight to the wagon bed.

With all their effort four men rocked it back and forth until it toppled off the wagon and landed with an earth-shuddering jar and rolled and slid twelve feet down the gravel-covered hillside.

From the engine, Barnes came back behind the engineer and his fireman, his rifle aimed at their backs.

"All you railroad men stay lined up," said Shear.

"You—you're not going to kill us, are you?" said Oaks, looking ill and shaky.

"Naw, don't be scared, *Ronald*," said Shear, as if he found the thought ridiculous. "We won't kill you, unless you force us to, that is. We've killed so many railroad hogs today, we're all sick of it."

One of the guards looked back and forth at how many men the outlaws were keeping covered. "This is humiliating," he said, stepping forward. "I won't stand for it!"

"I don't blame you, mister," said Shear. "Rudy, kill him."

Duckwald pulled the trigger on his rifle without so much as lifting it to his shoulder. The man slammed back against the express car and fell dead on the ground.

"If anybody else feels *humiliated*, now is the time to step forward and get yourself shot," said Shear. "The buzzards out here will thank you for it."

As Shear spoke, his men had climbed into the express car and began carrying heavy crates of gold coin and ingots out and stacking them on the empty wagon.

"Swean, show me something," Shear said.

The gunman broke open a crate lid with his pistol butt and raised a handful of gold coins and let them fall through his fingers.

"God, how I love stealing," Shear said, on the verge of getting emotional about it.

Papa Dorsey had walked to the engine, climbed up and fired blast upon blast of shotgun loads into the boiler lines, blowing them apart. He came walking back with a satisfied smile on his white-bearded face.

When the last of the crates were staked on the wagon, Shear's men gathered and mounted their horses, three of them carrying burlap bags full of firearms. Before turning to his horse, Shear held his Remington out at arm's length, the tip of it against Oaks' head. "Ronald, I wish I didn't have to do this—"

"Oh God, please! No!" the frightened man begged, sobbing, terrified.

"Get a grip on yourself, Ronald!" said Shear. "I meant, I wish I didn't have to *say good-bye*. You boys have been so hospitable."

The mounted men hooted and laughed as Oaks' trembling knees gave out and he fell to the ground. Shear climbed into his saddle and said to the railroaders, as he turned dead serious, "All of you remember, we could have killed you but we didn't. Think about that before you decide to come after us. We *will* kill you then."

Chapter 21

Sandoval had ridden a mile ahead of the gun wagon and found the massacre in the canyon along the rock-cut trail. But instead of riding back to tell Thorn and the ranger, he stepped down from his saddle and led his horse up a steep path to the cliffs from which Shear and his men had launched their attack on the wagons. At the top of the cliff trail, he looked back and forth, then down the canyon wall behind him.

The bodies of Calvin Kerr and Dent Phillips lay battered and broken twenty yards apart among the rock. Walking a few steps farther along the high trail, he spotted two loose horses milling in a narrow strip of pale wild grass, their muzzles to the ground. Farther along he saw a lone horse standing with a man's bloody arm reaching up from the ground, gripping its stirrup.

Sandoval walked closer, his rifle half leveled in his hands. Taking the loose horse's reins, he looked down and into the face of Tinnis Mayes. The wounded gambler struggled to raise his eyes toward him.

"Do—do you have . . . a drink, sir?" the gambler managed to murmur.

Holding the reins to the horse, Sandoval reached down and loosened Tinnis' hand from the stirrup. He pushed the horse's flank; it sidestepped out of the way. He stooped and rolled Tinnis onto his back and looked at all the dark blood on his side, his chest, his bloody right hand gripping the Colt Thunderer.

"I happen to have a bottle in my saddlebags," he said, reaching over and lifting the Thunderer from the gambler's grasp.

"I'll . . . just wait . . . right here," Tinnis said, looking up at him.

Sandoval retrieved the bottle and a rolled-up blanket. Stooping down again, he stuck the rolled blanket under Tinnis' head and uncorked the bottle. He held the man's head up a little more and guided him through a drink of the fiery rye.

"How bad is it?" he asked, noting that even in the gambler's weakened, wounded condition the whiskey went down smooth and effortlessly.

"Not . . . so bad," Tinnis said. He offered a weak half smile and added, "Want to . . . see my wound?"

Sandoval returned the half smile, going along with him, and said, "Sure, I'll take a look." He started to cork the bottle, but Tinnis wrapped a bloody hand around it.

"Do you mind?" he asked, sounding stronger somehow now that the whiskey coursed through him.

Sandoval turned loose of the bottle and unbuttoned the gambler's blood-soaked shirt and spread it open.

He saw the bullet hole just beneath Tinnis' right ribs. Fresh red blood still oozed slowly but steadily. He reached beneath the gambler and felt the bleeding exit hole straight through his side.

"There's no bullet in you," Sandoval said.

"Now, there's . . . a stroke of luck," Tinnis said wryly, struggling to raise the bottle to his lips. Sandoval helped him take another drink. This time he made sure to take the bottle from him and cork it and set it aside.

"You've lost lots of blood, gambler," he said.

"Us Lucases have . . . always been free bleeders." He struggled upward a little, craning his head like a turtle in search of the bottle.

"Keep still," said Sandoval, pressing him gently back to the ground. "You're not a Lucas."

"How . . . dare you, sir?" the gambler said. "Are you questioning . . . my mother's virtue?" His bloody fingers crawled across the dirt in search of the bottle, like some craving spider.

"I know your real name," said Sandoval, ignoring the gambler's quips. "It's Mayes . . . Tinnis Mayes." He reached over and set the bottle farther out of reach from Tinnis' hand. Then he loosened Tinnis' bandanna from around his neck for a bandage and shook it out. "Captain Thorn knew that all along."

The gambler's hand slumped on the ground, as if in surrender.

"I suspected as much," Tinnis said. "Thorn is . . . a crafty old fox. But I suppose . . . everyone in the corps has heard of . . . the infamous Rebel Marine."

"I had heard of you," said Sandoval. He ripped a

section of Tinnis' shirttail away, tore it into strips and tied the ends together. "But I wouldn't say your name was *infamous* or even tarnished."

"Oh?" said Tinnis. "Are you saying . . . time has . . . forgiven my transgressions?"

He watched the young bounty hunter lay the folded bandanna against the wound's entrance and press the gambler's hand down on it to hold it in place.

"Maybe time *has* forgiven. Maybe *you* haven't," said Sandoval, without looking up from his work. But he did see Tinnis' fingers crawl toward the bottle again, and he moved it even farther away.

"My God, man . . . pass me that bottle," Tinnis said. "That's something one marine . . . always does for another." He coughed and added in a strained voice, "What will it hurt, a drink before dying?"

"I don't think you're going to die," said Sandoval. "If the bullet had struck any vital organ, you'd have been dead before now." He reached up, loosened his own bandanna for a dressing to place on the exit wound.

"Hallelujah, then. Allow me . . . to celebrate," said the gambler. His fingers crawled again toward the bottle.

Sandoval stopped and looked down at him. As if reconsidering, he said, "You're right, what can it hurt?" He reached over, picked up the bottle, pulled the cork and pitched it aside. "Here, drink it. Drink it all. Maybe you'll be dead before my father gets here. He'd prefer seeing a dead marine to one drowning in self-pity."

Tinnis snatched the battle eagerly. But he stopped and said, "Your . . . father? Cadden Thorn?"

"Yes, he's my father," said Sandoval. "He's a *real* marine. He's never been afraid to take a knock-down blow and stand back up and rally a charge." He gestured with bloody fingers toward the bottle. "Drink up, Mayes. Drink it all. My father, the Captain, is an old salt. He might care. I'm a younger marine. Were it not for the honor of the corps that binds us one and all together, you never even existed."

"I'll drink to that," said Tinnis in a critical tone. He raised the bottle toward his lips with a weak hand. But before he could take a drink, the two of them spotted the gun wagon rolling onto the high trail, Thorn and the ranger having followed the hooves of Shear's men, rather than following the firewood wagon tracks into the canyon.

"Oh hell, now the captain . . ." Tinnis sighed, letting the bottle slump in his hand.

When the ranger and Thorn rolled up, stopped and climbed down from the wagon, the gambler eyed the Gatling gun and said, "I bet I can tell you where you acquired that wicked-looking contraption."

"I bet you can too," Thorn said. He looked down at the bloody bandanna bandage, then at the bottle in the gambler's hand.

"Don't even try taking this from me," said Tinnis, tightening his hand around the bottle.

"Not even for a drink?" Thorn said, reaching down with his gloved hand.

"This is not a trick, is it?" Tinnis asked warily. But upon seeing the look on Thorn's face, he relinquished the bottle to him and watched him turn up a shot and wipe a hand over his mouth. Tinnis looked a little surprised when Thorn handled the bottle back to him.

"Your son and I . . . had ourselves a . . . nice little chat, Thorn," he said. "He tells me you know . . . my real name and what happened to me at the war's end."

"I do," said Thorn. "You didn't get the pardon President Lincoln intended for you to have, but at least you didn't hang as a Southern spy."

"Better that I had hanged, Captain," the gambler said with a bitter twist to his voice. He looked away as if in shame. "I brought dishonor . . . not only to myself, but to the corps itself."

"No, you're wrong Mayes," said Thorn. "If that was true I wouldn't be talking to you right now. You're a Southerner. You chose to fight for the South. Nobody judged you harshly for it. You became a spy for the South. Nobody judged you for that either. The only thing your fellow marines ever judged you for was losing faith in them."

"I never lost faith in the corps," said Mayes. "I thought it was they who lost faith in me."

"It comes to the same thing," said Thorn. "Only *your* lack of faith would question the faith of your brothers."

Mayes raised the bottle toward his lips, but he stopped, considering what Thorn had said. He seemed to have grown stronger with some whiskey in his belly and the bleeding stopped. For a moment he stared at the bottle, lost in thought.

Finally he said, "What's the difference? I stopped being a marine . . . a long time ago. I'm a drunkard now."

Sandoval and the ranger watched in silence as the two continued.

"Indeed you are a drunkard, Mayes," Thorn said. "But you were a damn good marine—you always will be."

"Stow it, Captain," said Mayes. "I don't even . . . want to hear it. The past is dead and gone. Good riddance to it, I say." He raised the bottle as if in a toast. But Sam noticed he lowered it without taking another drink.

Thorn stepped closer and loomed over the wounded man. "Are you going to die any time soon, Mayes?"

The gambler gave a nod toward Sandoval and said to Thorn, "Ask my doctor."

Thorn looked at the younger bounty hunter. "What do you say, Sandy? Is Tinnis Mayes going to die from this wound today?"

"No, Captain," said Sandoval, "I believe he stands a good chance at living this day out. It would be better if he left the whiskey alone for a while."

"Aw, forget that," said Thorn, sweeping the possibility aside with his gloved hand.

Mayes raised himself up stiffly on his good side, the bottle still in hand. "What is your growing interest in whether I live or die, Captain?" he asked.

Thorn thumbed toward the wagon. "We have a Gatling gun, plenty of ammunition and all the bad men a fellow would ever want to shoot at." He stopped and let his words hang in the air.

"Are you asking me . . . if I'd like to join the three of you, Captain?" Mayes said. "Go fight Shear and Lord knows how many of his men?"

"Only if you think you can gird up and make a worthy showing for yourself," Thorn said. He stood with his hands down at his sides, waiting for Mayes to make a move to rise.

"Oh, I think once upon my feet, Captain, I might

even surprise myself," Mayes said, reaching his bloody hand up to Thorn.

"On your feet, then," said Thorn. He offered a hand and lifted him to his feet, giving no regard to the wound in the man's side, or the pained expression Mayes struggled to keep from showing on his face. The open bottle was still in his other hand, but he made no attempt to drink from it in spite of his pain of his wounds—both old and new.

"I'll pull the wagon over closer," said Sandoval.

"The wagon . . . ? Nonsense," said Mayes, "I'm perfectly able to ride this horse."

He handed Sandoval the whiskey bottle, turned, took hold of the saddle horn and pulled himself up, favoring his wounded side until he settled onto the saddle.

"Keep up the good work," Thorn said proudly to him. He stepped quickly over to the wagon and came back leading his horse. "I'll ride along beside you for a ways, if that suits you. We can rehash the battle that had taken place here."

"It suits me fine, Captain," said Mayes. "I always enjoy good company."

When the two had started off along the thin high trail, the ranger and Sandoval stepped up into the wagon and rode along a few yards behind him.

"Mayes seems all right now," Sam said, "but how's he going to do when we get off this trail onto the flatlands and start making some time?"

"We'll just have to see," Sandoval replied quietly, staring ahead.

"You said he was going to live," Sam said.

"I said he stands a good chance," Sandoval reminded him.

"What are his chances?" Sam asked.

"Fifty-fifty," said Sandoval, "probably no better or worse than for the three of us. But if I hadn't said what I did, Thorn would not have left a wounded man behind."

"So you told them what they wanted to hear?" Sam asked.

"I told them what they already knew," Sandoval replied. He slapped the horses' rumps lightly with the traces, keeping them moving slowly but steadily. "Anyway, it goes without saying, he'd prefer to die in a battle than bleed out drunk on a blanket. What warrior wouldn't?"

The ranger didn't answer. He only nodded and stared at the two riders in front of them. He saw the gambler slump sidelong in his saddle; and he watched Thorn reach over and help him straighten up.

They rode on.

In the brutal afternoon heat, as the four riders crossed the sandy flatlands toward Skull Rock Pass, they spotted in the distance two men walking unsteadily toward them. By the time Thorn had brought out his long telescope and raised it to his eye, gunshots began echoing across the broad expanse of desert. Through the circle of the lens, he focused just in time to see a dozen *Comadrejas* converge on the two lone strangers and shoot them down.

"Confound these desert heathens!" said Thorn, wincing as the *Comadrejas* jumped down from the blankets and saddles and began stripping the clothing and boots from their two hapless victims. A knife slashed across the top of one of the men's bare head; his scalp was pulled loose beneath a warrior's hand. The warrior danced about like a crazed demon, waving the loose flap of skin and hair back and forth wildly above his head.

Sandoval braked the wagon and stood up, staring hard through narrowed eyes. "Shall I mount up, Captain?"

"No," said Thorn, "they'll be gone before we get there. You and Mayes follow in the wagon behind the ranger and me. We'll see if either of these poor men has survived."

Even as he spoke, the ranger was down from the wagon and atop his stallion, joining the captain. Tinnis slipped down from his own mount and joined Sandoval on the wagon seat.

"Do you know how to fire one of these?" Sandoval asked as the ranger and Thorn rode away at a run.

"Yes," said Mayes, "I fire all things military."

"Then hang on," said Sandoval.

In spite of his wound, Tinnis checked the Gatling gun over good and squatted down beside it as the wagon jerked forward behind Thorn and the ranger.

Moments later as the ranger and Thorn rode up to the men lying naked and bloody in the sand, Sandoval swung the wagon wide around the grizzly scene; Mayes aimed the Gatling gun, but only in time to see the *Comadrejas* disappear over a rise in the sandy flatlands.

"Save our ammunition," said Sandoval to the gambler, who had already decided as much on his own. The young bounty hunter slapped the traces to the wagon horses' backs, circled and came to a halt in a rise of dust beside Thorn and the ranger.

Sam dismounted and kneeled over the man who'd been scalped, his body spasming in death throes. Behind them, Thorn gave Sandoval and Mayes a grim nod. Mayes stood up from the wagon seat. He now carried two Colt Thunderers in his waistband—the one given to him by Shear and the one the ranger had returned to him earlier on the trail. He lifted one from his waist and started to raise it toward the dying man. But in that second, the stranger stopped his spasming and fell limp and still on the sandy ground.

The ranger stood and saw the Colt in the gambler's hand. Mayes lowered it and shoved in back into his waist.

"It would have been for the best, had he done it, Ranger," Thorn said quietly.

"I know," said the ranger. He bent down and retrieved a leather wallet from the sand and shook it off. He pulled out a railroad identification card and a Great Western Frontiers detective's badge. He held it around for Thorn to see as the bounty hunter stepped closer.

"Another dead railroad detective," Thorn said. "No wonder the railroad is so intent on stopping Shear and his gang."

"These two were unarmed," said Sam. "They couldn't even put up a fight."

Thorn stared along the long line of wagon tracks and horses' hoofprints they had been following until they'd spotted the two men on foot. "How much farther to the Skull Rock Pass, Ranger?"

"Ten miles," said Sam, already turning to the stallion. "We best hurry. If Shear has left men stranded there with no horses or guns, these Desert Weasels will soon start skinning them alive."

The ranger, Sandoval and Thorn quickly loaded the naked bodies onto the rear of the wagon. Mayes sat slumped on the wagon seat, holding the horses steady, yet slumping more and more as the other three worked.

Back in their saddles, before heeling his horse forward, Thorn looked over at the wagon at Mayes, lying almost sideways in the wooden seat.

Climbing up into the seat beside the wounded gambler, Sandoval leaned Mayes the other way and took the traces to the horses.

"Is he going to be all right?" Sam asked, seeing the concern on Thorn's face.

Thorn's expression turned to one of pride.

"Oh yes, I believe he is," he said, "now that he's back among his own kind."

"I meant his *wound*, Captain," Sam said.

"Yes," said Thorn. He looked at Sam with the slightest smile on his weathered face. "So did I."

Chapter 22

When Ronald Oaks saw the wagon roll into sight from the same direction that Shear and his men had ridden in from, he stood and stared. A four-shot pepperbox hideout derringer hung in his hand. One of the men had managed to hang on to the small pistol throughout the robbery, and quickly turned it over to Ronald Oaks when the gang had fled.

"My goodness, have they come back upon us?" Oaks asked no one in particular. A dark streak of urine still lay damp down his left leg.

"Not from that direction, sir," said the young caboose guard, Dennis Sheplet. "Remember? They rode off that way, toward Alto Meca." He had seen his partner, the older guard, shot down by Papa Dorsey. He had seen action fighting the *Comadrejas* and found his own courage not lacking. His trousers were dry. . . .

"Of course I remember, Sheplet!" Oaks snapped. He took a breath and tried to get a grip on his fear for the men's sake. The wax in his mustache had melted away and left one of the sharp points drooping down the corner of his mouth.

From alongside the train two guards came back, one carrying a fireman's shovel, one an iron tool for prying loose stuck coupling knuckles.

"We have some lit oil lanterns we can throw on them, sir," one of the men said to Oaks. "I'm afraid that's the best we can do."

"Oil lanterns, shovel handles, rail tools against a Gatling gun?" said Oaks. "I think not. But stand by and be ready. We might have to sue just that, if we're hard pressed."

But as the riders and the wagon drew closer, Oaks saw the badge on the ranger's chest and looked relieved. "Thank God," he said.

"What is it, sir?" the guard with the shovel asked Oaks.

"It's a lawman," Oaks said. "Gather everyone and tell them to stand down."

The two guards looked at each other, recalling how excited and welcoming Oaks had become when Shear and his killers rode in.

"Are you sure, Mr. Oaks?" the guard asked.

"Blast it, yes, I'm *sure!*" Oaks snapped. "Now do as you're told, or I'll have young Sheplet here take your place. I'm *still* in charge of this train."

Riding up to the train ahead of the gun wagon, Thorn stopped a safe distance back. Sam rode few feet closer, his badge in view, and called out to the railroad me.

"Hello, the train," he said. "I'm Arizona Territory

Ranger Samuel Burrack. "We found two of your men, dead, back along the trail."

Oaks stood up and craned his neck and looked at the naked bodies lying bloody and pale in the sunlight. He winced and shook his head.

"The poor wretches," he said aloud to himself. "We were afraid of that," he called out to the ranger.

"We're riding forward," Sam said, seeing the hesitancy on the part of the railroad men.

"Certainly," said Oaks. "Pardon us, Ranger. We're most cautious right now. We were deceived by men arriving in two of our own firewood wagons. They took a Gatling gun from us just like the one in *your* wagon."

Sam and Thorn rode forward. Sandoval and Mayes rolled forward in the gun wagon, Mayes staying in the seat away from the big gun.

"That would be Brayton Shear and his Black Valley Riders," said Sam. "We confiscated this gun from his hideout."

The ranger, Thorn and the wagon stopped up closer.

"Step down, Ranger," said Oaks. In an attempt at being hospitable he said, "We have neither guns nor horses." He held up the pepperbox as if to prove their plight. "But we have food and water until our situation improves—provided the *Comadrejas* don't reappear and massacre us where we stand."

"That's a strong possibility," said the ranger, he and Thorn stepping down side by side. "If Clato Charo didn't know before that you're unarmed and horseless, he knows it now that he found two of your men unarmed and traveling on foot."

"Have you any spare guns you can lend to us?" Oaks asked humbly.

"Whatever we can rummage up among us, you're welcome to," Sam said.

The guard with the shovel stepped forward as other men stepped down along the big train and walked back to them.

"What about that Gatling gun too, Ranger?" he asked boldly.

"I'm the man in charge here, Bentley," Oaks snapped at him. "I'll do all the speaking on our behalf."

"Begging everybody's pardon—yours too, Oaks," said the railroad detective. "You're acting a little too shy to ask." He looked at Sam and said, "Ranger, we see what those Desert Weasels will do when they come back here, knowing we're armed. If we had the big gun, they wouldn't face us. If we had the wagon, we could send somebody for help."

Sam and Thorn looked at each other. "Having it with us would sure make up for our short numbers," Thorn said, between the two of them.

Sam considered it then countered, "Like you said, we can travel faster without it."

"It's your call, Ranger," Thorn said.

"I can't leave them out here defenseless," Sam said quietly. "Charo's warriors can get awfully ugly. *Co-madrejas* are all cowards, but they'll turn brave against a band of helpless men."

"Then leave it. We'll travel faster without it." Thorn gave a slight shrug. "If we need one we can take the one Shear has."

"Good thinking, Captain," Sam said with a thin, wry

smile. He turned to Oaks. "Have your men come move the Gatling gun and set it up. Keep the wagon and horses too."

Seeing and hearing what was going on, Tinnis Mayes managed to keep himself seated upright. He took the nickel-plated Colt Thunderer he'd been carrying for years and the same model Shear had given him and laid them both on his lap. With a sigh, he picked up the one Shear had given him by its barrel and handed it out to one of the railroaders who'd come to unload the Gatling gun.

"Anything for the *railroad*," he said with a hint of sarcasm in his voice as the man took the pistol from him and thanked him for it.

Evening shadows stretched long across the hills and rocky desert floor as Shear and his men pulled the two wagons up along a steep trail, five miles below the nearly abandoned hilltop town of Alto Meca. On the wagon seat sat Papa Dorsey and Rudy Duckwald. Beside the wagon, Brayton Shear looked down from his saddle at the wooden crates of gold coins and ingots.

"We lost three men back at that wagon ambush," he said pensively. "Sentanza, Kerr and Phillips."

"Four, if you count that half-ass gambler, Tinnis Lucas," said Duckwald from the wagon stopped beside him.

"I'm only counting ones that would have had a full cut coming from this gold," said Shear. "Lucas might've only gotten a half cut, him just coming in the way he did. I'm going to miss that damn gambler."

"I'll miss never getting to kill him," Duckwald said with disappointment. "I should have rode over and put a bullet through his head before we left."

"I saw him lying there with his side shot open, bloodier than a stuck pig," said Shear. "He looked as dead as any dead man I've ever seen."

"Drunks are hard to kill," said Duckwald. "That's a fact of science."

The group sat in silence for a moment, letting the horses rest before making the hard steep climb in front of them.

"I don't know about any of the rest of yas," Papa Dorsey said, finally, turning and looking around from the wagon seat. "But I could take my share right now and go my own way, be happy as a grinning fool in a pumpkin patch."

The men looked at Shear to see how he took the old man's suggestion.

"Papa Dorsey," Shear said to the white-bearded old wagon guard who had turned traitor to his fellow railroad employees, "I don't know how we would have pulled this off without you."

Dorsey smiled with satisfaction and looked back and forth among the gathered men.

"Keep that kind thought in mind when it comes time for us to settle up," he said. "I am not a man opposed to receiving bonuses either, for work well done." He grinned behind his white beard.

"It has *all* been taken into consideration," said Shear. "Believe me, if you were a Black Valley Rider, you'd get a full share, like all the other Riders."

"I understand," said Dorsey.

"But now is not the time to stop and part out the swag," said Shear.

"Why's that, Big Aces?" asked Dorsey.

Hearing an outsider call Shear "Big Aces" caused the men to fall tense and silent.

Shear kept his temper, but he warned the old man with a stiff smile. "Do not call me Big Aces, Papa," he said, his finger raised for emphasis.

"Sure thing, Big—I mean, Mr. Shear, that is," said Dorsey, correcting himself. "But let's get back to business. Why can't I get what's coming to me right now? I don't need to ride on into Alto Meca with yas. My work is done."

"I understand. But you not being a Black Valley Rider," Shear said, raising his voice a little, "I have to ask you this before we settle up." He leveled a questioning gaze at the old railroader. "Are you going to be riding with us some more in the future? Or was this just a onetime thing for you?"

Dorsey grinned. "Call this my railroad retirement pension," he said. "I'm going to take my cut and buy me a place up in Utah."

"Utah, eh, Papa?" Shear baited.

"Yep, Utah," said Dorsey. "I'll spend the rest of my days swilling whiskey on the front porch with no britches on, just to torment any Mormon neighbors who happen along."

"That's ambitious of you," said Shear. He turned his eyes to Rudy Duckwald sitting beside the old railroader. "Rudy, you're Mormon, are you not?"

"My folks were," said Duckwald, giving Dorsey a cold, hard stare. "They was tormented all their lives by drunks with no britches on."

"I didn't mean nothing by it," Dorsey said.

"They all said that when confronted," Duckwald replied.

"Pay him off, Rudy," said Shear.

Without batting an eye, Duckwald pulled the trigger on the rifle resting in the crook of his left arm. The bullet ripped through the old man's jaw, snapping his head backward at an awkward angle. His body jerked and flipped from the wooden seat. Dorsey hit the ground dead, the left upper part of his head missing, pouring blood.

"Anybody else want to settle up here instead of riding into Alto Meca?" Shear asked. "If so, ride up here and you'll get what's coming to you."

None of the men ventured forward.

"All right, then," said Shear. "We're going to stop outside of town at a little adobe that used to be a whorehouse. There's a woman still living there named One-legged Lilly Quid." He raised a hand for emphasis. "Call no attention to either Lilly's missing limb or her husband Freddie's head jerking. These are friends of mine. They will misdirect anybody who comes snooping around looking for us."

"I thought we got everybody shook loose from our trail, Big Aces," said George Epson.

"We did, George," said Shear, "but you never know who's going to show up these days. So treat Lilly Quid and Freddie Dupree right. We'll take some spending gold with us. But we'll leave both wagons hidden there on their place. We'll stick the gold wagon in their barn. They'll look after it for us."

The men looked at one another. "So, you trust these folks that much, do you, Big Aces?" Ted Lasko asked, trying to sound conversational about it.

"Oh yes, indeed I do," said Shear. "These people would sacrifice their own lives to see to it nothing happens to this gold while it's in their care."

Lasko squirmed uncomfortably in his saddle, but then asked in the same conversational tone, "Why is that, Big Aces?"

Shear turned and stared at him. "Ted, do you have a pencil and paper handy?"

"Uh, no, I don't," he said, the look in Shear's eyes making him nervous.

"You need to write all these questions down," said Shear, "so we can sit here and go down the list one by one instead of us riding on in, getting some gold and riding on to Alto Meca."

"Sorry, boss," said Lasko.

Shear looked all around at the other men. "I figure we'd round up some whores, throw ourselves a fiesta before we circle around and ride back to Black Valley," he said.

"Whoa! Yes, sir!" said Epson. The rest of the men grinned and nodded their approval.

"What about you, Ted?" Shear ask Lasko. "Want to ask questions or get on to Alto Meca and round up some whores?" His right hand rested on the butt of his big holstered Remington.

"No questions here, boss," Lasko said, with a cautious grin.

Stepping his horse around Papa Dorsey's body lying sprawled on the trail, Shear turned and rode off up the steep trail. Halfway up, Shear turned onto another trail that ran onto a stretch of flat hillside. He led the riders and the wagon across a wide flat stone surface to where a cabin made of pine log, stone and adobe sat nestled on the steep hillside.

Inside the cabin, One-legged Lilly Quid stood leaning on her homemade crutch, gazing out at the approaching riders through a wavy glass windowpane.

"Damn it, Freddie, are they ever going to get it through their heads I'm out of business?" Even as she spoke she touched her free hand to the side of her hair, checking it.

"I reckon not, Lilly," said Freddie Dupree. He put a small Uhrlinger hideout pistol in each of his front trouser pockets and kept his hand on them until he reached out for the front door handle. "Keep yourself out of sight, Lilly," he said over his shoulder. "If they see you in that blue dress, they'll go plumb loco."

Chapter 23

When Shear's men had half circled around the cabin, Shear rose a little in his stirrups and called out, "Hello, Freddie Dupree . . . Hello, Lilly Quid."

The men sat watching as the cabin door eased open and Freddie Dupree slipped out on the porch, barefoot, both hands shoved down inside his baggy trouser pockets.

"I'll be dipped and rolled dry," he said, squinting up at Shear in the dimming evening sunlight. "Is that you, Brayton?"

"It's me, Freddie," said Shear. "Now pull your paws up off those Uhrlingers before some bad memory comes to mind, and we start shooting each other."

Freddie slipped his hands up off the pistols but kept his thumbs hooked in his pockets. "He-heck, Brayton." His head made an uncontrollable jerk. "I got no *bad memory* of you. You—you were always square wi-with me." His head jerked again.

Shear's men gave each other a look, but sat in silence.

"Where's Lilly?" Shear asked.

"I'm right here, Brayton!" Lilly called out, swinging the door open wide and standing in the doorway in a pair of ragged miner's overalls she'd hurriedly changed into. "What in the world brings you up this way?"

Shear gave a quick look around the place as he said in a more guarded tone, "A wagonload of red-hot railroad gold, Lilly. We need a place to let it cool some overnight."

"Just like the old days, eh, Brayton?" said Freddie with a chuckle.

"Just about, Freddie," said Shear.

"Is anybody dogging you?" Freddie asked, his eyes slipping away to the thin trail on the other side of the flat stone shelf they stood on.

"Our trail is clean enough to eat off of," Shear said with a slight grin.

"You always was a careful one," Freddie chuckled. "Damn it! I'd give anything if I was in on it with you."

"You're not, though, so put it out of your head, Freddie," said Shear, his tone stiffening a little as his grin went away. "There's something in it for you, for keeping our wagons hid."

"Hell, I wasn't hinting at any gold," said Freddie. He shrugged. "You know me, Brayton. I just meant I'd like to have been in on the whole thing. I like that fire it puts in the belly."

Shear let out a breath and eased some. "Yeah, I know you, Freddie," he said. "Pay me no mind. It's been a busy day." He watched as Lilly and Freddie stepped down off the porch.

"Well, get down off those tired horses before they

fall," said Lilly. "We've got a barn you can stick your wagon in. Nobody comes here anymore except some crazy old coots now and then, thinking I'll still cock my ankles for them."

Shear gave his men a nod; they all swung down from their saddles.

"I'll go boil you boys a pot of coffee," Lilly said, excited at having so much company unexpectedly.

"What's in that barn, Freddie?" Shear asked. He gestured toward a large barn with a sagging roof.

"Nothing but dirt," said Freddie. "We keep our old buggy horse in a stall out back."

"Is there room for both of our wagons in it?" Shear asked.

"No," said Freddie, "but you can back one wagon under an overhang right around that hill turn." He pointed to where a trail rounded out of sight around a large tall boulder.

"Good enough," said Shear. "Freddie, do me a favor, go inside and help Lilly boil the coffee while me and the men divvy up some spending gold."

"Sure thing," said Freddie. He stopped first and said, "Are you riding into Alto Meca? Tonight?"

"That's my plan," said Shear. "I want to get there before dark and do some drinking, maybe chase down a whore or two."

"There's still a saloon for the drinking," said Freddie. "But there's not much in the line of women. Most all the young pretty doves flew off last summer." He shook his head in regret. "The pickings are slim and poor now."

"We'll make do," said Shear, undaunted.

At the rear of the gold wagon, he and his men gathered in a tight group. From the wagon bed, Duckwald pitched down a crate of gold coins, then jumped down behind it.

With the blade of a big bowie knife, Dave Pickens pried the lid off the crate and laid it over in the dirt. The men stared at the glittering unstamped coins in the evening sunlight.

"Jesus! Those are some pretty things," Epson said, almost breathless at the sight. "Unstamped, and waiting for whatever the *generalissimo* wanted to put on them."

"Most likely his head on one side," said Duckwald.

"His tail on the other," Epson chuckled.

The men stood waiting for Shear to stoop down before they followed suit. When all of them were huddled around the crate, Shear picked up a coin and hefted it on his palm.

"How much are they, Big Aces?" asked Longley.

"Twenty-dollar pieces at least," Shear said. He stopped hefting the coin and turned it back and forth on his fingertips.

"Yeah . . . ," Longley cooed.

"The *generalissimo* will never see gold this pure and clean in his whole life," said Shear. "I ought to be ashamed of myself." He grinned. "But I'm not."

He picked up four more coins along with the one in his hand and dropped all five onto Longley's eager palm. Seeing Longley look at the coins questioningly, Shear stopped what he was doing and stared coldly at him.

"Damn it, Ben," Pickens said to Longley, giving him

a shove. "If you spend that much on anything in Alto Meca, God help you."

The rest of the men laughed.

"Hell, I know it!" Longley said, falling away with a laugh, clasping his fist around his gold coins.

Shear's hands went back to the crate, counting out five gold coins to each of his gunmen.

When he'd finished disbursing the gold coins, Shear stood up and gestured for Pickens to put the lid back on. He watched closely as Pickens did so. When the crate had been passed upward and restacked by Duckwald, who'd climbed back onto the wagon to receive it, Shear turned back to the men.

"Two of you take this gun wagon around that turn and stash it under the cliff," he said. He looked up at Duckwald and said, "Put this gold wagon in the barn. Grain and water the horses, then lock the barn down good and tight."

"You got it, Big Aces," said Duckwald atop the gold wagon.

Shear turned to the other men and said in a quiet tone of voice, "Let's be real sociable. First, we'll have some coffee with Lilly and Freddie." He looked up at the afternoon sky, judging the length of daylight. "Then we'll ride into Alto Meca about dark and see what we can stir up for ourselves."

Two hours later on the cusp of darkness, Sam stood up from tracing the outline of wagon tracks and hoofprints with his gloved fingers in the dim grainy light. Behind him, Thorn sat atop his horse, watching him. Behind Thorn, Sandoval and Tinnis Mayes sat atop their horses, having left the Gatling gun and wagon with the stranded railroad men—the gun for protection, the wagon to send for help.

"The riders and the wagons turned here," Sam said, gesturing his hand toward the thin trail leading upward to their left. "The riders came back down, but the wagons didn't." He gestured farther along the trail. "It looks like they've headed for Alto Meca."

"How far?" Thorn asked.

"An hour and a half, give or take," the ranger estimated.

Thorn glanced back over his shoulder. "Mayes' side has started bleeding again. The wagon was easier on him than the saddle."

"I hear you talking about me, Captain Thorn," Tinnis said in a strained voice. He nudged his horse forward, his left hand gripping his side, fresh blood on his soaked and dripping bandage. "Be reminded . . . I did not sign on . . . for the short tour." He bowed slightly, in pain, as he spoke. "I am here . . . for the long ride."

Sam and Thorn looked at each other.

Sandoval looked up the trail where the hooves had first gone. "There must be something up there," he said. "They left their wagons there." Looking back at Thorn and the ranger, he said, "Mayes will be dead if we don't get him off of this saddle for a while."

"I say we . . . ride on," said the gambler, weaving a bit in his saddle as he spoke.

Sam and Thorn both ignored Tinnis and nodded in agreement with each other. They mounted, turned their horses and rode up the rocky trail between the wagon tracks.

When they reached the cabin, they stopped moments later at the stone ledge where the cabin sat against the hillside. Sam called out, "Hello, the cabin."

"Holy Moses and Mable!" Freddie said inside the window, peeping out from a lower corner of the wavy pane. In the fading evening light, he saw the badge on the ranger's chest. "Brayton told me that he wasn't being dogged!"

"Then he must've thought that he wasn't," said Lilly, in Shear's defense. "Now get the hell out there and tell them something."

"Tell them what, for goodness' sake?" said Freddie, spreading his hands helplessly.

"I don't know," Lilly snapped at him. "But get rid of them!"

"Damn it! I'll try," said Freddie.

"Hello, the cabin," Sam called out again, this time in a stronger tone.

Lilly cursed under her breath and stooped down and looked out the corner of the window herself. "He's an Arizona Ranger," she said. "He's out of his territory. What is he doing here?"

"I'll be sure and ask him," said Freddie, lifting one hand off the double Uhrlingers so he could open the door.

From the lower corner of the window, Lilly's eyes went from rider to rider, then stopped at the gambler, seeing him sway and barely catch himself from falling to the ground. *Well, I'll be . . .* , she said to herself.

The first thing the ranger noted when Freddie Dupree stepped out barefoot on the rough plank porch was the position of his hands, both shoved into his baggy trouser pockets.

"Raise them slow and empty," he said. He'd been holding his Winchester rifle propped on his thigh; he lowered the barrel until it stopped level to Freddie Dupree's chest.

"Hey, easy there, lawman," said Freddie. He raised his hands from his pockets and held them chest high. Both pockets sagged a little with the weight of the two small pistols. "You can't blame a man for being heeled out here. We've got *Comadrejas,* Apache, outlaws, Mexican *banditos.* Hell, you name it. We've got it up here."

"We know," Sam said coolly. "We tracked two wagons up here all the way from Skull Rock."

"You did, sure enough." said Freddie, sounding a little surprised, as if the wagon tracks and scars across the stone shelf weren't really there.

"You know we did," Sam said in a strong yet even tone of voice. "Where are these wagons, and where is Brayton Shear and his Black Valley Riders?"

"Uh-uh, wa-wait a minute, Ranger," he said, his head making a hard jerk. Over his shoulder he called out with urgency, "Lilly! Li-Lilly! Ge-get out here." He looked back and forth wide-eyed between Thorn and the ranger.

As the woman slipped out the cabin door onto the porch, Sandoval had looked down at the ground. He turned his horse and eased it away along the path leading to the second wagon.

On the porch, Lilly stood with her hands chest high beside Freddie Dupree. "What is it you want, Ranger?" she asked.

"Brayton Shear, ma'am," the ranger said. "Don't even waste your breath denying he's been here."

"All right, then, I won't," said Lilly. She stepped off the porch and walked toward the gambler, who sat slumped and half conscious in his saddle. "What are you trying to do, kill this one?"

"No, ma'am," Sam said, "he's one of us. He needs some tending—"

"I know who he is," Lilly said, cutting the ranger off. "He's Tinnis Lucas, and he's not one of *you*. He's one of Brayton Shear's informants."

The gambler opened his eyes and said with a weary smile, "No, I'm not . . . anymore, Lilly."

"Not what?" Lilly asked, a hand on her hip. "Not Tinnis Lucas, or not Shear's informant?"

"Neither," said Tinnis. He drifted and slumped farther.

Sam swung down from his stallion and hurried over in time to help the woman catch the gambler as he slid down his horse's side.

"This is a fine fix I'm in now," Lilly grumbled as she and the ranger carried Tinnis toward the cabin. "Brayton has been my friend since longer than I can remember, and this drunken gambler has always done right by me. Now he's sided with the law against Shear, and here I am, stuck right in the middle."

As they stepped onto the porch, Tinnis hanging between them, she shouted at Freddie Dupree, "Freddie! Get some fresh water and cut some clean bandage for me."

"Lay the guns on the porch first," said Thorn, still atop his horse watching.

Freddie hurriedly laid the two Ehrlingers on the plank porch, turned and ran inside behind Lilly and the ranger.

From around the boulder, Sandoval came riding back and stopped at Thorn's side.

"The gun wagon is around the turn, under a cliff," he said. Gesturing toward the wagon tracks leading to the barn, he added, "I predict that the other wagon will be in there."

Thorn looked at the two guns lying on the porch. Deciding that the ranger would be all right, he turned his horse and rode beside Sandoval to the locked barn.

Inside the cabin, the ranger and Lilly laid the gambler on a bed in the corner. The ranger stepped back to where he could keep an eye on both Lilly Quid and Freddie while Freddie tore cloth into strips for a bandage change.

"Tinnis," Lilly asked close to the gambler's pale face, "what have these lawmen done to get you to turn your back on your friends? Did they do this to you?"

"No, Lilly," Tinnis managed to say. "It's a . . . long story. . . ."

"Well, he's knocked out," she said, reaching around and taking the bandages from Freddie's hand. "Get me some clean water and a washcloth. I'll get this done while he can't feel anything." She asked the ranger, "What did he mean, saying he's not Tinnis Lucas?"

"His real name is Tinnis Mayes, ma'am," the ranger replied while she busily unwrapped the blood-soaked bandage from around the gambler's waist. "Like he said, it's a long story, and it goes back a lot of years."

Thorn and Sandoval entered and closed the door

behind them. Sandoval moved over to the window and peered out, keeping watch on the trail.

"You lawmen," Lilly said, shaking her head. "How can you face yourselves, turning a man against his own kind this way?"

"Ma'am," said Thorn, "Tinnis Mayes was one of *our kind* long before he took up with the likes of Brayton Shear and his men."

"Well . . . it just doesn't seem right," she said idly, appearing to only hear what suited her.

"Sandy found the Gatling gun," Thorn said to the ranger. "We found the railroad's gold on the wagon in the barn."

"We had nothing to do with any of it," Freddie cut in, walking to the bedside holding a pan of water and a washcloth. "We didn't know they were coming here, until all of a sudden here they were."

"Shut up, Freddie," said the woman. "These lawmen are not our friends, Brayton Shear is."

"There's no doubt they're going to be coming back for the gold," Thorn said to the ranger. "It looks like they grained and watered the wagon horses without unhitching them from the rig."

Sam observed Lilly peeling away the blood-soaked bandanna and saw dark blood oozing out of the wound.

"Yes, no doubt they're coming back," Sam replied to Thorn, "and no doubt Tinnis isn't going anywhere for a while. We'd best be ready for them when they return."

Chapter 24

When Shear and his men rode in to the dusty, all but abandoned, mining town, two old-timers stood up from rickety wooden chairs and stood staring at them. On a battered empty crate between the two chairs lay a worn and faded checkerboard, its pieces evenly distributed.

"It's time we called it a night," one of the men said, judging the dim evening light.

The street of Alto Meca lay strewn with tumbleweed and patches of pale wild grass standing at the corners of empty boarded-up buildings. A broken freight wagon, sandbanked up on its spokes, lay just off the middle of the street. Beneath a high porch, a lean bitch hound stood up with pups hanging and whining and dropping from her sagging teats. She barked once half-heartedly, then coiled back down as the men rode past at a walk.

Dave Pickens spat sidelong and said as he looked at the bitch and her liter, "I hope we haven't just witnessed the *whole* of entertainment this town has to offer." He ran the back of his hand across his lips.

"No," said Duckwald, his head raised to the dry dusty air, "there's whores around here. I'm sniffing two right now."

"Yeah?" said Longley, giving him a dubious look. "What color's their hair?"

"One's yellow," said Duckwald, still sniffing. "The other—hell, I don't know. She could be bald as an egg top and bottom. I don't care."

The two old men continued to stare in silence until Shear touched his hat brim and said, "Good evening to you, gentlemen."

"Likewise," said one of the old men. He pointed a finger along the empty street. "The saloon is open if you're looking for a drink. There's only two fellers drinking there, pilgrims like yourselves."

"Obliged, sir," Shear said with a sweeping gesture.

Tobias Barnes said quietly to Ballard Swean riding beside him, "What the hell else would a man be looking for in this pig-wallow?"

They rode on.

At a burning oil pot out in front of a clapboard building that stood badly tilted to one side, the men reined their horses over to an iron hitch rail and stepped down from their saddles. Shear ran a hand over the rump of one of two horses already standing at the hitch rail. The horse's flesh was dry. The animal looked rested.

Duckwald sniffed the air again and said to Ben Longley, "We're getting closer."

Longley just shook his head.

A face looked out from a dusty saloon window, then disappeared as the eight gunmen stepped onto a weathered boardwalk and walked inside and across a squeaking bare plank floor.

"Is this place getting ready to fall over?" Shear asked the short, stocky man standing behind the bar. The gunmen spread along the bar. At a corner table two men sat bowed over shots of whiskey. A half-full bottle stood on the table between them. They watched the gunmen out of the corner of their eyes.

"No, sir-*iee*, she's safe as your mama's arms," said the bartender. "Just built crooked from the start, is all." He grinned widely and tugged at his white-turned-yellow collar. "What'll yas have, gentlemen?"

"Whiskey, for openers," said Shear. "Beer, mescal, anything else you've got that's not poison." He laid a plain-faced twenty-dollar gold coin on the bar top.

"Say, mister, unstamped coins are a rare sight around here," the bartender remarked. "Am I being too nosy asking where you acquired them?" His hands adeptly snatched up three fresh bottles of rye from beneath the bar top as he spoke. He pulled the corks and slid the bottles along the bar, shot glasses right behind them.

"Damn right, you are," Duckwald cut in, catching a bottle and a glass for himself. He leered menacingly at the man. At the corner table the two men tossed back their shots of whiskey, grabbed the bottle and eased quietly out the front door.

"Easy does it, Rudy," said Shear, defusing the wild-eyed gunman. "Not too nosy at all," he said to the bartender. He raised another gold coin and turned it between his thumb and fingertip. "This is railroad gold. We robbed a train and took it from them."

The bartender froze. He stood staring, stunned into silence.

The gunmen also froze in silence, staring at Shear in disbelief.

Shear looked at the bartender, then at the faces along the bar. After a second he threw his head back in a hearty laugh. "Damn, fellows, I'm joking!"

The men laughed in relief. So did the bartender. His knees had gone a little weak. "Mister, you sure had me going there . . . ," he said. Still laughing, he pulled up empty beer mugs, three in either hand, knocked back a tall wooden tap handle and stuck the mugs under its spigot, filling them one at a time.

Duckwald leaned forward onto his elbows and said to the bartender, "On the way in here, I scented up some whores. Where are they?"

"All the whores left here over a year ago," said the bartender, "but it just happens that two young doves walked into Alto Meca a week ago. Apparently the gentlemen they were traveling with were no gentlemen at all. They left them stranded—put them out along the trail and left them seven miles from town."

"Oh my God," Longley said quietly. He gazed Duckwald up and down as if in awe. "What color is their hair?" he asked the bartender.

"One's a flaxen-haired little honey," said the bartender. "The other . . . well, I can't say. You'll have to judge for yourself."

"Oh my God!" Longley repeated in a louder voice.

Duckwald gave a rare smile of satisfaction. "Get them down here, bartender!"

"Oh, they're coming down, fellows, soon as they get powdered up," said the bartender. "They were excited to see yas ride in. They need to raise money for stage fare."

No sooner had the bartender spoken than a door at the top of a leaning stairs opened and two young women walked out onto the landing wearing short, scanty dance hall dresses and carrying feathered fans.

"Did I hear someone say they're looking for female companionship of an informal nature?" said a blonde with a suggestive expression, her feathered fan cocked beneath her right ear.

"My God, Rudy," Ben Longley asked, without taking his eyes off the two women, "how long have you been able to do this?"

"All my damned life, Ben," Duckwald said. He pushed himself back from the bar and hurried over to the tilted stairs, catching the sassy blonde in his arms as she threw herself forward from the bottom stair.

Watching, Shear took out a cigar and stuck it into his mouth, hearing the woman squeal with delight. He grinned and raised a fresh shot glass of whiskey in his hand.

"Ah," he said, "these are the moments to enjoy. If only we had some music now, I'd call this a perfect celebration."

"Say, mister," said the bartender, "I just happen to have a Missouri squeeze box in the back room."

"Do you indeed?" said Shear. He tossed two more old coins on the bar top. Along the bar, some of the men did the same, until a sizable amount of gold lay glittering in the lamplight.

"Well, go get it, friend. Let's make this a night to remember," said Shear.

Late in the night, after the men had taken their turns walking up and down the tilted stairs, Shear stood at the corner of the bar, whiskey bottle in hand. His shirt blared open down the front. His string tie hung loose; his gun belt hung over his shoulder where he'd forgotten and left it hanging after his earlier trip upstairs.

Above the bartender's accordion music, the blonde, an Illinois girl named Emma Fay Wheatley, said in Shear's ear, "Cleary and I are only six dollars shy of bypassing Denver and going on to San Francisco."

"Bless both your hearts," Shear said. He tipped his shot glass toward them. "I'm only happy we could help in some small way."

"Is there anything else we can *both* do for you?" she cooed.

"Girls, I'm good as a man can get," Shear said. He threw an arm around each of them and pulled him to his sides.

"Anything you'd like to *watch* us do?" the other girl, Cleary Jones, asked in his other ear.

Shear chuckled at her offer. "So that's how it is, eh?"

"It is if you want it to be," Cleary replied.

Before Shear could answer, the bartender's accordion playing abruptly ceased. The drunken outlaws along the bar turned. The two men who had left so quickly earlier in the evening now stood in the middle of the plank floor, each wearing a tied-down holster on his hip. The butt of a Colt revolver stood near each gun hand.

"Brayton Shear?" said one of the men, a slim young fellow with a drooping mustache and a scar across the bridge of his nose.

Shear's gunmen stood straighter at the bar.

"Who's asking?" Shear replied.

"I'm Patton Clark," said the young gunman. "This is my brother, Noland. "You've probably heard of us—the Clark brothers, out of Nogales?"

"I can't say that I have," said Shear. "But then I don't get around to the cattle spreads or the sheep ranches."

Duckwald stifled a laugh, and stared hard at the two young toughs.

"We're neither cowhands nor sheep men," said the other man, stepping up beside his brother. "We do gun work, and we do it well." He stared at Shear. "Want to see some right now?"

The half-drunken gunmen stiffened along the bar. Their hands went to their gun butts. Shear stood firm, but ready to set them into action.

"Whoa there," said Patton Clark, "that ain't what he meant!" He held a hand up in a show of peace. He gave his brother a tense, angry look.

"No," said Noland Clark, "I meant I'd show you some friendly, but slick, gun handling—maybe shoot a mug or two off the bartender's head."

Shear grinned and perked up and said in a mock but friendlier tone of voice, "There you go. That might be fun. What say you, bartender?"

"Good Lord, no!" said the bartender, the accordion squeezed tightly shut between his hands on a sour note.

He gave the young gunmen a fiery stare. "Have you lost your damn mind, young fellow?"

"Well, there goes that idea," Shear said to the Clark brothers. He shrugged. "Is there anything else we can do for you before you head back to the bunkhouse?"

"I told you *we're not cowhands*," said Noland.

"We wondered if you need any help," said Patton, cutting his brother off.

Shear gestured toward the women hanging on his sides. "Do I look like I need any help here?"

Noland started to say something more, but his brother grabbed his arm and pulled him back.

"Come on, brother," Patton said. "We're not welcome here."

"You finally got it, eh?" Duckwald chuckled. The other men joined in as the two young men turned back toward the front door.

Patton stopped and said to Shear, "We saw the moon and star on your vest earlier. We were told you Black Valley Riders are square shooters. But maybe we were told wrong about it."

"Hang on, Clark brothers," said Shear as the two started toward the open front door. "Don't get your bark on with Black Valley Riders, unless you're tired of living."

The two turned again and stared at Shear.

Shear gave them a thin, flat smile. "Hell yes, I've heard of the Clark brothers, everybody has. I was just testing your iron."

The tension eased.

"But who told you about *us*?" Shear asked.

"Mingo Sentanza," said Patton. "We know Mingo."

"You used to," said Shear. "Mingo is dead. He took a bad fall over in the hills. He wasn't the only one. I lost a few men there."

"That's too bad," said Patton.

Shear shrugged. "Too bad for them, but maybe a good thing for the Clark brothers."

"We're all ears," said Patton.

"Have a drink," said Shear. He jiggled both young women under his arms and. "Either of you need a sweet young whore?"

"We had them earlier," said Noland. "A drink sounds good, though."

"Right, business, eh?" said Shear, appraising the two. "I like that. Set them up, bartender," he ordered, "then get back to the squeeze box while me and the Clarks have ourselves a little talk."

"Obliged, Mr. Shear," said Patton.

Noland nodded his thanks.

Shear lowered his hands and gave both doves a friendly slap on their backsides. "Go perch on somebody else's shoulder, gals," he told them.

While the bartender once again started filling glasses and mugs and playing the accordion, Shear and the Clarks stood at the corner of the bar and discussed the two young gunmen riding with him and his men. By the time they slid an empty whiskey bottle back across the bar, the music had changed from playing high-spirited Irish reels to squeezing out slow, soulful Spanish ballads.

The bartender stopped playing and asked, "Another bottle for the three of yas?"

"This one's for the trail," said Shear. He took out

more gold coins and spread them on the bar. "You sure know how to squeeze that thing, barkeep," he said, nodding at the accordion.

"Thank you, sir." The bartender smiled and lowered his head in modesty.

Shear called out to his men along the bar, "Everybody get up some more gold for this wonderful man, show some appreciation before we leave."

The men weaved and swayed drunkenly, their hands going into their pockets. But in a second, the sound of coins jingled in the air.

Seeing the glimmer of gold in the lamplight, Emma Fay said to Cleary, "We'd be dang fools to jump off this wagon."

"I was just thinking that myself," Cleary whispered back to her, the two sitting up on the bar edge, one on either side of George Epson.

Emma Fay eased down off the bar and walked toward Shear. "Hey, big fellow, if you're leaving, can Cleary and I ride along with you a ways?"

"Are you sure? It's a rough trail we ride, little dovey," Shear warned her.

"Sometimes a gal likes it rough," said Emma, a hand cocked on her hip.

Shear looked at his men and saw the eager look on their whiskey-lit faces. He grinned. "Well, what the hell? You gals grab what you're taking. Let's ride up out of here."

"Who're they riding with?" asked Longley with a hopeful look.

The men all moved forward toward the two women. Emma held up a hand and said, "Easy, fellows. Cleary and I will sort of switch from one of you to the other and make do."

The bartender shook his head and hurried along the bar raking gold coins into his palm. Somewhere on the empty outskirts of Alto Meca, a thin rooster crowed in the blue darkness.

Chapter 25

During the night, the ranger and the bounty hunters had moved the Gatling gun from beneath the cliff overhang and set it up inside the barn doors atop the gold wagon. Atop the tall boulder, Sandoval had laid out a folded wool blanket and arranged his Swiss rifle and ammunition alongside Thorn's battered naval telescope. From his higher position the young bounty hunter could watch the winding trail that Shear and his men would ride back on from Alto Meca, without being seen himself.

Without disturbing the lock on the front barn door to which Brayton Shear carried the key, the three had managed to gain entrance through a small rear door. When they'd finished setting up the big gun, its barrels pointed at the front doors, they had even swept away any sign of their footprints. They had hitched their horses out of sight behind a large stone sticking out of the hillside.

It was almost daylight when the ranger stepped out

of the cabin through a short side door and carried a cup of coffee over to Thorn inside the barn.

"You read my mind, Ranger," Thorn said, taking the hot tin cup from the ranger's gloved hand into his own.

"I poured a canteen full and carried it up to your son," Sam said.

Thorn sipped the coffee through a gust of steam. "I know, I saw you. Obliged," he said. "How's Tinnis Mayes doing in there?"

"He's awake, sitting up," said Sam, "keeping watch on Lilly and Freddie. I wouldn't be out here otherwise. Those two are apt to do anything to let Shear know we're waiting for him." Sam looked at the stacks of ammunition laid out beside Thorn in the wagon bed. "You're all right firing and reloading for yourself?"

Thorn just looked at him.

"I'll get back inside," Sam said, "before Freddie or Lilly decides to take advantage—"

Sam's words stopped short as two shots were fired from the front porch of the cabin.

Running out the back door of the barn, Thorn right behind him, the ranger saw Freddie Dupree lying in the dirt out in front of the cabin. Tinnis stood behind him, his Colt Thunderer in his right hand, his left forearm gripping his wounded side. Pushing the gambler aside, Lilly ran screaming down to Freddie and pulled him to her heavy bosom. "You son of a bitch!" she shouted back at Tinnis, who slumped over against the door frame.

Stopping over Freddie, his own Colt drawn, the ranger looked down and saw the smoking derringer lying near his hand. Freddie groaned and opened his eyes.

"I knew that wasn't the sound of a Thunderer I heard," Sam said, stooping, picking up the small hideaway derringer.

"I thought you'd shot him, Tinnis," Thorn called out to the gambler as he pulled Lilly to her feet. Freddie groaned and rubbed the back of his head.

"No . . ." The gambler had to take his time and catch his breath. "I cracked his head . . . but I caught up to him too late to stop him . . . I'm afraid."

"There's no way Shear didn't hear the shots," Thorn said. He looked at Sam with disappointment.

"Good! Good!" said Lilly. "I hope he did, you dirty sonsabitches!" she shouted at the three. She spun toward Tinnis. "And to think I used to consider you a friend."

Sam helped Freddie to his feet. "Both of you get back inside."

Freddie managed to cackle with glee even as he rubbed the welt on his head. "Did I do good, Lilly, ol' gal?"

"Damned good," Lilly said. "I'm proud of you."

The two walked arm in arm past Tinnis, back into the cabin. As Sam walked in, Tinnis said, "I don't know where he . . . got the pop gun, Ranger. But he broke for the door before . . . I could stop him."

"I should have cuffed them to their chairs," Sam said. He shoved the derringer into his belt. "Freddie had this hidden somewhere in here, just waiting for his chance to use it."

"Damn right," Freddie called out proudly from the corner of the cabin where he stood beside Lilly. She stood gently rubbing the back of his sore head.

"Well . . . what do we do now?" the gambler asked Thorn and the ranger when they'd passed him and stood in the middle of the floor. He left the open doorway and stood beside them.

"Same as before," said Sam. "It's gone too far to make any changes now. Shear has more gold waiting here than most thieves like him see in a lifetime of stealing. He's not going to turn and ride away, gunshots or not."

"He could be here any second," Tinnis said, his voice sounding stronger now, out of necessity.

"Sandy has us covered," said Thorn. "They won't get any closer than his telescope range without him warning us."

Shear and his men were less than two miles from the cliff side when they heard the two pops and a long echo in the distance. Several of the men straightened in their saddles and turned toward Shear, who rode along in their midst. Duckwald raised his face from between Cleary Jones' breasts.

"What does that mean, Rudy?" Cleary asked, sitting straddled over his lap, facing him, her short dance hall dress pulled up over her pale thighs.

"Cover up, sweetheart," said Duckwald. It means the party's over." He lifted her, turned her and sat her down in his lap facing forward.

Beside him, his brother-in-law, George Epson, said over his shoulder at Emma Fay sitting behind his saddle, slumped against his back, "That goes for you too. The party is damn sure over." He shot Duckwald a sidelong glance. "Besides, I'm a married man—to his sister."

Emma sighed and sat up from against him. Her arms had been encircling him, her hands down inside his unbuttoned shirt. She grumbled but drew her hands away.

"Now get down from here," Epson said.

"And do what, *walk*?" Emma said in protest. "Cleary didn't have to get down."

"I don't give a damn what Cleary did or didn't have to do," said Epson, "get the hell down."

"Hey now! Easy there, George," said Shear, riding in close and reaching out and taking Emma in his arm. He lifted her over onto his lap. "Let's not let a couple of gunshots cause us to lose our manners."

"What do you suppose those two shots meant, Big Aces?" Dave Pickens asked, sounding concerned.

Shear looked back, making sure the Clark brothers were far enough back not to hear him. The two sat scanning the hill line ahead in the grainy morning light.

"They were warning shots from Freddie," Shear said in almost a whisper. "I slipped him my double-barreled derringer, told him not to fire it for any reason, unless somebody rode in off our trail."

Emma cut in, sounding scared, ready to slide down from his lap. "So you mean there's somebody—"

"Shut up," said Shear, shaking her a little, holding her firmly in place. "You wanted a ride, now you've got it."

"Who do you figure?" Duckwald asked, moving his

horse over closer to Shear, the other men doing the same. At the rear the Clark brothers looked at each other and nudged their horses forward.

"I don't know," said Shear. "It could be anybody, maybe railroad gunmen. But whoever it is, they're not getting away from there with *our* gold."

"What if it's the law?" Duckwald asked. "They'll want us more than they'll want the gold."

Shear didn't answer. Instead he half turned with Emma on his lap and looked at the Clark brothers as they came to a halt up closer.

"It's time to prove yourselves, Patton . . . Noland," he said. "Get this done and you'll be wearing a moon and star of your own."

"Let me guess," Patton said, unconcerned. "You want us to ride ahead and scout for you. If anybody gets killed you want it to be us, the newcomers."

"Damn good guess," said Shear.

"A moon and star sounds just fine to me," said Noland. "But I figure there ought to be something more, in case we do run into a railroad posse or the like."

"A smart man, your brother," Shear said to Patton Clark, "and greedy too." He gave them a flat, tight grin. "I look for those traits in new men."

"It's a fair question," said Patton. "What else do we get if we ride into trouble?"

As Shear spoke his right hand came to rest on the butt of his black-handled Remington. "Ordinarily I'd say it's not what you'll get for *doing* it, it's what you'll get if you *don't*." He let out a breath. "But not this time. I like you fellows. How about five hundred in gold coins, along with your moon and star? All you got to do is scout ahead for us, to a cabin sitting up on a cliff side."

The two looked at each other, then back and Shear. They smiled. "Consider it done," said Patton.

Atop the boulder, Dee Sandoval sat scanning the lower trail with the naval telescope as the first rays of sunlight peeped over the horizon. In the circle of lens, he spotted the two riders moving up the trail through a lifting morning haze. Staying crouched on the rock, he held up two fingers for the ranger and Thorn to see from where they stood out in front of the cabin.

While both men watched, Sandoval gave Thorn a straight wave of his hand. Thorn gave him a wave of acknowledgment and turned to the ranger.

"There's two riders coming up," he said. "Sandy says they're traveling alone."

"Shear and most of his men pulled back when they heard the shots," Sam said. "These two are scouts."

"Makes sense," said Thorn. "But Shear won't be far behind, even if he thought the Seventh Cavalry was waiting here. He's not giving up this gold."

The two looked at each other. Sam said, "We've lost our element of surprise. But tell Sandoval to hold his fire and let them in closer."

Thorn gave Sandoval a hand signal, then said to the ranger, "He's got the message. I'll get back to the Gatling gun. When they all get in close I'll blast the doors open from inside."

Inside the cabin, Lilly and Freddie lay handcuffed together in a corner against the thick pine cabin wall. The ranger had taken the feather mattress from the bed and thrown it over them. On the front porch, the gambler stepped out and looked down at the ranger as Thorn hurried around to the back of the barn.

"I've got the cabin covered, Ranger," he said, holding his Colt Thunderer down at his side. He gave a weak, spent grin. "Ready when you are."

Sam looked him up and down. "I'm covering the cabin with you."

"I assure you . . . it will not be necessary, Ranger," said the gambler. He gave a feeble but sweeping gesture toward the door with his gun hand. "But your company is always welcome."

As he walked up onto the porch and into the cabin, the ranger gave a look back toward the top of the boulder where Sandoval lay in wait, and toward the barn where Thorn sat behind the Gatling gun.

As if reading the ranger's thoughts, Tinnis said quietly, "It's true our lives are in each other's hands, Ranger. Yet I can think of no hands I'd trust as much."

"I know they're both seasoned fighters," Sam said, walking inside, the gambler right behind him.

"Seasoned fighters to say the least," Mayes assured him. "And if the good captain told you he can walk on water, do not bet against him."

Chapter 26

From atop the boulder, Sandoval held an aim on Patton Clark, the first of the Clark brothers to ease his horse up onto the flat stone surface. Noland lagged back, rifle in hand, covering his brother as Patton nudged the horse forward at a walk. Patton prowled all around the front of the cabin, the locked barn doors and along the base of the large boulder at the turn in the trail.

Upon his return to the front of the house, he called out, "Hello, the cabin," and sat with his Colt in his hand, cocked and ready.

Sam opened the door slowly and stepped out onto the porch, his big Colt also cocked and ready.

"Who the hell are you?" Patton Clark asked.

"I'm Arizona Territory Ranger Samuel Burrack," said the ranger. "I'm here reclaiming the gold Shear and the Black Valley Riders stole from the railroad."

Patton looked all around. "All by yourself?"

Sam saw no reason to keep the numbers a secret. He and the bounty hunters wanted Shear and his men

to come face them. "There's three men with me," he said
coolly, "two bounty hunters and a gambler."

"Oh, so this is about bounty money?" Patton asked.

"Tell Shear we've got the gold. Everything else he
can figure out for himself."

Patton gave him a knowing look. "I'll tell him," he
said, backing his horse. "We'll be seeing you again *real*
soon."

Turning his horse, he rode over and turned it and sat
beside Noland for a moment, the two staring at the
quiet, peaceful cabin. "Did you hear that?" Patton asked.

"Oh yeah, I heard it all," Noland replied in a lowered voice. "Let's go."

The two backed their horses slowly and turned them
to the trail, guns still in hand. "We showed Shear that
our blood doesn't run yellow," Patton said.

"Yeah," said Noland, "and we got ourselves joined
right up with the Black Valley Riders." They gigged
their horses as one and rode away down the trail.

Atop the boulder, Sandoval eased the rifle butt down
from his shoulder as he watched the two lope down
out of sight among the rock and pine.

Less than a mile down the trail, at a wide spot, Shear
had moved his man forward and waited; Patton and
Noland Clark reined over and stopped.

"Well?" said Shear.

"There's a ranger there named Samuel Burrack,"
said Patton. "He said there's two bounty hunters and a
gambler backing his play."

"Son of a bitch," Shear cursed. He glared at Duckwald.

"*I* never said they were dead. Fisk said it," Duckwald said in a strong tone, his gun already in hand ready to fire.

Shear saw it. Even if he managed to get the drop on Duckwald, he realized this was no time to kill off one of his best gunmen.

"Those two damn-blasted *sailors* turned bounty hunters, and Tinnis Lucas," Shear said, pushing up his hat. He shook his head.

"The ranger said to tell you they've got the railroad gold, and you can figure out the rest for yourself," said Patton Clark.

Shear didn't even have to consider it. "All they want is a straight-out confrontation," he said. On his lap, Emma Fay squirmed a little. He gave here a short squeeze to settle her while he continued to think.

"Are we going to give it to them, Big Aces?" Duckwald cut in, his arms around Cleary, who sat slumped back on his lap, a hand stroking his knee, his thigh. He'd drawn his rifle and held it lying across her bare thighs.

Shear said with a slight scoff, "One *ranger*, two *sailors* and a drunk? You're damned right we are." He drew his rifle from its boot.

"Can I get down now?" Emma Fay asked.

"Not a chance," said Shear. He laid the rifle across her thighs as well. "Haven't you ever wanted to see a gun battle up close?" he whispered with a dark chuckle, close to her ear.

Emma understood his intentions. She shrieked and squirmed and tried to get free. Beside them on Duckwald's horse Cleary did the same.

"Let me down!" Emma screamed at Shear. She threw a clawed hand back into his face, going for his eyes.

But Shear reached a big hand around, squeezed her throat until she began to turn purple.

"See, it doesn't matter to me," he said in her ear. "You can ride into this dead or alive." He eased his hand around her throat and felt her gasping for breath. He gave a dark grin. "Now you just relax. Try to enjoy the ride."

Beside them, when Cleary had begun to struggle, Duckwald had simply raised his rifle from her lap and with a short hard blow cracked her in the jaw with the bottom of the barrel. She lay limp against his chest, blood running down her cheek.

Shear laughed and said to the men, "Rudy always had a more *direct* way with women." He looked around and called out in a raised voice, "Let's go get our gold wagon, before it gets away from us!"

The men looked at each other, questioning Shear and Duckwald using the women for shields; but the thought of the gold wagon getting away from them quickly won out. They turned their horses and fell in on the steep trail toward the cliff-side cabin.

Here they come. . . .

Sandoval watched through the telescope as the men rode into sight on the steep trail. There was no need to give a signal to the ranger and his father. His first shot would tell them everything they needed to know.

He scanned from rider to rider, seeing the two women, one with a look of terror frozen onto her face, the other lying unconscious, lolling on the outlaw's lap, her legs flopping against the horse's side.

Lowering the telescope, Sandoval raised the big

Swiss rifle to his shoulder. On the trail the sound of hooves had begun to rumble up along the hillside as he moved his rifle sights away from the women.

On the trail, Epson, having realized too late the benefit of keeping one of the young doves on his lap, kept as close to his brother-in-law's side as he could at the head of the riders. Yet, as they rounded a turn, he was forced to veer away from Duckwald's side for just a moment; and that moment was all it took.

Sandoval's first bullet appeared to have exploded inside the outlaw's head. The impact picked Epson up from his saddle and flung him backward in a wide spray of blood, bone and brain matter. His spooked horse stumbled and fell, forcing the other riders to swing wide, dangerously close to the edge of the trail and the gaping valley two hundred feet below.

Ben Longley's horse didn't make it back from the edge. Instead its hooves found loose breakaway rock and gravel; both horse and rider flew out off the edge and soared down out of sight, their legs still running, seeking purchase in the thin air.

Sandoval methodically reloaded, knowing the success of his first shot. He had taken out one man and left the rest scattering and struggling to right themselves as they topped the edge of the stone cliff surface and made for the cabin.

Shear and Duckwald drew back, keeping the two women against them for protection for as long as they could. Cleary had awakened from the crack Duckwald had given her with the rifle barrel, but she was half dazed. Shear shouted into Emma Fay's ear as the fighting raged, "How do you like it so far?"

Once the rest of the outlaws were on the flat stone surface, Sam and Tinnis Mayes opened fire from the front windows of the cabin, making their position the outlaws' most likely target. Atop the boulder, Sandoval scanned with his rifle sights until he took aim at Dave Pickens, who had ridden wide of the others and managed to get closest to the cabin. Pickens' Colt blazed at the front window where the ranger stood firing back with his Winchester.

Just as the ranger swung his Winchester toward Pickens, he saw the outlaw flip backward from his saddle beneath a red mist of blood, Sandoval's rifle resounding from above them.

The outlaws, seeing they needed cover more than they needed horses, flung themselves from their saddles and hit the ground. They dived flat to the ground or ran left and right in a crouch toward the cabin and the barn.

As the three reached the front of the barn, Thorn opened fire with the Gatling gun. Two men fell dead in a hail of bullets mixed with splinters and ripped boards from the closed barn doors. The third man, Ballard Swean, raced away. But a bullet from the gambler at the cabin window nailed him solidly in his back.

"There goes my moon and star pin," Tinnis said in mock regret, smoke rising from the barrel of his shiny Colt Thunderer.

The ranger only had time to glance over at the gambler. He turned back to the window as a bullet thumped into the frame near his head. Running toward cover in the yard near the cabin, Patton Clark, seeing that his shot had missed the ranger, took another aim.

But Sam's Winchester stopped him short, sending a bullet tearing through his chest.

Beside Patton, his brother, Noland, let out a cry of rage and fired at the ranger's window. But the ranger levered his Winchester quickly and fired. His shot hit Noland Clark dead center just as Sandoval's Swiss rifle took the top of the outlaw's head off.

Over the edge of the stone surface, Shear noted the steady thumping of the Gatling gun fall silent. He looked at Duckwald as a lull in the rest of the fighting became noticeable. With the young dove trembling against his chest, Shear said, "Rudy, it looks like you and I are going to be splitting that gold between the two of us."

Duckwald looked around at where their horses had run to after they'd jumped down from their saddles with the women as shields. "We could make a run for it," Duckwald said.

"Without the gold?" said Shear. "Nonsense! We're taking it. I won't be beaten by these jakes."

"Jesus, Big Aces," said Duckwald, "it sounds like they've killed everybody but us!"

"All because we've got these sweet little doves," said Shear. "Can't you see, they're our passage out of here, Rudy, gold and all." He grinned. "I might keep one pinned to my chest every job from now on." As he spoke he loosened his trouser belt, pulled it from his waist and wrapped it a turn around Emma Fay's neck.

Inside the cabin, Sam and the gambler looked at each other in surprise as they heard Shear call out, "Hold your fire, Ranger. We're coming up. I have some gals here I want you to meet."

Sam looked out and all around at the dead strewn on the stone surface in pools of blood. Their spooked horses had raced away up the trail around the large boulder. Dust from their hooves still loomed in the air.

"That was fast," Sam said. He eased down and watched from the corner of the window frame as Shear and Duckwald eased into sight, the woman pressed to them. Shear held a firm grip on the belt around Emma Fay's neck.

"Whatever you think you're going to do, Shear, it's not going to work," Sam called out, seeing the women, one with Shear's belt circling her throat. He stepped away from the window and walked over to the door, Tinnis right behind him. The two stepped out onto the front porch.

"Oh, but that's where you're wrong, Ranger," said Shear. "Unless you and your sailor friends want to scrape enough of these young ladies back together to give them a decent burial, you better get my gold wagon out here, pronto!"

"And give us the Gatling gun, too," said Duckwald, easing up beside him, Cleary hanging loose and wobbly against him, his arm crooked around her neck.

On top of the boulder, Sandoval moved his sights back and forth from one outlaw to the other, looking for his best and safest shot.

Thorn swung the front barn doors open and stood in the open doorway, his left hand resting on the handle of his sword. One of the badly bullet-riddled doors broke in half and crashed to the dirt.

"Be a man, Shear. Turn the women loose," Thorn said in a commanding voice.

"Well, well," Shear said, "at last I get to meet one of the sailors I've heard so much about."

"Marine," Thorn said.

"Whatever," said Shear. "You have some damn nerve, thinking you're going to do this, coming out here in *my* country, and collect blood money for killing the Black Valley Riders."

"It's already done, Shear, look around you," said Thorn. "Now turn the women loose. At least die like a man, instead of like a snake."

"Huh-uh, it's not done, *sailor*," said Shear. "These men lying here aren't half the Black Valley Riders—not even a third."

"Good, we can make some more money hunting the rest down and killing them too," Thorn said matter-of-factly.

Sam and Tinnis saw what Thorn was doing, goading Shear into facing him man to man without the women as shields. Sam looked up at the top of the boulder to where he knew Sandoval was watching. Sidelong he whispered to the gambler, "Stay here." He gave a short nod toward Rudy Duckwald. "I'm getting on this one's other side."

As Sam eased around to the other side of Duckwald, the outlaw turned right along with him, but still not enough to give Sandoval a clear safe shot.

"You've made all you're going to make off killing me and my men, *sailor*," said Shear. He twisted Emma Fay around and stuck the barrel of his Remington against her temple. "If I go down, she's going with me. Now get the wagon out here, sailor. I'm through talking."

Thorn seemed to not hear him. He stepped sidelong

away from the barn doors as if partly allowing Shear to gain entrance. "I have seen lowly cowards take innocent hostages all over this world, Shear. But this is the first time I have ever seen it here, in these United States of America."

"I see what you're doing, sailor. It isn't going to work," said Shear. "I'm going to count to three—"

"Do you really suppose that we are going to allow you to step onto that wagon with a woman in tow and ride away from here?" said Thorn, cutting him off. He almost grinned. "Are you so scared you're not thinking straight? Is that it?"

"I told you it's not working, sailor," said Shear, moving sidelong toward the open barn doors. "Come on, Duckwald, we're leaving."

"This is not going well, Big Aces," Duckwald said.

"You're right," said Thorn. "And it's only going to get worse." He held a hand up, signaling Sandoval. "Watch this."

Above them on the boulder, Sandoval saw Thorn's hand go up. He saw the position of everyone involved. Sam had moved around to be able to take out the other outlaws as soon as he made his shot. *All right, here goes. . . .*

He looked down the sights at the thin two inches of space he had between Shear's head and the woman in front of him. But then he lowered the sights away from Shear. A head shot wasn't what this called for. As Thorn's hand dropped, Sandoval aimed the rifle lower and squeezed the trigger.

Shear and Duckwald stood twenty feet apart with

their hostages. The big rifle resounded overhead and kicked up a five-foot spray of rock chips and dirt on the stone surface halfway between them. Each outlaw turned and jerked his hostage around toward where the shot had hit. In doing so, Cleary Jones, who had regained her consciousness, tore herself free from Duckwald's arm, fell and scrambled away on hands and knees.

Sandoval had his shot now, but he waited, seeing the ranger call out to Duckwald, "Over here, Rudy."

Duckwald swung around, his Colt up and cocked. But the Ranger's shot hit him in the heart and knocked him back onto the stone shelf.

Shear had given Thorn a clear target as he'd spun toward Sandoval's rifle shot. Thorn's Colt bucked once in his hand. The bullet sliced past the woman as she tried to pull away, and punched through Shear's left shoulder.

The impact threw Shear sideways, pulling the woman around with him as he managed to stay on his feet. But in the end he had to turn the belt loose to keep from falling himself. As soon as the belt left his hand, Thorn recocked the horse pistol and stepped forward, intending this next shot to be his last.

Shear's Remington had fallen to the ground. He dropped onto his hands and knees and tried to reach it, his wounded shoulder not helping. "It's over, Shear," said Thorn, stepping closer and closer, the horse pistol aimed down at him.

"This is . . . crazy," Shear lamented. With all his strength he began raising the Remington. "I can't be dying here . . . killed in the high desert . . . by a *sailor* of all things?" His bloody thumb managed to cock the hammer.

"Marine. . . ." Thorn's pistol bucked again while the smoke of the first shot still curled from its barrel.

Shear collapsed dead, the morning sunlight reflecting off the moon and star pinned to his vest.

Epilogue

—————

In moments the two shaken young women had been helped to their feet and led inside the cabin. Sam flipped over the feather mattress and helped the old couple to their feet and took off their cuffs. He said to Freddie, "If you want to do something for your friends, gather them up. These men will be taking them to town and turning them in for their bounty. That's better than dragging them off for the buzzards."

"By myself?" said Freddie. "I'm an old man. They weren't that good friends anyway, now that I think about it."

"Go gather them up Freddie," Lilly demanded. "I'll boil these two doves some coffee."

"How—how did you know we're doves?" said Cleary Jones, still trembling, and her eyes red from tears.

Lilly gave a wry smile. "Oh, just a wild guess."

"I'd rather have whiskey," said Emma Fay, "if you've got any."

Lilly chuckled and shook her head and walked to

the hearth. "No hard feelings, Ranger," she said. "Shear was a friend when he was alive, but now that he's dead, he's just one more *dead* outlaw."

"I understand," said Sam, punching out empty shells from his Colt and replacing them with bullets from his belt.

The gambler seated himself at a battered table and clutched his forearm around his wounded side. When Sandoval walked inside, his Swiss rifle in hand, Tinnis looked back and forth between Thorn and his son and asked either of them, "So, this is what you're planning on doing for a living now, hunting bounty?"

Before Sandoval could reply, Thorn said, "Not my son, Mayes. Sandy's going back to his regiment." He gave Sandoval a look. "Isn't that right, son?"

Sandoval looked surprised that Thorn even knew the idea had been on his mind for a while. He hadn't mentioned it.

"I might," he said, "if that fits in all right with your plans," he said. "I mean, I don't want to leave you short-handed?"

Thorn looked at Tinnis and said to Sandoval, "I don't think I'm going to be shorthanded. I believe the gambler here is just itching for this sort of work, once he's sober and his side is healed."

"Really, now?" said Tinnis. "What makes you *suppose* that I'm just itching for this *sort of work*? Do you think I'm crazy, Captain Thorn?"

"A little, perhaps," said Thorn. "But more importantly I believe this is the best use of your training and talent. The question is, can you stay sober enough for me to count on you?"

Tinnis considered it. "Most of the time, yes, I believe I can do that."

"Then it's settled," said Thorn. He looked at Sam. "Ranger Burrack, I considered recruiting you to join me, but I believe you have been a ranger too long for me to turn you into a marine."

"Obliged, Captain," Sam said. He eyed the older bounty hunter. "I considered asking you to join me, but I decided you'd been a marine too long for me to ever turn you into a ranger."

Thorn smiled. "Good return, Ranger," he said.

Sandoval walked over to the ranger and held out the big Swiss Husqvarna rifle. "Ranger Burrack, I've seen how you look at this rifle of mine. I'll be going back to my Springfield when I rejoin my regiment . . . so, this is yours. I know you'll only use it for the best of purposes."

The ranger stood speechless for a moment; then he took the rifle. "Dee Sandoval, I am much obliged. I only hope I can one day shoot it as well as you do. . . ."

The four men turned silent for a moment as if paying tribute to something they now all held in common among themselves.

An hour later, the ranger had broken down the big Swiss rifle and placed it in its wooden carrying case. The two bounty hunters and Tinnis Mayes stood on the porch as he tied the wooden case down beneath his bedroll and stepped up into his saddle.

When he'd backed the big Appaloosa stallion from the hitch rail, Sam looked down at Thorn and Sandoval, who had followed him out onto the porch. Mayes stood in the open doorway, leaning against the frame.

"Until we meet again, best to each of you," Sam said.

As he turned the stallion, Mayes raised a three-finger gesture with his hand.

Sandoval said, "Adios, Ranger."

"Keep an edge on, Ranger," said Thorn. He jiggled the handle of the big sword at his side. *"Semper fidelis."*

"Aye, aye, Captain," Sam replied. He tapped the stallion into an easy gait and touched his fingertips to the brim of his sombrero. *Semper fidelis . . . ,* he said to himself. And he put the stallion forward, out, across the stone cliff, down the high trail, toward the badlands, where sunlight and sand wavered and swirled as far as the eye could see.

Don't miss a page of action
from America's most exciting Western author,
Ralph Cotton

CITY OF BAD MEN

Coming from Signet in February 2011.

Little Ester, the Mexican Badlands

Lawrence Shaw rode the dusty switchback trail upward nearly a mile, then stepped his big bay over onto a rock ledge and looked down, checking his back trail. Beneath him the speckled bay chuffed and shook out its damp mane in a gust of dry, warm wind. Overhead lay a wavering white-hot sky. Below, a desolate, broken world of stone, gully, hilltop and cut-bank lay carpeted over with sand—a harsh, unaccommodating fauna that showed no welcome toward humankind.

Home . . . he told himself wryly.

The bullet wound in his head had mended slowly but steadily for the past four months. The doctor who had most recently examined him declared Shaw's being alive a miracle of medical science. Shaw supposed it was true. Leastwise, he himself had never known anyone to take such a shot and live. As far as it being a miracle, he couldn't say. Miracles didn't come around much, the way he saw it.

He wasn't even completely certain who had shot him, and, for some reason he himself did not understand, he didn't care. *It was the young woman though,* an inner voice told him. He gazed out from his saddle across endless rolling hills bathed in a harsh glare of sunlight and wavering heat. Deep inside, he knew it had been her.

Now put it away . . .

Being a gunfighter, being known as the *fastest gun alive.* There were more people wanting to kill him than he ever cared to think about. Getting shot was something he'd learned to take in stride long ago, a part of the life he'd chosen for himself. So was getting killed if it came to it, he reminded himself, watching a big, lone hawk swing in a lazy circle high above him. He tried not to make a big thing of it, getting shot. It happened to everybody now and then.

His memory was not clear on what circumstances had drawn him back here to the fiery Mexican badlands, but it was good to be back all the same, gunshot wound or no. His pal U.S. Marshal Crayton Dawson had called this *his* kind of place—"Gun Country," he'd said. And he'd been right, Shaw realized. There was solitude here. This was a good place for a man like himself. Anyway, here he was . . .

The bay scraped a hoof and tossed its head. Shaw touched back on its reins.

The bullet had hit him at almost point-blank range, so close that the blast of powder had burned his hair off. But instead of entering his skull, the big .45 caliber slug had only fractured it. Oddly enough the bullet had flattened and crushed its way upward and bored a path across the top of his head. It split his scalp like a dull hatchet, leaving in its wake a long furrow of cracked skull bone along the way, and came out on the other side. He winced, thinking about it.

A miracle? Maybe . . .

He turned the big speckled bay and rode back onto the dusty switchback, reminding himself once again not to think about it. But more than likely, it had just been a bad bullet, a weak load. *Hell, who knew . . . ?*

The bullet wound had not left him unscathed. Even now he went about his day-to-day life with much of his consciousness still partially mired in a dark, dreamy numbness that refused to turn him loose. Peculiar though he found it to be, there were days, even *weeks* at a time that he could not account for. Then, out of nowhere, his memory seemed to catch up with him in some jumbled, unsteady fashion, as if he'd been traveling somewhere far ahead of it.

It was strange, he told himself, nudging the bay forward. But he'd gotten used to *strangeness* in his life a long time ago.

Home . . . he told himself again, this time without the irony. Finally, he forced himself to dismiss all thought on the matter and gazed off across the rocky hilltops and into the endless breadth of earth and sky. He took a deep breath and let it out.

"We've still got a long way to go," he said down to the bay. Yet, in truth he had no real destination in mind, only a deep, persistent need to keep moving.

He wore a long corduroy riding duster with leather-trimmed pockets and collar. Beneath the open duster front, his big Colt stood in its holster on his right hip.

His headwear was a large black bandanna pulled back and tied at the base of his skull beneath a tall sand-colored sombrero. The sombrero was plain, but with a fine line of green embroidery the color of pale wild grass on its high, soft crown.

His boots were *caballeria* style, high-welled, battered and scuffed to the desert hue. The right boot was plain seasoned leather, but the left boot bore a wraparound carving, tooled in fine detail, of two wild stallions locked in a death battle.

When he arrived at Little Ester, the first town in a string of ancient Spanish-settlement remnants, he stepped down from his saddle beside a short stone wall surrounding the town's watering well. He hitched the bay to a thick iron ring attached atop the short wall. Reaching down under the bay's belly, he loosed its cinch and let it drink.

As the thirsty horse drew water, Shaw pulled a gourd dipper up from an oaken bucket sitting atop the stone wall and drank from it himself. Behind him an elderly man appeared from the dark shade between two adobes, a frayed straw sombrero in his knobby hands.

"*Bienvenidos a Pequeña Ester, señor,*" he said. Welcome to Little Ester.

"*Gracias,*" Shaw replied. He wiped a hand across his lips and dropped the gourd dipper back into the bucket.

The old man paused, looked Shaw up and down, taking particular note of his finely tooled boot.

"May I ask what brings you to Little Ester?" he asked in stiff English.

Shaw turned facing the smiling old man. "Passing through," he said.

"Aw, *sí*, passing through," said the self-appointed town greeter. "I understand." His eyes went back to Shaw's boot, then back to his face. "Always when men come to Little Ester from the east, they are passing through." He offered a smile, seeing that Shaw had little conversation for him. Shaw glanced at the shade between the two adobes the old man had walked out of.

But as the old man turned to walk away, Shaw said out of the blue, "Tell me, *senor*, is there a witch here who carries a covey of trained sparrows?" As soon as he'd asked, he'd realized it had been a mistake. But it was too late; he had to let it play itself out.

"A *bruja*?" the old man said, curiously. "With trained sparrows?" He considered the question and he rubbed his goatee for an answer.

"Never mind," Shaw said, wanting to let it go. It had been over a year since he'd seen the witch and her covey of dancing sparrows. And it hadn't been here in Little Ester. It hadn't even been close. These were the kinds of things that concerned him about himself lately. This was his head wound talking, he thought.

But the old man did not know what the term *never mind* meant. He studied the question for a moment longer, then raised a thin knobby finger and said, "Ah, wait! But, yes, I do know of such a *bruja*."

"You do?" Shaw said. Then he said quickly, "It's not important."

"She does not come here," the old man continued all the same. "She travels the hills south of here across the desert basin."

"Yes, *gracias*," said Shaw, "I remember now." He didn't manage to hide the look of concern on his face.

The old Mexican tilted his head and asked, "May I ask why you seek her, *senor*?"

"I'm not seeking her," Shaw said. "I was just curious, is all."

"Oh," the old man said, only appearing to half believe Shaw. "I thought you seek her because she is from your country."

"From *my* country?" That got his interest. "She's American?"

"*Sí, Americano.* Did you not know that about her, *senor*?" the old man asked.

"No," Shaw said, "I didn't know that." He stepped over closer to the bay and loosened its reins from the iron ring.

"It is a good day when a man learns something new," the old Mexican said, grinning over bare gums.

He wanted money.

Shaw reached into his trouser pocket.

It had been in the dusty adobe village of Valle Del Maíz that he'd seen the old witch wrapped in a ragged black cloth. She had tossed her covey of paper-thin sparrows upward in a circle of glowing firelight and appeared to orchestrate their movements with the tips of her bony fingers. *An American . . . ?* That was a surprise.

"Tell me, *amigo*," Shaw said, dismissing the witch and her sparrows, "have two American lawmen passed through here?" He took out a small gold coin and placed it on the old man's weathered palm.

"*Americano* lawmen . . . ?" The old man closed his palm over the coin as he gave the matter some thought.

"Yes," Shaw said, "one is called Dawson. The other one is called Caldwell—some call him *Undertaker*. They track outlaws along the border." He reached down under the bay and fastened its cinch.

"Ah, yes, I have heard of these men," the Mexican said, tapping a finger to his head. "But no, they have not been to Little Ester. This I would know, if they had."

"You're certain?" Shaw said. He tested his saddle with a gloved hand.

"*Sí*, I am certain," he said. He stepped back from Shaw as if in caution. "Are they hunting *you*, maybe, these lawmen?"

"No," Shaw said, not wanting to offer any more about himself or the two lawmen than he needed to. He swung up into his saddle. "Maybe *I'm* hunting them."

"Oh...," the old man said. Shaw saw the man's eyes go once again to the tooling on his left boot, then back to Shaw's face as he turned the bay and put it forward along the stone-lined trail.

No sooner had Shaw ridden out of sight than three gunmen walked out of the same dark shade where the old man had stood before venturing to the well.

"Who is he, old man?" a young Mexican named Dario Esconza asked. He stood expectedly with a bottle of mescal in one hand. He held his other hand loosely shoved down behind his gun belt, close to the big bone-handled Starr revolver holstered low on his hip.

"He did not tell me who he is," the old man said, having buried the coin out of sight inside his ragged clothes. He rubbed his bristly chin as if trying to recall what Shaw had told him. "I cannot remember why he said he came here." He grinned sadly. "My mind does not work as well as it used to. Life is hard."

Esconza scowled at him, knowing the old man was fishing him for money. "If you think life is hard now, imagine how much harder it will be when I stamp my boot down on your throat." He took a step closer.

"*Por favor*, Dario! Please, no," the old man said, raising his hands as if to protect his face. "I will tell you what he said."

Esconza stopped and stared at him. The other two gunmen, both Texans on the run from the law, looked on, liking the way Esconza handled things.

The old man said, "He searches for an old *bruja* who carries a covey of trained sparrows in her bosom."

"A witch with sparrows in her bosom . . ." Esconza said staring flatly at the old Mexican.

"*Sí.*" The old man shrugged, knowing how unlikely it sounded.

Esconza and the two gunmen looked at one another. Then Esconza turned back to the old man and took a deep breath, running out of patience.

"That's real good, old man," he said, stepping forward again. "Now I'm going to kick you back and forth in the dirt for a while. Then we'll start over."

"It is the truth, Dario. I swear it," the old man said, speaking hurriedly now. "He asked about the *bruja*, and I told him she does not come here. Then he asked about the two lawmen you told me to look out for, the ones who you said are hunting down the Cut-jaws gang."

"The two lawmen, eh?" said Esconza. "Now we're getting somewhere. What did you tell him?"

"I told him they have not been through here." The old man shrugged his bony shoulders. "Because it is true—they have not."

Esconza turned up a drink from the bottle of mescal and passed it to one of the other two gunmen. He stared along the rise of dust Shaw's horse stirred in its wake.

"What else?" Esconza asked. "Is he running from them?"

"He did not say," the old man replied. "I asked if they hunt him, and he said maybe he is hunting them."

One of the gunmen, a Texan named Ollie Wilcox, lowered the mescal bottle from his lips and passed it to the other gunman. "That's no answer," he said.

The third gunman, a Tex-Mexican named Charlie Ruiz turned up the bottle, swigged from it, then lowered it and said, "Yep, he's on the run, if you ask me."

"Yes, I think he is," said Esconza.

He furrowed his brow in concentration and added, "I know this man . . . I have seen him before somewhere."

"Yeah . . . ?" said Wilcox. He just stared at him.

Esconza nodded his head in contemplation. "It will come to me."

Ruiz grinned at Wilcox and asked Esconza, "So, what do you want to do? Chase him down and tell him you know him from somewhere?"

"We are looking for good men, eh?" said Esconza. "If he is hiding from the law and he is good with a gun, we will invite him to ride with us, I think."

Ruiz grinned again. "What if he's hiding from the law but is *not* good with a gun?" he said. "What if he has toes missing from being so bad with a gun?"

Esconza shrugged and reached out for the bottle in Charlie Ruiz's hand. "Then I will kill him, and we will ride away." He looked at the old Mexican and said, "See how life is *not so hard* for those of us with a bold nature?"

"*Sí*, I do," the old man said. Then he fell silent and stood staring at the drift of dust above the trail.

"A writer in the tradition of Louis L'Amour
and Zane Grey!"
—*Huntsville Times*

National Bestselling Author

RALPH COMPTON

**Available wherever books are sold or at
penguin.com**

No other series packs this much heat!

THE TRAILSMAN

Follow the trail of Penguin's Action Westerns at

Charles G. West

**"RARELY HAS AN AUTHOR PAINTED THE
GREAT AMERICAN WEST IN STROKES SO
BOLD, VIVID AND TRUE."
—RALPH COMPTON**

War Cry

Will Carson is the best scout at Fort Dodge. Then he
saves the life of Sarah Lawton, a lovely widow with
her young daughter, both helpless under Indian fire.
And by doing so, he's made mortal enemies with the
Cheyenne—who are now out for his blood...

Also Available
Storm in Paradise Valley
The Blackfoot Trail
Shoot-out at Broken Bow
Lawless Prairie

Available wherever books are sold or at
penguin.com

S805